THE
DOWNSIDE

THE DOWNSIDE

MIKE COOPER

MYSTERIOUSPRESS.COM

OPEN ROAD

INTEGRATED MEDIA

NEW YORK

Copyright © 2017 by Mike Cooper

Cover design by Drew Padrutt

978-1-5040-4461-5

Published in 2017 by MysteriousPress.com/Open Road Integrated Media, Inc.
180 Maiden Lane
New York, NY 10038
www.mysteriouspress.com
www.openroadmedia.com

For my father,
an inspiration and a model, always

THE
DOWNSIDE

PROLOGUE

The hobo was no particular surprise, but when Finn saw a dust plume coming up the canyon, he knew they had a problem. They were deep in the New Mexico desert, railroad tracks disappearing into mirage in both directions the only mark of civilization.

"What the fuck?" Jake's voice crackled in Finn's ex-military Racal headset.

"Don't know."

Air brakes hissed and couplers banged as seventy freight cars' worth of slack bunched up. The train jerked to a rough, grudging stop on the siding. Finn figured the engineer probably would have done a better job if Jake wasn't pointing a gun at him.

"Two guys here," said Jake over the comm. He sounded calm, which didn't mean much. Finn had known Jake since high school, a million years ago, and had never seen him rattled. But he was surely in control. Even with his face covered up—probably using a bandanna, romantic that he was—Jake had *People* magazine looks and charisma to spare.

"That's all of them." Finn ticked a mental box. Like all the big railroads, Union Central kept their crews at a minimum. "Put them out of the way." Jake would plasticuff them in a corner and stay in the locomotive to handle any calls from the dispatcher.

The hobo had found a nice spot on the deck of a grain car, shaded by the hopper's slanting steel wall. By coincidence, the grainer was only two cars away from the ore gondolas. So when the old guy stuck his head out into the bright desert glare, the first thing he saw was the Deere excavator, still chained down to its flatbed, pulling up right alongside the track.

Finn jumped down from the flatbed's cab, leaving his door open. A blast of diesel sounded as Corman, who was sitting at the excavator's controls, swung its arm up and over the gondola. Corman was a huge man, his partially bald head almost brushing the cab's roof. But his hand was delicate on the levers.

Another rumble as Asher pulled up in the open-trailer semi. His own style was less careful, and his truck slammed to a stop alongside the flatbed. Still, close enough. The excavator's scoop rose, full of molybdenite, and Corman swiveled it around to dump into Asher's trailer.

Asher stuck his head out the cab window to look back. No mask. Finn grimaced. It probably didn't matter—no one was around to see and Asher could always shave off his ridiculous musketeer's beard if he had to change appearance—but still. Asher did things his way, fuck you anyway.

Thirty seconds, and they were already unloading. Finn organized a tight schedule and generally managed to make it stick. His own version of just-in-time logistics.

Guys on a payroll could fuck around. When you were *stealing* the delivery, efficiency mattered.

"Get off there," Finn called over the engine noise to the hobo. The man crawled out, obviously stiff from sitting on the jouncing metal platform for hours.

"This ain't Alamogordo." Grime had worn deeply into his face. Apart from the mainline and a battered metal shed, the siding was surrounded by emptiness—dirt, sand, and scrubby yucca, with a few low mountains purple in the distance.

And the dust from an approaching vehicle. Only a few minutes away now.

"Nope." Finn himself wore a painter's mask and sunglasses—the practical outlaw. "Sorry to do this, old-timer, but you got to go sit out of the way. There's some shade by that shack down there."

The hobo reached back to get his bindle off the grainer's porch. Finn noticed he had a metal spoon, the handle bent over and tied to his belt with frayed twine, and a plastic soda bottle filled with water.

"You're robbing the train, ain't you?" He cackled briefly. "I didn't think that ever happened anymore."

"On your way, now."

"Sure, Butch." He started to walk toward the shack but turned his head back. "Can I ask you something?

"No."

"Is there a lot of money in that? In a truckful of rocks?"

Finn shook his head. "Don't pay any attention to us."

Back in the truck's cab, Finn pulled his binoculars from the pack and peered at the unexpected company, coming up fast. His hands were sweaty inside the latex, but combat gloves were fingerless, which was an obvious problem.

"Two pickup trucks," he said over the radio. "Or . . . no. One pickup and an SUV. I can't see faces."

"Say who they are?" Asher's voice.

"Not *la migra*." Border Patrol vehicles were white with lightbars. These were black and unmarked. "Keep loading."

"I locked the engineers in the toilet," Jake said on the radio.

"Stay there and keep your head down." Finn wished he had a long gun, but they only carried sidearms. Big weapons were just a pain in the ass.

Until you needed them, of course.

A half minute later, he put the binocs down because the trucks were now clear enough.

"Uh-oh." Asher wasn't paying attention to his job.

"Shit."

"Motherfuck."

Well, Finn couldn't blame them. Three men were standing in the bed of the pickup, holding the roll bar as the truck bounced along the dirt road. The SUV had a sunroof, and another man stood through it, arms and torso free.

All four held assault rifles.

"Keep working," Finn radioed as he opened the door.

"What are you doing?" Asher didn't sound happy.

"They don't look like law enforcement to me."

"All the more reason not to talk to them." Jake was the voice of reason, as usual.

"Maybe we have common interests."

Finn walked out with his hands halfway up in the air and stopped about a hundred feet from the train. A minute later, the pickup skidded to a halt on his right. The SUV continued another dozen yards, then stopped abruptly. Dust blew across the scrub. Four rifle barrels pointed over.

A moment of silence. Behind him, Finn heard the diesel engines idling. Corman and Asher were obviously waiting to see what happened.

"*¿Quién diablos eres tú?*" one of the new arrivals called from the pickup.

"Sorry," Finn said. "How about in English?"

"*¡Tú, hijo de perra!*"

Well, it was obvious enough now. Somewhere in these seventy railcars was an undeclared shipment, FOB the middle of fucking nowhere. Customs in El Paso couldn't inspect every car even if they wanted to, and the railroads weren't going to cough up for extra security. If Finn's crew hadn't arrived first, these jokers probably would have simply bled a brake line for a ten-minute delay, unloaded their bales of whatever, and disappeared before the engineers even noticed.

The man who'd spoken now hopped lightly from the pickup's bed and walked closer. He wore a baseball cap backward on his head and an Abercrombie T-shirt tucked into faded black jeans. Just like any NMSU college student—except for the M16.

"What are you doing?" A mild accent, and he seemed more curious than upset.

"Transferring cargo." Finn looked back at the gondolas for a moment. "You, too?"

"We're not interested in rocks. Will you take that mask off?"

"Sure. Can I tell my guys to go back to work?"

"Are you in a hurry?"

"No more than yourselves."

Just a couple of general contractors working out a problem. And Finn still thought everything would be fine. They could make an arrangement and go their separate ways, never to meet again—because, really, they were in completely different lines of business. The guy even offered him a cigarette while they stood there, talking it out.

Jake, a quarter mile down at the front of the train, must have heard the new problem first.

"Uh, boss?" he said quietly into the radio. But it was too late. Heads were turning in the pickup, and a moment later Finn recognized the sound.

A helicopter.

"¡Desgraciado!" Finn's new friend swung up his M16. "¡Oye, eres policía!"

"No!"

The guy might have pulled the trigger, but they both noticed new towers of dust on the other side of the train. The choppers were approaching in an attack vector, three abreast, and suddenly, a line of vehicles was banging out of some hidden canyon, red and blue lights flashing.

Finn ran toward the flatbed, expecting a shot in the back any moment. Gunfire sputtered, almost lost in the rapidly increasing noise of the chopper. Sirens rose in volume, dopplered by the speed of the approaching cars.

The cavalry had arrived.

"Shut it down," Finn said into the radio before rolling under the truck, arms over his head.

He hoped the hobo had sense enough to stay out of the way. He hoped his guys wouldn't do anything stupid. Two months of planning shot to hell, but forget that; they'd be lucky if they didn't spend the next decade in prison.

Bullets spat into the dirt around him. An explosion. Dust flew everywhere, raised by rotor wash and vehicles skidding near the train. A man shouted nearby, the words lost.

Finn closed his arms over his head, holding back an urge to burrow into the dirt. In the chaos, trying to figure out what was happening, his mind couldn't let go of one nagging question: Had the police arrived for them—or for the narcos?

And if it was Finn's crew, how had they *known*?

CHAPTER ONE

P ostrelease counseling."

The clerk slid a photocopied sheet of paper through the slot under his reinforced window. The lexan was scratched and nicked, making the clerk's face blurry. A circle of quarter-inch drill holes in the window had been covered over with a newer slab of polycarbonate, held in place by lag bolts. Finn wondered what exactly some inmate had shoved through the holes when they were open.

He looked at the sheet, two columns of nearly unreadable small type. "What's it say?"

The clerk shrugged. "Don't fuck up, or we'll see you back here."

"I hadn't thought of that."

"If you can't read, you can listen to a recording."

State law must have mandated counseling. Socorro Correctional was a contract prison, run for profit, and they tended to follow the minimums. New Mexico legislators certainly didn't care.

"I don't think I forgot how yet," said Finn.

Behind him, the escort guard grunted and leaned against the door, clunking it against the wall. The clerk had turned away, digging through a heap of paper and plastic on his side of the counter. He found a one-gallon ziploc and shoved it through the slot along with another form.

"Sign the paper and give it back," he said.

The bag bulged with a wallet and phone and loose change and a length of light steel chain. Finn's name had been scrawled on the outside in heavy marker.

"What about my clothes?"

"Sign the form," said the clerk again. "We only store clothing eighteen months. You can keep what you're wearing."

Finn looked at him a long moment. "Okay." Cheap denims, a long-sleeved T-shirt, and canvas shoes. Before pocketing the wallet, he looked inside: a few hundred dollars and nothing else.

He never carried anything but mad money on a job. Nothing that could fall out of his pocket for a CSI tech to find later.

"Are you closing your commissary account?" asked the clerk as he took the paper Finn slid back to him.

"Of course."

The clerk shrugged again. "Some guys, they figure they're coming right back, they don't bother."

"Maybe they just can't believe how little they made." Finn studied the check the clerk passed him. At thirteen cents an hour, seven years of prison labor had netted him $841.31. "You withheld *taxes*?"

"We do things right around here."

The guard led him out one more corridor, through two final sets of electronically sealed gates, and then pointed at a simple metal door.

"Out you go," he said.

Finn felt an unexpected rush of emotion—elation, fear, uncertainty, adrenaline. Through a window alongside the door, he could see a parking lot, dusty and white in the desert heat, with riot wire fencing the perimeter and an empty road stretching into the scrubby badlands.

"When's the bus?" he asked.

"*Haw.*" It might have been a laugh. "You ain't got nobody picking you up, you can walk. Turn left—town's four miles."

"Right." Finn took a last look: a concrete floor, blank walls with broken holes leaking gypsum. The guard didn't offer to shake hands. "Have a nice day, you hear?"

Outside, he walked away from the building, tipped his head back, and closed his eyes. The sun blasted down, maybe 110 degrees of shadeless heat, with a few slight puffs of breeze. Behind him, faintly, the sounds of a compressor, some window air conditioners in the administrative offices, a pair of tractor trailers idling somewhere. In front of him, a slight rustling as wind pushed across the desert, and nothing else.

A car door slammed. Footsteps.

"How are you, Finn?"

A female voice. His eyes snapped open.

Dark hair, not too long, silky white shirt tucked into jeans. Average height, shorter than him. Easily the most beautiful woman he'd seen outside a magazine for a very long time.

"Who the hell are you?"

She grinned. "You're late."

"By about seven years." He looked around the parking lot: a few SUVs, some four-doors—nothing too small or Japanese. The cars were all empty. "I wasn't expecting to be met."

"I don't have much time." She held up a key ring. "Come on, I'll drive you to town. We can talk in the car."

"Who are you?" he said again.

"Emily Hale." She held out a hand.

Her grip was firm and surprisingly calloused. Out of practice, he had to remind himself to let go.

"Sorry."

"You have anything?" She looked past him at the prison's entrance, like the bellboy would be pushing out a luggage cart any second.

"Like what?"

"Okay then." She began to walk toward a white sedan parked under the DO NOT PICK UP HITCHHIKERS sign. When Finn didn't follow, she looked back.

"I work for Wes Schiller," she said.

He kept his face still, empty of reaction. Seven years *had* given him plenty of practice at that.

"I'm done," he said. "Out."

"Wes just wants to talk."

"No more jobs. It's over."

"Scared straight, were you?" She put a hand on one hip but seemed amused.

"Something like that."

"You don't know what he wants to talk to you about."

One of the tractor trailers at the receiving dock rumbled to life—diesel coughing, a tap on the airhorn. It turned left and faded down the road.

"I don't remember you," Finn said.

"No reason you would."

Which was true. Wes didn't exactly invite him in for office conferences. "How long have you worked for him?"

"Less than you've been on the state's nickel." She lifted her sunglasses and looked at him with the deepest, greenest eyes Finn had ever seen. "You don't really want to walk to town, do you?"

For a long moment, Finn pretended he couldn't decide, then shook his head slightly and said, "I guess not."

Her rental was an anonymous four-door, new and somehow rounder and more bug-eyed than had been the style when Finn went in. She beeped the lock and he opened the door, but he paused before getting in.

Four people had known that Finn planned to rob the ore train. Jake, Asher, and Corman were three of them, of course. But all of them went to jail, too, just like Finn. In seven years, he hadn't been able to think of a single reason why any of them would have turned.

The fourth person was Wes.

CHAPTER TWO

F ive minutes later, the air-conditioned rental brought them into
town: dusty streets, dusty buildings, shuttered storefronts with
dusty plate glass papered over. Emily parked on an angle on the main
street, near what seemed to be the single stoplight. A check-cashing
outlet, a lottery-and-cigarettes hole-in-the-wall, and a diner.

"Something to eat?" she said.

"Who's paying?"

"It's on account."

He *was* hungry.

An hour past lunchtime, the diner was almost empty: one
woman behind the counter and an old guy in overalls on a stool. A
radio on a shelf blared an argumentative talk show. Finn looked at
the menu, unable to decide.

Emily watched him. "Nothing you want?"

"Just haven't had to make choices for myself for a while," he said
but managed to order a pork sandwich and fries. They were in a
booth at the end, alongside streaked plate glass.

Emily sat straight, hands together on the table. "I read up on
you. Wes plays it close, you know? So I did my own research."

Wes ran investments, mostly commodities. They'd cooper-
ated on two occasions, after a chain of unlikely intermediaries had
brought them together. Finn had highly specialized, even unique,

skills, but to exercise them fully, he needed setup money. His kind of jobs couldn't be run on the cheap. Wes, in turn, had the money, over in the legitimate world—at least, as legitimate as superrich Wall Street investors could be—and he was always looking for what he called "exotics." Unusual investment opportunities. High-risk/high-return ventures. Lots of alpha and zero beta, whatever that meant.

A match made in heaven.

"You can't believe anything they write in the newspapers," Finn said.

"Court transcripts." Emily had an amused look again, mouth quirked up on one side. "Investigative records, including some private detective's backgrounder."

"Ah."

"Let's see. An autorack of Mercedes S-Coupes. An entire industrial machine line, just after it was installed, before they even started using it. Five containers of copper scrap on its way to China." She shook her head slightly. "Did you ever steal something that weighed less than twenty tons?"

"I've never done a day of time for anything except the molybdenite."

"A truckload of rocks."

It was all public information after the trial. But those green eyes watched him steadily, observing, measuring . . . judging.

"Two trucks," he said. "Seventy tons of ore. At the time, molybdenite was going for six fifty, seven a pound. The roaster wouldn't have paid full price, of course—not for a delivery at the back gate in the middle of the night."

"Roaster?"

"Only three plants in the United States take the raw ore and cook it down into molybdenum. We had—" He cut himself off.

Emily raised an eyebrow.

"Hypothetically," Finn said. "Some other ore thief might have negotiated all that ahead of time. Maybe a forty-percent discount. You can do the arithmetic."

She barely paused. "Six hundred thousand dollars."

Finn nodded.

Wes had funded the job, and he would have taken one-third right off the top. Maybe Emily knew that, maybe she didn't.

The waitress arrived with food, setting down the plates and drop-ping silverware rolled in napkins and two straws with the iced tea.

"Anything else I can get you?" she said cheerfully, stepping back.

Emily looked over, but Finn was still reacquainting himself with being politely asked his opinion on things. "Um . . ."

"We're fine, thanks."

The sandwich was unbelievably good. Even if it wasn't, Finn would still have eaten it as fast as he could. Prison habits.

"Wes has a problem," Emily said. Her hamburger sat untouched.

"I told you—"

"You could help." She paused. "You're probably the only person in the world who *could* help."

"Thanks."

"Wes is doing quite well."

"Good for him."

"But if this . . . problem . . . isn't solved . . . then his business becomes very, very difficult."

"Not interested."

"What I'm saying," she plowed on, "is that Wes is *extremely* motivated to have you on board. No messing around."

"Really?"

"He's desperate."

"Uh-huh." Finn spoke through a mouthful of sandwich. "In my experience, desperate people make the absolutely worst partners."

"Fair point. 'Desperate' might be overstating the case."

Sunshine glared through the window beside them.

"Before, I always talked to Wes directly." Finn raised one hand as Emily started to speak. "That's not the point. I'm retired. Tell him I'm sorry."

"Retired." Flat.

"Seven years I was in there." He paused long enough to drain his iced tea. "The world's different now. Bernie Madoff, you remember him? Goldman Sachs? All those fucking banks? The guys stealing a million dollars today, all they have to do is hit a few keys on a com-puter. Change a couple of decimal places. Done. And it's probably legal, too, the way the game is rigged. The only people actually steal-ing *things* anymore are junkie bank robbers and celebrity shoplifters."

"I don't know—"

"I'm a dinosaur," Finn said. "I'm not looking for one last glorious raid, then off to Bolivia. I'm going to sit on a lawn chair somewhere, listen to baseball. Thanks but no thanks."

Emily finally took a bite of hamburger. After a while, she said, "I told you, I read the court transcripts. From your case."

"The whole thing?"

"All three hundred pages."

"Huh."

She looked up at him. "The prosecution called nine law enforcement officers. County police, state troopers, the New Mexico Mounted Patrol—whatever that is—and the FBI."

Finn didn't say anything.

"The DEA was never mentioned. The drugs, yes. The drug smugglers, the stateside gang—guilt by association, I suppose. But actual drug enforcement agencies? Not a single reference."

"They didn't have to explain how they knew to ambush us," Finn said. "Not in the trial. Or at least not in *my* trial. I don't know what they said at the others."

"There wasn't a trial for the drug gang. They all pled out."

For seven years, Finn had been thinking about this question.

"We weren't bycatch," he said.

"No." She nodded. "*They* were."

"The FBI knew. They knew exactly when and where we were going to hit the train. So the obvious question is . . ." He let it hang.

"Well." Emily put her hands together on the table. "There are only a few possibilities. Did *you* tell them?"

He smiled. "No."

"Nothing in the transcripts even hinted at a prior investigation."

"My lawyer tried to bring it up, and the judge shut him down. Immaterial."

"True enough. But the question remains, and the likeliest possibility—well, you've no doubt thought it through."

"Yes." Seven years.

"So." She studied his face. "Who?"

"I don't know."

"Your three partners. One of them dimed you out."

Finn waited, wondering if she would—

"Or Wes," she added.

She would.

"He didn't know," Finn said. "I mean, he knew *what* we were doing—hell, he funded it. But I never told him where or when."

"The other three had no reason, either," Emily said.

The waitress dropped the check on her way past. The old guy at the counter started a conversation with her—grazing rights, politics, something. He did most of the talking.

"Thanks for lunch," Finn said.

"What are you going to do now?"

He shrugged. "Look up some old friends, maybe. You know. Catch up."

"Yeah." Emily gave him a knowing look as they stood from the booth. "One thing."

"What?"

She recited a phone number starting with 917. "Don't write it down, please."

"What if I forget?"

"I read your file, Finn. You don't forget anything."

"Whose is it?"

"Mine." She held out her hand again. This time Finn was quicker on the draw. They held on a few seconds longer, and when she let go, the sensation of warmth and pressure stayed in his hand.

"Have a safe trip back."

"I was wondering . . ." Emily said.

"Yes?"

"You could have given Wes up. Any time before sentencing, it probably would have cut those seven years back some."

"They asked."

When Finn didn't say anything more, Emily nodded. "Call me sometime if you want to talk."

"To Wes?"

"Whoever." Her crooked smile flashed again, and she was gone.

CHAPTER THREE

Two days later, Finn stepped from an almost-empty GCT bus into a humid Georgia morning. The bus spewed exhaust and ground away, disappearing into Gwinnett County suburbia. Finn yawned and rubbed grit from his eyes, squinting in the bright sunshine.

And frowned.

To the extent he had a plan, it wasn't complicated. He was going to talk to Jake. Then talk to Asher. Then Corman. And then he figured he'd know.

After that, there were options, but first, he had to *know*.

Of course, to travel around the country looking up his old pals, he needed money. Driver's license long since expired, no relatives still talking to him, the eight hundred bucks evaporating faster than he could keep track. When did everything get so damned expensive? Five dollars for a cup of *coffee*?

Fortunately, he had a safe-deposit box here at Gwinnett Trust Bank. It was the only one the prosecutors didn't find—even his lawyer didn't know about it, thank God, or Finn would truly be down to nothing. But here, in the anonymous Atlanta suburbs, he'd hidden away sixty thousand dollars. Once, it hadn't seemed like so much, not when he was knocking down three or four times that on every job. But now—a fortune.

The problem was that Gwinnett Trust Bank no longer seemed to exist.

Finn frowned.

The building was as he remembered, faux-Federal brick with a drive-through. The sign on the facade, however, read NORCROSS NATIONAL CREDIT UNION. A recent change; lighter patches in the brickwork's pointing revealed where the earlier, larger sign had been attached.

He hesitated another moment, then brushed his hands on his pants and went inside.

"You'll have to contact the state's abandoned property office."

The bank officer was a woman about Finn's age. She smiled apologetically. "I'm sorry."

"But—what do you mean? They just shut my bank down?"

"Almost five years ago. The FDIC came in Friday afternoon, and it was under federal receivership by Monday."

"I don't understand." He looked around, out the glass walls of the woman's tiny office. "It all looks the same. Same counters, same teller row—"

"We didn't acquire Gwinnett Trust." She made a serious face. "No one did. Too small and too bankrupt. So the regulators had to act. Of course, no one lost any money. You should have received a notification—did you have an account with them?"

"Just the safe-deposit box." Finn was still stunned.

"Even so. They would have contacted you. If you didn't respond, the box's contents would have been turned over to the state."

Of course they wouldn't have been able to contact him, since he'd used a false ID. He started to put his face in his hands, stopped.

"Georgia's had more bank closures than any other state." The woman sounded sorry. "But I have to say it's been good for credit unions. We opened this branch after Gwinnett Trust folded."

"You think Georgia will give me my money back?"

"Oh, certainly. There's a whole appeals process. Of course, they're backed up some, I hear. But you should be able to recover everything in about eighteen months."

Finn stared at her. "A year and a half?"

"More or less. As I say, they're kind of overwhelmed now."

"But I need my money now!"

"I'm sorry." She appeared unfazed. Probably, she had to announce bad news to penniless, homeless, former members of the American middle class all day long. "It's just how things work."

Outside, he stood in the humidity, headache thrumming.

Thinking.

It took half an hour to find a pay phone, a battered relic outside a dry cleaner's in a fading strip mall. The handset, black and in the sun, was almost too hot to hold. It demanded three quarters before grudgingly providing a dial tone.

Finn had no trouble remembering the number, but he paused, hand hovering above the hook for a moment. *Desperate people make bad partners*, he'd said to Emily.

Actually, they tended to make bad decisions, period. But an image of her face rose in his mind.

He dialed and listened for the ring.

CHAPTER FOUR

Kayo drifted to work at his usual time, around two p.m., breakfast in one hand and a cigarette in the other. The take-out French toast was folded around syrup, powdered sugar, and slices of orange, which he knew Millz would give him shit about, but fuck him anyway. Millz usually had a churro, and what was that, fried dough, right? Same thing.

"Yo." Millz was already inside Port Authority. It was a typical day for early November—damp, cold, sleeting—and they certainly weren't going to stand around outside. Kayo didn't care much one way or the other, and he had a good coat. Blue and black, some kind of mountain climber waterproof shit; he ever got tired of hustling bridge-and-tunnel farmboys, he could go be a K2 sherpa. But the point was, only the desperately fucked up were willing to transact in thirty-seven-degree rain, not to mention the goods got all wet. Better to be inside and dry.

"Nico get you the new cards yet?" Kayo asked.

Millz shrugged. "Dunno."

"Guess it don't matter." The place to sell fake Metrocards was outside the station, naturally, not inside. Not business for today.

Kayo finished his French toast and dropped its foil wrapper into a massive, bombproof trashcan. They meandered down the corridor. Humanity flowed along with them: students carrying instrument cases, working men in damp canvas jackets, business-men in shined shoes. Almost no one wore a suit anymore. Country going to hell.

On the main concourse, they split up. Kayo found an eddy in the stream of people, where the crowd slowed to maneuver a corner. He planted himself there and began the low, monotonous pitch, just loud enough to catch someone's attention if they wanted it to be caught: "Oxy, silver star, hydro. Weed? Got oxy . . ."

Not that he *really* had any of that. Anyone dumb enough to hand over a twenty, he'd nod to Millz across the concourse all secret agent–like, and Millz would be more than happy to pass them a little bag of catnip or twenty fake Adderall pills. Not a lot of money to lose, and though it wasn't a lot to earn, either, you mostly didn't go to Rikers.

Business was slow. The afternoon wore on.

Millz wandered over, parting the crowd. He was tall and wide and slow-looking, and people tended to get out of his way.

"Fuck it," he said.

"Yeah." Kayo nodded. "Maybe we go check out the buses, huh?"

They went down and watched the gates. Luck must have turned. Five minutes, and they both saw the guy at the same time.

"Washington just got in," Millz said.

"He didn't have to get on there."

The man was average height, stubbly, in an obviously new pair of plain tan pants and a short-sleeved white shirt. Underdressed for the city in November. He carried a small plastic handle bag and a bottle of water. He looked around, eyeing the platform, the advertising, the masses of people and the bustle, hesitated, then moved away.

They followed.

He stopped at a souvenir shop, deep in the subterranean Port Authority warren, and bought a Giants windbreaker and cheap ball cap. Loose cash from his left pocket—Kayo taking mental notes. A few words with the vendor, who gestured down the hall.

But not toward the exit. Deeper, and down one more level.

"This gonna be too easy," Millz said.

The man went into a bathroom fifty feet ahead of them. Millz and Kayo lingered near the door for a minute, not exactly blocking it, but casually discouraging anyone who might suddenly be inclined to take a piss. Not that this bathroom saw much traffic. Tourist restrooms were upstairs, clean and shiny.

This one was more of a . . . business center for the informal economy.

Inside the man was brushing his teeth at the sink. Brushing his *teeth*! Kayo stifled a laugh. He glanced sideways. The stalls all had their doors removed. In one, a guy slept clutching a dirty suitcase tied with plastic twine.

Millz went left, Kayo right, and they stopped six feet from the man's back. He saw them in the metal mirror, spat, rinsed the brush, and turned around. He left the plastic carry bag on the sink's edge.

"How you doing?" Kayo put up a big grin.

"No."

"Got a cigarette?"

The man looked at him, and Kayo frowned slightly. The guy showed absolutely no sign of fear, just stood there all relaxed.

"Then how about a dollar." He didn't make it a question.

"No."

A long moment stretched out. The sleeper stirred, scraping his suitcase on the stall partition. No one looked his way.

"Okay," Millz said, and stepped forward—

But Kayo put a hand in the air. "Hold up."

Millz caught his tone and stopped. "What?"

"Look at his hand."

The man still held his toothbrush, but reversed: handle out, thumb along the edge, the end poking from his fist. He flicked his eyes between them, started to smile. Kayo checked his feet, saw one forward, one a little back and turned out, knees bent just enough.

Close up he didn't look so runty, either. Rangy. Some muscle there.

Kayo nodded. "Toothbrush," he said.

"Uh-huh."

"Used one like that before, have you?"

Millz grunted. "The fuck you talking about?"

The man glanced his way, then back to Kayo. "Not exactly," he said. "Didn't have a chance to sharpen this one."

Someone walked in behind them, turned, and left immediately. Footsteps and rumbling from the corridor outside echoed off the ancient ceramic tiles. Kayo crossed his arms.

"Where?" he said.

The man shrugged. "New Mexico."

"Federal?"

"State."

"Just get out?" After getting a nod: "What you doing here?"

"Came to the Big Apple to make my fortune."

Kayo decided. He turned to Millz and said, "Ain't worth it."

Millz didn't move. "Fuck him."

"How much you think he's carrying? Five dollars, I bet."

"Six," the man said. He seemed amused. "And change. Twenty-three for a hoodie? That's highway robbery."

"He threw in the cap, though."

For the first time, the man seemed impressed. "You were watching."

Millz looked at Kayo. "Motherfucker knows."

"Don't matter." He backed a couple steps. "We leaving you in peace."

"Thanks." Still calm and relaxed. "I thought they cleaned up this city. Broken windows, all that? No offense, but you guys are, like, 1978."

"Getting by. Just getting by." Kayo grinned again. "Like everyone else."

But before they were out the door the man called after them. "Hey."

Kayo looked back. "Yeah?"

"Maybe you can point me the right way. Being Welcome Wagon and all."

Millz growled, but Kayo didn't take offense. You had to like someone that confident. "What, you need some show tickets? Dinner reservations? Carriage ride at the park?"

"Six bucks, like I said. That's not going to get me a room at the Plaza." He pocketed the toothbrush. "Got any recommendations?"

CHAPTER FIVE

The vehicle was a vintage Land Rover—one of the old ones, painted in surplus military drab. Round headlights between oversize wheel wells. Like something out of a 1960s *National Geographic* documentary, jouncing across the Sahel, oryx and gazelles scattering.

But here it was on East Forty-First, pulling to the curb in front of Finn. Nine a.m. Saturday morning. Up close, he could see it had been immaculately maintained: the finish smooth and unblemished, window glass tinted dark as obsidian. The spare tire, mounted on the hood, was factory new, washed clean of any possible speck even between the treads.

The Rover was authentic in the same way as a ten-grand distressed leather bomber jacket.

Emily leaned over, one hand on the steering wheel, and pushed open the passenger door.

"Good morning."

"Thanks." Finn climbed in. The seats looked original, stiff and upright, but were upholstered in soft leather. "Nice ride."

She laughed. "It's his."

"Doesn't look like he actually goes on safari, though."

"Two hundred forty thousand dollars and a custom rebuild? I should think not."

"Nice that he gives you the keys."

"I'm a careful driver."

She looked as good as Finn remembered. A warm, pale-blue sweater, black pants fitted like tights, dark scarf wrapped just so.

"Where are we going?"

"Long Island." She glanced at him, then lowered a pair of sunglasses back into place and turned her attention to the road. "He prefers to be inconspicuous."

"In *this*?"

The Land Rover accelerated into traffic, engine loud and not very smooth. Totally overhauled maybe, but still original. "You'll see."

Whatever Wes wanted, it would be on the wrong side of the law. On the other hand, Finn needed the money. Anyway, perhaps Wes felt he owed Finn something. Maybe he was going to offer a briefcase full of cash to make up for the seven years of Finn's life lost.

Sure.

Emily turned right onto Second Avenue. Light traffic, but it was the weekend. Cold November sunshine glittered.

"Where are you staying?" she asked.

"With friends."

"That's good."

In fact, he'd checked into the Bellevue Shelter just before they closed for the night. Kayo—that was the would-be mugger's name—gave him directions. It sounded like he knew the place better than he admitted. The facility was huge and filthy, the intake processing slow, the mass of men noticeably unwashed. His bed was clean and surprisingly comfortable, but twenty cots had been pushed into a room sized for half that, and the guy next to him had coughed endlessly.

"What exactly do you do for Wes?" he asked. "Besides driving his cars?"

"*Hmm.*" Like it was a hard question.

"Manage investments? Keep the books?"

She thought. "Let's say, ah . . . chief compliance officer."

"What? Compliance with law and regulation?" Wes certainly didn't care—maybe he had to hire someone who did.

"Not exactly." They entered a line of cars, all slowing for the Midtown Tunnel portal. "More like making sure that *reality* complies with Wes's *desires*. If you see what I mean."

Once inside the tunnel, their speed increased again. The Land Rover was noisy, its suspension stiff. Finn leaned back in the hard seat, trying to get comfortable. When they emerged a few minutes later, back into bright daylight, he closed his eyes.

They drove for fifty minutes, out 495 and then south on a series of smaller but well-paved and fast-moving roads. Finn dozed, lulled by the Rover's rattle and road noise. Emily seemed to feel no need for conversation.

When she slowed, turned right, and braked to a stop, Finn came back alert, straightening in the seat. A stoplight, red. The area was suburban, with large houses and lawns concealed by stands of trees. At the next corner, a gas station and a chain coffee shop. Emily drove the speed limit, glancing at her phone once or twice.

"There," she said. They topped a rise and she slowed, reading the signs.

"No," said Finn. "Really?"

"Yes."

It was a hospital. Large, busy. The main building was seven stories, with newer additions on both sides and more office-park glass visible behind. The emergency entrance to the left, sheltered under a broad colonnade, two ambulances parked nearby. The main doors were opposite, before a broad expanse of parking lot.

"Okay," Finn said. "How sick is he?"

Emily laughed. "Not at all."

She didn't enter the main parking area but went the other way to an overflow lot across the street. It was up a small hill, cleared from a stand of forest that no doubt shielded views from neighboring manors. Emily nosed into a parking space at the far corner shaded by evergreens and looking directly down at the hospital.

"It's a charity road rally," she said. "Rich people driving fancy cars on a three-hour course. They end here."

"And what, they're expecting casualties?" But when Finn studied the lot, he saw that half the spaces had been set off with cones and fluorescent tape. A temporary awning sheltered a long table and a dozen chairs. From two hundred yards away, the details were hard to make out, but a number of people stood, talking with one another or staring at their phones.

"It's a fund-raiser for the hospital, duh."

"Ah. And Wes is driving?"

"He should be here soon. They left Jones Beach at ten o'clock."

Finn considered. "I thought you said a three-hour route. It's not a race, is it?"

"No." Emily checked her phone. "Still, Wes hates to lose."

"But if they're not racing—"

"And he's not the only one."

Far away, flashing lights caught his eye. An ambulance, topping a rise a half mile away, barely more than a blue-and-orange strobe at the distance.

"A fund-raiser," Finn said. "How much is Wes donating?"

"Nothing, I expect."

No surprise. "How does that work?"

"A thousand dollars per car. But Wes sits on the board." Emily glanced his way. "Charity is kind of *theoretical* to Wes, you know?"

"I'll keep that in mind."

As the ambulance approached, a car appeared behind it—a shiny silver blur, low to the ground. The car eased right, looking to pass, but the blacktop was narrow, solid yellow lines down the middle.

"Huh." Emily sounded surprised. "That's not Wes."

The silver car abruptly pulled out, accelerating past the ambulance. Finn tried to estimate speeds—sixty, seventy miles an hour? Slow for the Indy 500, but way too fast for—

"There."

A red car shot into view, passing the ambulance on its right. There wasn't even a breakdown lane—not on this suburban, half-residential road—just a wider bit behind a white line.

The ambulance jinked left, its driver caught by surprise, then immediately back when the silver car's horn blared. For an instant, all three vehicles were abreast, tearing toward the hospital at three times the speed limit.

The silver car pulled ahead and started to return to its lane. The red car blew its own horn and cut in. The ambulance braked hard, starting to fishtail, wheels squealing, falling back as the two cars converged in front of it.

"Jesus," muttered Finn.

A two-second game of chicken. The silver car ran a length ahead, but the red car was moving faster.

A cross street ahead of them, stop signs and a white SUV approaching. The ambulance hit its full range of sound effects: siren, whoops, blares. The two sports cars accelerated, inches apart, flashing through the intersection as the SUV slammed to a stop.

The silver car gave up, fading back and falling in behind.

Five seconds later, the red car entered the final curve, still far over the speed limit. Finn heard Emily's breath catch. At the last instant, brake lights glowed and the car screamed sideways, sliding into a long skidding turn that somehow put it through the hospital's lot entrance with about an inch to spare. Two hundred yards of smoking rubber.

And then it stopped, right at the first orange cone. A few seconds later, the silver car entered, still too fast but far more carefully, and pulled up alongside. Everyone in the lot turned to stare, all conversations halted.

Behind them, the ambulance turned into the emergency entrance loop, sirens off.

"Wes, right?" said Finn. "In the red car."

"It's a Lamborghini."

"Of course."

Emily laughed and pulled out her phone. "I'll let him know we're here."

CHAPTER SIX

Finn had to get into the rear seat, cramped and even less comfortable than the front. Emily stayed behind the wheel. Wes pulled the door shut and sat sideways.

He looked the same to Finn, even after seven years: broad shoulders and iron-gray hair in an old-fashioned flattop, a discreet gray jacket over a white button-down. He still wore his driving gloves.

"Finn." They shook hands awkwardly over the seats. "You look good. Real good."

"Clean living and exercise."

"How was it in there? You see stuff on television. The internet."

Finn shrugged slightly, said nothing.

"Anyway, sorry to bring you all the way here," Wes said, not appearing sorry. "Always better to talk in private."

"That was some entrance."

"Wasn't it?" He grinned. "Frank was driving like an asshole. Couldn't let that go."

Emily sighed. "Might want to get to the point, boss. They're all probably wondering what you're doing up here."

"Fuck 'em." But Wes reached into his jacket and passed Finn a small, dull silver bar. "Take a look at this."

It was surprisingly heavy, though lighter than gold would have been, cast with smoothed edges and corners. No markings. "Platinum?" Finn guessed.

"Rhodium."

Finn waited. "Okay."

"Know what it's worth?"

"No idea."

"About nineteen hundred an ounce today in the spot market. Better than gold. Gram for gram, rhodium is the most expensive metal on the planet."

Finn looked at the ingot in his palm. "This feels like a couple of pounds—"

"A shade under one kilogram."

"Which means it's worth, um . . ."

"Sixty thousand dollars." Emily did the math in her head in less than a second.

"Holy *mother*."

"Nice, huh?" Wes held out his hand and Finn passed it back, reluctantly.

"You're in the market?"

"Yes. My guys, they think the price overcorrected. When China comes out of its slump, the sky's the limit again. So we went in and bought." His smile disappeared. "A lot."

"Too much?"

"No." No hesitation. "We're absolutely going to make money. We just have to wait a year or two."

Finn considered. "Where is it? Stacked in your garage?"

"That's an excellent question," Wes said. "We keep our inventory in a third-party vault. Fifty million dollars' worth."

"Ah." The first indication of where Finn might enter the conversation. "That dollar value, if rhodium weighs about the same as gold, works out to be, um . . ."

"Seven hundred and fifty kilograms." Emily had the answer first again.

"Right."

Wes turned the ingot over in his left hand, his right withdrawing a heavy awl from another jacket pocket. "Here's the issue," he said. "Watch."

He held the awl firmly and scratched a rough gash in the metal. Finn leaned over the seatback to peer more closely.

Under a surface layer of matte silver, the interior seemed to be different: dull black and perhaps softer.

A pause. "Counterfeit," Wes said finally. "Not the only one, either."

Finn raised an eyebrow. "So it's not worth sixty grand after all."

That earned an unamused snort. "No."

"Why did you buy them?"

"By mistake, of course!" Wes ran a hand through his buzz cut. "One of my guys was in the vault, checking counts before the auditors went through. Somehow he dropped one, and it scratched off a corner."

"How do you counterfeit an ingot?"

"Cast a block of lead and dip it in melted rhodium sponge." Wes shook his head. "Hard to believe it's that easy, but lead's density is close enough for the control scales they use in the vault."

Finn didn't see the problem. "So call up the seller and complain," he said. "Send it back."

"Yeah, well, that's not so easy. We were buying all over the place—mostly South Africa, but Russia, too. Zimbabwe. You know how it goes."

"Uh-huh." Shady sellers, illegal deals, tax evasion, maybe violation of foreign ex-im controls. In those countries, bribery and subornation were simply how business got done. Of course, US prosecutors didn't always see it that way. "No recourse, huh?"

"Even if it were possible, the very last thing I'm going to do is announce to the world that we got screwed." Wes glared. "Every vulture out there would start circling."

"Well . . . then just sell off the bad ones yourself. Buyer beware and all that."

"Reputational risk." Wes shook his head. "A black-market operator in Harare doesn't give a shit, but if *I* sell bad metal, then either I'm a dupe or a fraud or both. The fucking hyenas would pick us clean."

They fell silent. Outside the Rover, sunlight reflected painfully from the parade of expensive, exotic, low-slung cars filling the lot below them.

"Not to mention," said Emily, "what do you think happens if news breaks that some rhodium stock is counterfeit? What's the market going to do? Not knowing how *much* is affected, or where?"

"Ahhh." Finn nodded. "Everyone but everyone is going to sell. Right? Immediately. Because they might be sitting on a pile of lead, too. Dump it as fast as possible. And then—"

"Prices will freefall."

"Exactly." Wes looked deeply unhappy. "Right after we've built up a . . . very substantial position. That *cannot* be allowed to happen."

Finn looked at him and started to figure out how why he was here. "You can't sell it," he said slowly. "You don't want to sit on it."

"The fakes are the problem."

"You need to make them go away."

"Yes."

"You want *me* to make them go away."

Wes nodded. "You're the best in the business."

The Rover's interior had become cold. Emily stirred herself and switched on the ignition, blowers starting up again.

"Aren't you insured?"

"Doesn't matter." Wes's grin came back, though at lower wattage. "You're only going to move the counterfeits."

Finn thought about that. "Move?" he said. "Not steal?"

"Yes."

"Hmm." He remembered now how much Wes liked a tricky plot. "Where?"

"To the neighbor's."

The way Wes explained it, the vault provided different options, depending on how much material you intended to store. Small amounts could stay in oversize safe-deposit boxes—double-keyed, heavy minisafes—but larger volumes required more space, so you could also rent your own five-by-five square of real estate. The cages were separated by floor-to-ceiling bars—"so the cameras can see everything," Wes said—and locked.

"We have one of the larger units, sixty square feet. Thing is, right alongside, someone is storing exactly the same material—racks of rhodium ingots."

"That's some coincidence."

Wes shrugged. "It's another commodities firm, and I know the guys there—when I started building up stock and needed to find a place, they recommended it. There aren't *that* many storage facilities specializing in long-term metal. Once, I happened to be inside at the same time they were, and we joked about it. Right through the cage."

Finn started to get the picture. "So what you want—"

"Sneak in and swap the bars. One to one. Do it right and no one will ever know."

"This other company—they might be upset if they find the counterfeits."

"Probably." Another shrug. "I sure was."

Undoubtedly true.

"The way you've described it." Finn stopped. "I don't know if it's possible to get in and out undetected."

"No, no, that's the great thing about this idea." Wes leaned sideways in his seat, hands chopping the air with enthusiasm. "If there's a problem, you just finish the switch and leave quick. Hell, you could even trip an alarm on the way out if you wanted. The rent-a-cops will flood in—and discover that *nothing was actually taken*."

"No harm, no foul." Finn squinted. "Talk about it like that, it's almost legal."

"Exactly!"

"And a few weeks later, you sell everything off, right? Because not only are you the only trader who knows there might be counterfeits in the supply, but you're also now certain that your stock, at least, is one hundred percent good."

"Or maybe we hold out, like we originally planned." Wes nodded. "Either way, we're good."

"If you don't need anything stolen, why do you need me?"

"Because even if nothing leaves the vault, it still requires a degree of, ah, specialized talent that's damned hard to find." He twisted around and looked intently into Finn's eyes. "And because I trust you. Anyone else might fuck it up."

Finn didn't say yes, and he didn't say no. "How much?"

"Seventy-five thousand dollars." He said it slowly, like a dramatic reveal.

"What?" Frowning.

"For a little planning and a few hours' work, maybe?" Wes moved his hands apart, like, *come on.*

"And the chance of going back to jail for another decade." Finn shook his head.

"Seventy-five's already a substantial risk premium, but all right. A hundred."

Suddenly, they were bargaining. Finn kept his exterior calm—prison had been good training—but possibilities unfolded in his mind.

It was awfully fast to be getting back in, already talking about another job. He was still readapting, finding his way in a world that—even after just seven years—was faster, harsher, and less forgiving. And to think about signing up with Wes again, that was just *stupid.* Still, one fact of his personal situation stood above the rest.

He needed money.

"Six hundred, and another fifty for expenses," he said. "Up front."

The negotiations went on a few minutes, though it felt pro forma. They'd worked together twice before, and Wes didn't press hard.

The elephant in the room was that Finn and his partners had paid a much, much higher price for the last job. Maybe Wes felt an obligation, maybe he didn't, but he seemed willing to pretend. It didn't take long before they ended up at four fifty.

Seven times Finn's retirement fund, which had been stolen away by the State of Georgia.

They didn't shake hands. "I'll think about it," Finn said.

"Not long." Wes pocketed the ingot and the awl. "The more time passes, the riskier it becomes for me. Emily will show you the setup, tell you the details. You figure out if it's even possible. Might not be, I guess."

A little obvious, that. Finn looked at Emily. "You know where the vault is?"

"Yup."

"Going forward, Emily's your contact," Wes said. "Tell her what you need, but—you know—keep it brief, right? We all have different jobs. They don't need to intersect any more than necessary."

He got out, closed the Rover's door carefully, and walked back toward the lower lot. Halfway down, he waved to someone, jacket blowing open in the winter breeze. He'd never removed his driving gloves.

Finn moved back to the front seat. He looked at Emily.

"What do *you* think?" he said.

"Seems a little complicated, doesn't it?"

"Yeah."

She withdrew a plain folder from her bag and handed it over, then put the Rover in gear. "The vault. Take a look, but you can't keep it."

"First Federal Depository, Inc." He read from the first page. "They're in New Jersey."

"It's . . . eleven forty. I'm clear the rest of the day." She backed out of their parking space and turned toward the exit. "What do you say? Want to go take a look?"

CHAPTER SEVEN

A t first, the vault appeared easy.

They drove across the lower tip of Manhattan—not too bad, midday—into the Holland Tunnel and through Jersey City. Skirting the vast Newark port facilities, Finn began to wonder, and his skepticism verged on disbelief when Emily slowed down.

"Inside," she said, pointing over a long fence topped with razor wire.

"That's a *railroad* yard." Stating the obvious. The side road was slightly elevated, looking down into an elongated bowl more than a mile across. Through the fence, they could see rail sidings filled with hundreds of freight cars. Sunlight reflected from the mirrored glass of a control tower. A pall of diesel drifted from innumerable, rumbling locomotives.

"That's right." Emily got the Rover moving again. "And the storage facility is . . . right there. See that concrete building?"

It wasn't much—single story, windowless, nondescript. It sat fifty yards in, separated from them by the fence, a gravel access road, and two tracks running along the edge of the property. Compared to the warehouses lining the avenue across from the yard, it looked like a gardening shed.

"Maybe this is a dumb question," Finn said, "but what the *hell* is a precious-metals vault doing in there?"

"Happenstance. When the financial crisis hit, everyone but every-one started buying gold. If you're not a wacky bird, you don't store it under your bed, and the commercial vaults started filling up."

"'Wacky bird'?"

She ignored him. "The railroads already carry valuable stuff, now and then—high-end industrial ceramics, lab chemicals, plati-num, whatever. Pennsylvania Southern was doing enough that they needed a secure building for transshipment."

"Huh."

"When the company figured out they could make real money renting out vault space, they expanded it, added high-tech security, and started advertising." Emily slowed again, approaching the yard's entrance. "Being inside an already-controlled perimeter made the service even more attractive."

A slow lane had been added along the fence, ending at a gate-house with a guard and a striped boom. One vehicle was in front of them, a battered white pickup with Penn Southern's logo on the door. The guard waved it through, then lowered the boom again. Emily came to a stop and opened her window.

"Emily Hale, Heart Pine Capital," she said. "We have—"

He interrupted. "ID?"

She handed over a driver's license. He studied it and tapped at a keyboard. Finn sat quietly, watching.

"Your plate's not in the system." The guard gestured slightly toward the front of their car.

"It's a company car."

"Get it registered before next time, please." He pushed a control and the boom raised. "Go straight in. You're not authorized out of the vehicle except at the vault."

"Thank you." She eased the car forward. They passed the control tower and admin building and continued straight into the yard.

"You know," said Finn, "ever since 9/11, security is totally out of control on things like, oh, for instance, rail yards. You got feds, you got the state, you probably got like a billion taxpayer dollars buying drones and guns and armor to protect the trains in here."

Emily nodded. "And the vault itself has three-foot concrete

walls, reinforced of course, and an even thicker floor. It's mostly underground."

"You have the plans?"

"Due diligence." She parked in a smaller lot in front of the bunker. "Before Wes started putting inventory there, he asked for an overview. Not blueprint level but thorough."

A truck ramp descended to an underground entrance alongside the parking lot. Finn tried to get a look without being too obvious. Spike strips, heavy pylons, possibly an overhead portcullis . . . He shook his head.

Inside, another guard in a neat blue uniform took their IDs—Finn's, too, this time—ran them through a scanner, and printed temporary badges.

"Make sure they're visible at all times," he said.

And now the vault began to seem impossible. Through an electronic turnstile to an elevator—wide as a freight elevator, but clean and shiny—from which they debarked into a second reception zone. Two guards, one behind bullet-resistant glass, examined their badges, cross-checked, and waved them into a mantrap.

"One at a time, door will close behind you, five seconds, door will open at the other side." The guard had obviously repeated the refrain many, many times.

Emily went first. Finn followed—and they still weren't in. Another anteroom, one more guard.

"Cubby nineteen," he said, looking from his computer monitor. "I'll escort you in."

Cameras absolutely everywhere. Heat sensors. Motion detectors behind light mesh screens.

The final door was total Hollywood: an enormous slab of steel ten inches thick with locking pins thicker than Finn's wrist that fit into matched holes around the frame. Two metal hatch wheels and an electronic display—LED digits, soft blue glow—completed the picture.

The door hung open, as it probably did throughout the working day. The guard led them through.

The vault's interior was surprisingly open, maybe five thousand square feet, somewhere between a bodega and a small grocery. The cages—*cubbies*, Finn amended to himself—were separated by half-inch tempered steel rods, set vertically two inches apart and crossed every six inches by a flat containment bar.

The guard unlocked their door. Medeco keyways. Finn sighed to himself. Probably to impress the customers, but come on, couldn't they have cheaped out *anywhere*?

He stood idly, pretending not to study every detail he could see, while Emily puttered at the racks. Wes was nuts—absolutely nothing about this would be easy, if it was possible at all.

Finn caught Emily's eye. She smiled and crooked an eyebrow, like, *What do you think? Nice, huh?*

Half a mil wasn't near enough to fix Wes's fuckup for him.

He hadn't thought it through.

Show up at Jake's doorstep, or brace Asher in some bar, or haul Corman out of a gym—the guilty one wasn't going to just up and confess. Fantasies of confrontation and truth were just that, fantasies. Prison time had toughened Finn, sure. Probably too much. But it hadn't made him into some kind of human lie detector.

On the other hand, suppose they all got back together, back for one more job. Especially one as hard as Wes's vault—they'd be living on top of one another for weeks, even months, setting it up. All that time together and *something* would slip. All Finn had to do was pay attention and be patient.

Which, as it happened, were two skills that prison had taught him.

Did Wes really think he'd do it for the measly payday on offer? Or did he think that Finn would break in and then rob the place anyway? Maybe that was the plan—get his problem fixed on the cheap. Look at it that way, Wes might figure he wouldn't have to pay Finn at all.

Lots of balls were going into the air.

Not to mention one other consideration. One other reason Finn was maybe a shade too keen to step up. One other possibility that he'd found himself thinking about far too much over the last couple of days.

Perhaps the most important one of all—or so it felt.

X   X   X

Emily dropped him off at the Exchange Place PATH station.

"Sure I can't drive you back into the city?"

"No thanks. Things to do."

"You know, to me, it looked impossible."

"Nothing's impossible."

"That door, like two feet of solid steel? All the guards?"

Finn laughed. "The door is pure theatre. The *walls* are what matter. As for the guards—their uniforms said 'Stormwall.' I'm sure that's a private firm."

"So?"

"So they were probably low bid. Those guys look good, but it's just more showbiz."

Emily watched him for a long moment.

"Where did you get the driver's license?"

"What?"

"No fixed address that I know of. You were in jail less than a month ago. How'd you manage a legitimate license?"

"You pay attention, don't you?" *Have to be careful*, Finn thought. He'd always been a sucker for a smart woman. "Watch the details, think about things."

"Yeah. Just like you."

"You notice the state it was from, too?"

"Georgia."

"Yup." He nodded. "Boardinghouse I was in. I kind of faked up a lease. That was good enough for residency. Had to take the driving test, though. Almost failed the parallel parking."

"You were a little rusty?"

"Yeah, you could say that."

A car blew its horn behind them. Emily was in a drop-off zone, but people were always impatient.

"One other thing . . ." she said.

Finn had unclicked his seat belt. "Yes?"

"That license has your real name on it." She continued to study him with a somewhat unnerving intensity. "And you weren't careful inside the vault—opened handles, touched things, handled the racks."

"Oh, that." He looked back at her. "What do *you* figure?"

"You left fingerprints and DNA everywhere."

"Uh-huh."

"So maybe you don't care, because you have no intention whatsoever of taking Wes up."

"Maybe."

The moment stretched.

"But *maybe* . . . say you do it after all, and CSI goes through with a microscope, and they find all kinds of physical evidence." She nodded. "You have an alibi. You were already there."

He smiled. "Even a bad lawyer couldn't lose that one."

"Easier than, I don't know, a pair of gloves?"

"The technology they have today—it's really, really hard to avoid leaving a trace for the detectives. And juries love that stuff."

"Really?"

Finn paused. "Well, that's what I heard, anyway. Sit in prison for a few years, it's just one extended seminar in practical lawbreaking."

"You're saying you could do it."

"Actually, I'm not sure," Finn said. "But it sure looks fun."

CHAPTER EIGHT

FOUR DAYS LATER

Finn drove a nine-year-old Ford F-150 down Milnor Street in northeast Philadelphia. He squinted through streaks and smears of rainwater on the windshield, checking signs and parking lots. A cold fog had turned slowly to drizzle as the day wore on, and the wipers were shot. Finn had bought the truck out of the ten grand Wes advanced him. He still had most of it left.

Now he slowed, figuring it had to be close. Coolidge Steel Fabricators. Baltic Plumbing. Blank cement or cinder-block buildings, barbed-wire fences around cracked asphalt.

The pickup bumped over a rough patch, and he saw his destination: Perricona Tooling & Precision. It sat small between a metals recycler on one side—a large yard of rusting junk—and a hot-dip galvanizing operation on the other. The galvanizing shop was a three-story building of corrugated metal siding, eye-watering vapor wisping from the cracks.

Two vehicles sat in front of the machine shop. One was another pickup, rust edging the wheel wells and PERRICONA on the door. The other . . . the other was a beat-up little hatchback with an OBAMA 2008 bumper sticker and what looked like a child's car seat sticking up in the rear.

Finn kept going. A hundred feet on, he found a place to park on the far side of the recycler. He backed in, killed the engine, and sat, peering across a lot full of ancient, flaking radiators packed together like overcrowded tombstones.

It *was* a toddler seat.

Not what one might expect for a customer of Perricona Tooling. Finn had worked blue-collar trades his entire life, and he knew what was important. A guy would go without housing, without food, without beer, rather than show up in what looked like his girlfriend's car.

He waited. The drizzle turned to rain.

Six minutes later, Perricona's door opened, and a young man emerged holding a small cardboard box. Plain dark pants and a work jacket over an unmarked T-shirt—not so different from what Finn was wearing. Twenty years old, maybe. He frowned at the rain, then stepped quickly to the hatchback. The vehicle sagged noticeably from his weight when he got in, then coughed to life and drove off.

Finn waited another twenty minutes, but nothing happened. When the rain slackened, he got out and walked past the radiator graveyard. Grime spattered off gravel in Perricona's lot.

The machine shop was dim inside. Tools filled the space, as familiar to Finn as an old pair of boots: lathes, shapers, planers, presses. Everything quiet and faintly covered in dust.

A man with safety glasses pushed up on his head stood at a screw machine, studying a pair of calipers. He glanced at Finn, did a double take.

"I'll be fucked." He dropped the calipers and swung forward, grinning.

"Hiya, Jake."

"Jesus, Finn, no warning . . ."

What the hell, the handshake turned into a man-type hug, hands slapping backs. After a few seconds, they let go simultaneously.

A little less hair, a little more gut, but Jake appeared about the same as the last time Finn had seen him, sitting on the witness stand, refusing to meet anyone's eye. They'd worked together for two decades, close as brothers or soldiers, but when the New

Mexico prosecutors started offering deals, Jake had cracked
straightaway.

As a reward, he was released five years earlier than Finn.

"Come on in, man, sit down." Jake pulled some metal chairs
from the computer table. "I wrote you a letter when I got out, that's
how you found me, right?'

"They weren't real good about passing on the mail."

"I felt bad."

Finn nodded. "Not your fault."

"I know what you said, but still."

Finn always told them, if something goes wrong, you do what's
right. We don't shoot anybody, we don't knock people around, we're
just picking stuff up. No one's getting thirty years for a pile of scrap
metal. The authorities want you to talk, go ahead and talk.

"You only gave them the one job," Finn said. "And I was the one
in charge, so fair enough."

"Seven years." Jake sighed. "I'm sorry, man."

He found some Stewart's Root Beer, popped the bottles open off
the edge of the desk. Rain drummed on the roof.

"Shop looks nice," Finn said.

"There's a reentry program." Jake handed him a bottle. "This vol-
unteer used to come into the pen, help us write résumés and shit.
She told me about it. They helped me get the licenses, all that."

Starting the business would have taken cash, too. Jake had
always been careful with his money, putting some aside after every
job. Planning ahead. No surprise he'd done a better job than Finn
hiding it from the law. Sure.

Or maybe Jake had gotten paid on the side for turning them
in. Finn still couldn't figure out why he would have done it, but the
suspicion nagged.

It blunted the pleasure of the reunion.

"Gone straight, then," he said. "Congratulations."

"Aw, you know."

"Who's Perricona?"

"Guy I bought the building from. Easier to leave the sign up."

"You're doing good."

The shop wasn't busy, though. Stock shelves in the rear had bar and plate steel, but Finn didn't see half-finished projects anywhere. The welding table sat empty. And Jake was alone, on a weekday afternoon.

"Getting by."

"Yeah?"

"Not much manufacturing around here anymore. Everything's gone off to China or Vietnam or some fucking place."

"Hard to make the rent, huh?"

"Some months." Jake drank some soda. "Okay, most months."

"Sorry."

"Nah. So what are you doing now?"

"Not sure yet. Looking at things."

"It's tough." Unexpectedly, he grinned, taking Finn back—Jake, always the devilish charming one, always ahead of the joke. "We're *old*, man."

"You? And I'm not even forty."

"You're not?"

"Fuck you." Finn laughed. "Getting close to forty, I admit, but not over the line yet."

"I dunno." Jake's grin faded. "What'd you think about it?"

"Think about what?"

"Being inside, all those other fuckups all around you every minute? You ever seen so much plain *stupid* in one place before?"

"You got a point there."

"I ain't going back."

"Uh-huh." Finn looked away, studied Jake's rack of shaping tools. "That go for your customers, too?"

"Huh." Jake took a long pull at his Stewart's and set the bottle on the floor by his chair. "Sitting outside awhile, were you?"

Finn's turn to shrug. "Whatever bit of tooling you made for him, he wasn't taking it back to a worksite. Not in that car."

Jake laughed. "I know, man, I *know*. I told him that, too, but he says it's perfect camouflage everywhere else. Park anywhere and no one looks twice."

"And where does he park?"

"Here and there." Jake leaned his chair back. "Down the street from rich people's mansions, sometimes."

"Ah." Finn nodded. "Special tools, then."

"Custom work. You can always charge a good premium for custom."

Finn thought about it. "You're not making picks, are you? House-breaking tools? Because, I mean, even seven years ago you could get all that stuff on the internet. No reason for someone to come all the way out here, you can just order it from Amazon."

"Sure, you can do all that. Of course, you have to know how to hide your tracks online, in case the cops go looking for some reason. Plus you need a mail drop. Plus a credit card, preferably with a fake name." He picked up his root beer. "Guys like Joey, it's easier for them to come here."

"Uh-huh." Finn thinking, hard to get much more small-time than *that*. Jake couldn't be more than scraping by.

"Anyway, he's a good kid."

"Wouldn't sell you out, would he, this Eagle Scout?"

"Course not."

The steady drum of rain on the roof had eased, and Finn could hear a heavy engine starting up next door. A front loader, maybe, moving scrap metal around. The smell of the machine shop had worked its way into his subconscious, a familiar tang of oil and metal. He felt . . . at home. Back where he belonged.

"They did a good job rehabilitating you," Finn said.

"Yeah, well. How about you?"

"Put it this way: No one's hiring."

"No shit."

"I thought I was done." Finn sighed. "But it's not that easy."

"What have you got?" Jake was serious now.

"One last job," Finn said.

The shop was on the cold side. Okay for work but not for sitting. Finn shifted deeper into his jacket.

"What is it?" Jake's interest was undisguised.

"It's impossible. It's the hardest target you can imagine, protected by unbreakable security. No one's worried because infiltration is lit-erally inconceivable. You'd need a million dollars and a James Bond arsenal just to get started."

"Do you have a million dollars?"

"Nope. The arsenal, though . . ." He gestured slightly at the machines.

Jake stood up, not saying anything, and walked back to his bench. He moved a few tools, straightening up, then turned and leaned against the edge, arms crossed.

"A big one," he said.

"It could be."

"Risky?"

Finn couldn't help smiling. "It's the destination not the journey."

The door rattled and a pair of men ducked inside, their coats dark with rain. One carried a plastic blueprint tube, the other a scuffed leather folder.

Maybe Jake wasn't quite at rock bottom. The tiny nagging suspicion . . . Finn couldn't read him, not like he used to.

"Hey, Jake," the first man said. "Brought the plans over." He looked at Finn. "This a good time?"

"Sure." Finn was already standing, and he set his root beer on the desk. "We were just wrapping up."

Jake came over for a departure handshake. "Good to see you, man."

"You busy tomorrow morning? Early?"

"Not sure."

"We'll take a look at the job site. You tell me what you think."

"Maybe."

"No harm in it." Finn nodded to the newcomers. "Still raining, huh?"

"All day long."

"It's that time of year." He looked back at Jake. "Early, like I said."

"Okay, man." The grin. "Can't hurt to look."

CHAPTER NINE

At dawn, the industrial park lay quiet, none of its hardscrabble manufacturers working a third shift. Security lights flickered off as the sky lightened. An inland breeze picked up, bringing the smell of salt marsh and the cawing of waking birds. Chemical plants and tank farms ran right to the edge of the wetlands, a porous barrier of asphalt and chain link between them.

David had arrived an hour earlier, slipping noiselessly to his chosen vantage and easing his ballistic carryall to the ground. Since then, sipping broth from a black thermos, he'd seen only a few vehicles drive past. None entered the park. He was careful not to look east, where the sun's first rays might dazzle his eyes. The previous day's rain had cleared the air, and the day was forecast bright and cloudless.

Fifteen minutes beforehand, he extracted his equipment from the padded case, softly clicking it together with practiced ease. By habit that probably revealed his age, he sighted in with the optical rangefinder before activating the digital readout. A hundred and fifty meters, close enough. He ran through the rest of his checklist automatically, every step critical.

You only get one shot.

He looked at his watch—another old guy's habit, since the digital screen carried a min-sec stamp in the corner—and capped the thermos. He knew the schedule as well as the operators themselves. In the distance, a train whistle sounded, clear in the dewy air, and David nodded to himself. The grade crossing at Route 16, exactly on time. He bent to his eyepiece, breathed out, and focused. His hands, resting lightly on the controls, were perfectly still.

A few wisps of predawn fog remained in the shadow of the nearest chemical tank. The single-track feeder curved from around back. Just as the lead locomotive thundered into view, a flock of wading birds rose, squawking and flapping around it. It was an extraordinary sight—a dark blue SD70M in full roar, banked on the curve, a dozen pink, black, and white herons caught in midflight above it. In that split second, David knew he had the shot of his life . . . Then a pickup slammed over the curb behind him, spraying gravel as it skidded to a halt, one door ricocheting open. David fumbled, his fingers slipping off the grip. He straightened up and began to swear, loudly.

"I knew you'd be here!" The driver was a young guy, military haircut, big grin. He came over as the locomotive hammered past, the train making so much noise that neither man tried to say more. David shook his head, looking sadly at the camera in his hand.

When the train had gone and silence returned, David said, "This better be good, Sean."

"The CEO's coming in this morning."

"So?"

"So you have to be there. They've been calling all around trying to find you. Where's your phone, anyway?"

"In the car." David glanced at his gray Interceptor parked farther down. Three antennas and a lightbar made it look police, but the door logo was Penn Southern's. "Didn't want the interruptions."

"I figured."

"It's so important, they could have told me yesterday. What's the big meeting about, anyway?"

"Dunno. Too secret for me."

"Really?" David felt a stirring of interest. "Who's in?"

"You and Boggs. Don't know more than that."

"Is there a problem someone forgot to tell me about?"

"Not that I know of."

"All right." David packed up the camera, careful with the lenses but not wasting time. "I'll follow you back. They waiting now?"

"Boggs is with the dispatchers, making everyone nervous."

"I bet." He stood up, case in one hand, tripod in the other. "Call ahead and send someone over to Tip Top Donut. Boggs likes the ones with cream inside."

"Will do."

At the car door, he paused. "You really have no idea?"

Sean shook his head. "Something big."

"Of course." David slung the camera gear into his passenger seat, next to the shotgun. "But Boggs doesn't always get the priorities right."

David Keegan loved his job because, first and last, he loved trains. And always had. He'd grown up so close to the New York Central, he could watch the signalmen in their tower next to his backyard. At ten years old, he recognized the reporting marks of a hundred railroads and could distinguish a GP7 locomotive from a GP9 with one glance at the radiator screens. In high school, he built a Heathkit scanner, mounted it in his Dodge, and soon knew as much about operations as the yard's trainmaster. Unlike many railfans, a mostly law-abiding and conservative lot, he even hopped freights, hoboing around the country during summer breaks.

But for all that, he never wanted to be an engineer. You could go deaf rattling around on your bedroll in a freezing boxcar, and fifteen-hour shifts in the cab didn't seem like enough of an improvement. So he avoided drugs and hippies and the counterculture generally—albeit not without an occasional wistful glance—and joined the police academy straight out of high school. An occupational exemption from the draft was a bonus. In 1972, while his friends went to love-ins and Vietnam, David became a special railway agent on the Pennsylvania Southern.

Four and a half tumultuous decades later, through mergers, abandonments, deregulation, the collapse of most major roads and the consolidation of the rest, Penn Southern somehow survived—and so did David. Almost at retirement, he was now special agent in charge for the railroad's busiest district, centered on Newark. He and a few dozen officers patrolled eight yards, two thousand miles of track, and more vandals, thieves, vagrants, criminal rings, and white-collar fraud than anywhere else in North America. He had solved murders, broken up gangs so organized they could strip a container bare in fifteen minutes, and recovered three million dollars stashed in a Caribbean bank by a bent procurement executive. He had saved lives and, once, killed a drug-addled squatter who attacked him with a bowie knife under a trestle.

His phone buzzed. It took a moment to find it on the seat, under the camera case. Driving one-handed, he swiped open the connection.

"I had a call from the yard." Sean's voice. "Wondering where the hell you are."

"Guess we better step on it."

"Code three?" Sean's voice perked up.

"What the hell." David found the dashboard switches without looking and flicked on his lightbar. "Skip the siren for now, though, okay?"

"You got it."

Sean's truck accelerated, his own blue lights strobing. Morning traffic was heavy with commuters, but they got out of the way fast enough when they saw his big grille in their rearviews. He used the air horn at intersections, clearing a path. David stuck right behind, content to let the kid have his fun.

They drove through the Ironbound, the old industrial docklands. Huge freight cranes loomed in the distance, trundling stacks of containers on and off cargo ships. Less than a minute later, Sean turned onto Caleb Street, which ran alongside the southeast perimeter of Penn Southern's yard.

Halfway down the long block, he noticed a cluster of people standing in front of one of the industrial buildings across the street. It was an old warehouse, empty since a freight forwarder went broke in the last recession. Two men and a young woman were on the truck lot in front, looking up at the building. A shiny, old-fashioned Land Rover was parked alongside. The males wore unremarkable work jackets and boots, while she was dressed for business—nice skirt and coat—and a looker to boot. No doubt she was the real estate agent. The other guy was on his cell phone.

David thought it would be nice to see the economy finally picking up again. Railroad traffic had been holding its own, but the customers were always hurting.

Sean had gotten way ahead, already turning the corner a quarter mile down. David put his attention back on the road, making a mental note to see who ended up leasing the warehouse.

Keeping track of the neighbors was all part of the job.

When the two police vehicles disappeared into the rail yard, Jake looked at Finn.

"Code three," he said. "Wonder what that was about."

"Just a reminder."

"What?"

Finn put his hands in his pockets. "Not to relax. They've got a decent-size police force in there."

"That wasn't police," Emily said. "Just railroad security guards."

"They have guns and radios. Makes the question of arrest authority kind of moot, in our case."

The sun was up, illuminating the sides of the buildings in a golden glow. The contrast of the deep blue sky above, barely tinged with Newark's inevitable smog, looked like a nineteenth-century romantic's oil painting. The breeze, which had started out light, began to rise.

Finn turned back to peer at the rail yard. "Like I was saying, it's that cinder-block bunker all by itself there. Just inside the fence."

"Doesn't look like much." Jake fiddled with the small laser rangefinder he'd pretended to be making a call on when the prowl car drove past. "I'm getting . . . one hundred seventeen meters."

"Plus another ten or so this side, into the warehouse."

Jake studied the building. The wind blew scraps of paper from the road's curb.

"Hard to say anything from here," he said.

They walked over. The business door was solid metal and solidly locked. Around the side, three truck bay doors were actually welded shut, but two had small safety-glass windows at eye level. Jake squinted through one.

"Can't see shit. Wish we had a key."

"The broker can show us, but we don't really need to get inside yet. You know what it'll be like—empty."

"Concrete floor?"

"I assume."

Emily was on her phone, swiping through email. "You don't need me anymore, right?" she said.

"No, we're good."

"Nice meeting you," Jake said.

Emily walked to the Land Rover. They watched her back out, wave once, and drive down Caleb Street.

"That is one fine-looking young woman," said Jake.

"Don't even think about it."

"Why, are you—?"

"Because this is a *job*, you moron."

"Just saying." He paused, a slow grin starting. "You reacted kind of strong there, man."

"Oh, fuck off."

The breeze continued to freshen, beginning to kick up dust.

"You have a time frame?" Jake asked.

"End of the year."

"That's tight."

"Every day we wait, there's a chance the problem gets discovered. Then everything goes into screaming lockdown, and we really *are* done."

"Still."

"I'm thinking the holiday week," said Finn. "Quiet time. Hardly anything going in or out—except us, a few hours one night."

"New Year's Eve?"

"Yeah, maybe." They went to the back of the building, where Finn's truck was parked out of view from the street.

"Still risky," Jake said. "Lots of security in there."

"We'll set up a distraction. Keep 'em busy with something else."

"Like what?"

"I don't know. They're a railroad—how about we steal a train?"

Jake groaned. "Oh, sure, that worked *great* last time."

"Well, I'll think of something." Finn blew on his hands. "What do you say?"

"Thinking about it." Jake went around to the passenger side. He'd parked a few miles away, and Finn had driven him over. No need to concentrate risk further than necessary. "It's not impossible?"

"Of course not."

"December thirty-first."

"Yeah."

Jake pulled open the door. "That sure ain't much time."

CHAPTER TEN

David eased out of the cruiser, favoring his left leg. The doctor said he might want an artificial knee, but that seemed far too dramatic a step. He sighed and pulled himself vertical, using the door as a prop before slamming it shut.

The classification yard's dispatch center was a forbiddingly blank building of '60s-era brick and aluminum, topped by a 360-degree glass tower. It doubled as Penn Southern's administrative office for the district. David had his own rooms around back, including a holding cell and a well-secured gun locker. Sean's truck was parked at the end of the small lot, with one slot left for David's prowler.

The executive spaces up front were filled, Boggs's company Escalade prominent among them. A driver sat inside, staring idly at his phone, with the engine running.

Of course, that didn't mean Boggs would necessarily be leaving soon. He just liked his vehicle kept warm.

Inside, David greeted the desk man.

"He's waiting for you in the conference room," the guard said.

"Sean there already?"

"He took the doughnuts in."

"Hope you got one."

The man grinned. "Chocolate sprinkle."

The conference room was on the second floor, with ancient linoleum and an imitation-wood-grain table that carried decades of dings and cigarette burns. A long row of windows looked out over the yard—the same view the dispatchers had in their aerie one floor above.

"Good morning, sir," David said.

Boggs irritably slapped shut a leather portfolio at the table's front. "About time," he said. "Let's get started."

"One sec." Sean was crouched at the AV cart, fiddling with cables. "Sorry, I can't get your laptop connected."

"I don't need it." Boggs stood up as Sean sat down. The CEO was easily the best-looking man in the room, all dark hair and white teeth and a fine suit.

Being twenty years younger than David helped, of course.

"First of all," he said, "this topic is confidential. You can take notes, I don't care, but don't go talking about it outside. For now, you two are the only ones who are going to know, and I want it kept that way."

David looked around for doughnuts but saw only an empty cardboard plate, dusted with powdered sugar, near Boggs's chair. "Fine by me," he said. "But if it has anything to do with operations, we might need to make arrangements."

"We'll get to that. I just want to emphasize again, *top secret*. If even a whisper gets out, it's going to make the whole thing much, much more difficult."

"Got it."

"Thank you." Boggs had his most serious face on. "It's very important." He cleared his throat, taking his time, preparing the reveal.

"So," said David. "Is this about the Chinese excavator?"

There was a long pause.

"How," said Boggs slowly, "did you know that?"

"NYPD's intel section called me last week."

Boggs glared. "The deputy commissioner swore up and down he'd keep it secret!"

"Wasn't him." David leaned back, his chair scraping the linoleum. "They have informants out in the activist groups. Some environmental bunch is upset."

"Guys in the barn were talking about it, too," said Sean. "One of the mechanics has a brother-in-law at Leveret Steel, something like that. Are they really shipping it on a special?"

Boggs stared at him. "Jesus Christ."

David coughed. "Actually—"

"What else, some dumbshit posted pictures on Facebook?"

"No, what I was going to say is I don't actually know that much about it."

Boggs raised his hands like he was surrendering and looked at Sean. "Why don't you tell him? At least we can see how accurate the rumors are."

"It's the Antarctic mining project," Sean said.

"I heard that much." David's holster was digging into his side, and he shifted it to a more comfortable position in the chair.

"So the Chinese are breaking the treaty, going in for platinum and chromium and I don't know what. It turns out one of their scientific stations is sitting right on top of the biggest seam in Wilkes Land—quite a coincidence, that. But apparently digging platinum out of the coldest place on Earth is trickier than West Virginia, and they're buying some of the equipment from Leveret. In particular, the excavator, which is going to be the third-largest piece of earth-moving equipment ever built." He hesitated. "Ice-moving?"

"Whatever." Boggs took back the conversational reins. "None of this matters to us, except that they're shipping the excavator out of Port Elizabeth—and they're bringing it here by train. *Our* train."

David considered that. "How big?"

"What?"

Sean crossed his arms. "The biggest component is the bucket-chain arm. I think they said thirty-seven meters."

"Leveret's in Pittsburgh." David ran the routes in his mind. "And that's huge. Articulated flatcars?"

"Custom built."

A train horn blew, and they all turned instinctively to the window. Nothing exceptional—cars coasting into the retarders, switching engines at work, a full train moving slowly out the mainline.

"The problem isn't how big this thing is," said Boggs. "It's the demonstrators."

"That's what NYPD was worried about." David nodded. "Not Earth Liberation Front—like them, but more radical. They're expecting direct action."

"Then you've got the anti-China protesters," said Boggs. "Free Tibet, that kind of shit."

"They don't sound too bad."

"Plus, there's the matter of Leveret's ownership structure." He paused, looking around. "Oh, the lunch table hasn't reviewed that in detail, too?"

David raised his eyebrows. "Ownership structure?"

"They were bought out by private equity a few years ago. There were some internal deals . . . At this point, the largest owners are Goldman Sachs, Carlyle Group, and I think some unit at J.P. Morgan."

David laughed, not happily. "Oh, that's awesome. So Occupy Wall Street's joining the party, too?"

"Some bunch of commies or another. Who can keep them straight?" Boggs shook his head. "And don't forget the extremists who'd rather go to war with China than sell them stuff. They'll probably have the guns."

"How long is the excavator going to be on the property?"

Boggs shrugged. "At least one shift to unload the damn thing and truck it over to the port. Probably need a special hauler."

"No doubt the protesters will figure that out." David sighed. "So for a day, maybe a day and a half, we're going to have a big angry mob at the gates. Think they'll chain themselves to the track?"

Sean shook his head. "Nah."

"Good—"

"Nowadays they use bicycle locks."

"I need an action plan," said Boggs. "We're going to be ready for them, no matter what. Newark has already told me they can send out their Special Operations division."

A year before, David had participated in a joint drill with NPD's crowd-control unit. The armored trucks and mounted water cannons certainly were intimidating, not to mention the dozens of assault paramilitaries in black helmets and body armor.

"If a riot starts," he said, "which you're making sound all too likely, it's going to affect everyone. I'm sure we can keep it contained outside the yard, but we might not be able to send trains in and out on schedule."

"That's why we're doing it on New Year's Day." Boggs looked pleased with himself, so it was clear where that idea had come from. "Number one, it's one of our slowest periods anyway—everything's rush, rush, rush to the end of the year, then all the shippers take a break. Number two, everyone's hungover—including, I'll bet, most of those hippie protesters. We'll schedule the transfer for early morning, say four a.m., and that alone should cut the crowd in half. Number three . . ." He paused, looked at his fingers. "I know there's a number three."

David had hoped to have the holiday off himself. Visit the grandchildren, watch some football—forty-four years of seniority, he ought to get real vacation time now and then.

Boggs wrapped up the meeting in a cheerful mood. "I'm sure we can make this work," he said, picking up his portfolio and buttoning his suit coat. "But let's try *extra* hard to keep the actual day from slipping out, all right? I know you think it will leak, but the longer we keep it under our hats, the more trouble the protesters will have organizing themselves."

"I'll tell everyone not to call the *Star Ledger* just yet."

"Good, good."

After he'd sailed out of the room, David and Sean looked at each other.

"You know, scheduling it during vacation week just means more people will have time off to come down and join the fun. And if Boggs is serious about four a.m., they'll be coming straight from the bars."

"Carrying noisemakers and party hats," said Sean.

"On the other hand . . ." David eased up from his seat, knee hurting, and pushed himself standing with the chair back. "He's right about one thing—it *is* the quietest day of the year. Nothing else will be going on at all."

CHAPTER ELEVEN

Finn drove across the Ironbound, keeping to the speed limit. The wind had picked up, gusting against the truck and swirling grit off the streets.

"What I don't understand . . ." Jake said.

"Yeah?"

"So the way you describe it, this guy Wes wants us to break in but not actually *take* anything."

"Right."

"An incredibly well-protected vault filled with precious metals. Could be anything in there—millions and millions of dollars' worth. *Tens* of millions."

"Or even hundreds. Yup."

"We break our backs getting in—I mean, you can come up with a plan and all, but it sure ain't going to be easy—and then we stand there, surrounded by more treasure than we could spend in ten lifetimes . . ."

"Uh-huh."

"And then we just walk away."

"That's Wes's proposal."

"But the payout, the only way we actually get any money out of this for ourselves—Wes has to *pay* us. We're completely dependent on him."

"Like I said, that's his proposal."

Jake crossed his arms. "I don't like it."

Finn slowed for a light.

"Me neither," he said. "That job would be stupid. All risk and no reward."

Jake started to smile. "I *knew* it!"

"Wes just needs the break-in to cover up his problems with fake ingots—not for us to actually steal anything. If we get caught and somebody talks, then he's got huge potential problems. So he wants us in and out as quick as possible."

"But we're smarter than that," said Jake.

"We're not leaving empty-handed, no."

"How much?"

"What?"

"How much are we going to take out?"

Finn nodded. "Everything," he said.

They pulled into the Home Depot parking lot where Finn had picked Jake up earlier. It was a good place to meet and switch vehicles: busy in the early morning, filled with small-time contractors who looked no different from themselves coming and going. Finn had checked, and the store's cameras all seemed to be on the building itself, not at the far end of the lot.

Wind buffeted the truck. Jake didn't get out immediately.

"So you're in?" Finn said.

"Now that I know you're serious." Jake patted his pockets, looking for something. "Work-for-hire's bullshit, but if we can offload a few million dollars of untraceable metal, then damn straight I'm in."

"You might be thinking too small."

"Fucking awesome, man."

Down the row from them, two guys were hoisting a stack of plywood onto a panel van's roof rack. The wind kept lifting the wood sheets, threatening to send them across the lot like a tornado. Even through the closed cab, Finn could hear them swearing and shouting at each other.

Jake found what he'd been searching for, a round chewing-tobacco tin. "Want some?"

"I quit when I was inside." Finn felt the nicotine pull but resisted. "Don't need the mouth cancer."

Jake shook the tin and it rattled. "Me, too—I just store my gum in here."

"All the same."

The pair of carpenters finally secured their plywood by having one guy climb up and sit on top of the stock while the other tied the ropes around it. Elsewhere in the lot, carts were shoved sideways by the wind, hats blown away, a swirl of dust and paper and rubbish kicked up in a minicyclone.

"Feels like a storm is coming, even though the sky's clear," said Jake.

"Can you talk to the galvanizing shop today?" The plan wasn't detailed inside Finn's head, but he could see the contours.

"Yeah, but he's going to wonder."

"Tell him you need to get rid of a body."

Jake laughed. "I think he might do that on the side anyway."

He shook out a few Chiclets, threw them into his mouth, and zipped his jacket back up. "I got to get going."

Finn nodded. "Thanks."

As he opened the door, Jake paused. "We're going to need a railroad man," he said.

"I know."

"A *good* one."

"I already called him," said Finn. "Just waiting to hear back."

CHAPTER TWELVE

I don't want a fucking *garbage* train! Not today!"

Corman looked down at him. The guy was a Cross-Harbor vice president. What the fuck did he think the company *did*? Half their business was carrying trainloads of trash to faraway landfills.

"Three times a week," he said. "Per contract."

"Send them back!"

"Back?" The wind gusted again, hard, and Corman zipped up his slicker. It was small on him—Corman was the approximate size of a grizzly—but better than nothing. "The switcher shoved off an hour ago. The gons can sit there or come off the float, but they ain't disappearing anywhere."

They stood on the edge of Brooklyn, at the far reaches of the Sunset Park piers. Ancient pilings stood like broken teeth in the water. An abandoned warehouse stood to one side, empty windows staring blankly at Cross-Harbor's floating dock. Iron rails led to the platform's end, where Corman had snugged in the barge with a four-foot wrench. Four gondolas had already been pushed aboard the barge on tracks that could accommodate six cars altogether. One more sat waiting on the dock.

Tarps were tied over the open tops, but nothing could disguise the stink.

"That engine can take them away." The Cross-Harbor VP pointed at the ancient GP9 behind Corman.

He sighed. "The geep's yard-only," he said. "Not rated for traffic. Probably up and die anyway, we tried to move the entire cut."

"You're not understanding me." The VP breathed heavily, apparently trying to keep his nose closed off. "We have *visitors* today. Potential investors. They're going to arrive in five minutes. We want to show them a clean, well-managed, high-functioning shortline railroad. Not a goddamned . . . reeking . . . dump!"

Corman had spent ninety minutes coupling and uncoupling the gondolas, wrench slipping off the heavy iron where it was fouled by unspeakable slop. His boots and gloves stank wretchedly.

"I ain't sure we should be running a full load over now anyway," he said. "Weather's kicking up."

The VP glanced at the harbor. Jersey City was three miles away, clearly visible across the water, but the waves looked rough.

"If you can't get *them* off the barge, then get *it* off the dock," he said. "Now."

"That's up to the captain."

The tugboat had already tied onto the barge, waiting for Corman to finish loading. He'd cabled down the four cars and had been setting out the last one when the VP's black Mercedes G-Class bumped across the yard's broken asphalt.

"Now!" the VP repeated.

Corman looked at him for a long moment. The guy was probably half his age, clean-shaven and glaring, collar turned up on a fancy oilcloth jacket.

It would have been easy to swing the wrench, nine pounds of cast steel, and knock the VP right off the dock. For a moment, Corman could *feel* the impact, hear the dumbfuck yelling, see him tumble into the filthy, seething water.

Instead, he nodded, set down the wrench, and found his cell phone.

The VP stepped to the shelter of an open shed—some angle iron and a few sheets of galvanized metal that made up Cross-Harbor's operations center. After a minute's discussion with the captain, Corman trudged over.

"He says it's too dangerous."

"Fuck him." The VP shook his head but took the phone. "Captain? Yes . . . No, I don't need to hear that. No, I don't see any whitecaps. Look, I've sailed a Radford yacht in thirty-knot winds, you can't tell me anything about fucking *currents*. Throttle up and get that pile of shit moving away from shore!"

Corman walked off.

He needed the job. Barely more than minimum wage, cheapskate health insurance, and no possibility of advancement since he and one other hogger made up the entire roster of rail personnel. Not to mention the sheer indignity of moving garbage scows thirty feet at a time. But his days on the union list were long gone. After four years inside, he was lucky to be employed anywhere.

The captain must have lost the argument, because in a few minutes, Corman got the signal to unhook the barge. He recovered the wrench, walked to the end of the dock, and started to unbolt the rail lock.

The barge and the floating dock rose and fell on the swell. It seemed awfully rough to Corman, and glancing past, he could see the first foamy bits appearing on open water. He stopped to look at the tugboat's bridge, raising both hands as if to say, *Really? Are you sure?* The captain leaned out to wave and gave a short blast on the whistle, so Corman bent back and finished the job.

The tugboat's engine rumbled, and a gap opened. Black water splashed and whooshed in between the barge and the dock. Slowly, the rail float moved into the harbor.

Corman walked back and retrieved his cell phone from the VP, who was sheltering under the shed's lean-to roof. The wind was loud on the corrugated metal.

"Still looks dicey to me," he shouted.

"Thank God he's moving away." The VP turned toward the entrance. "They're here."

A silver SUV pulled alongside the Mercedes and three men got out—suits, dress coats, shiny shoes. Their approach over the broken ground was slow.

The VP made a shooing motion. "Disappear."

"What?"

"I told you, this is a *money* opportunity. Not your conversation. Go . . . shovel some ballast or something."

Corman nodded slowly. "Right."

He found a spot under the eave of the deserted warehouse, fifty yards away. Years of graffiti covered the bottom seven feet of the wall, archaeological layers of Krylon.

The wind slackened, gusted, blew heavily again. The suits stood in the shed. Corman could see the VP gesturing emphatically.

Out in the harbor, the barge seemed to be making little progress. Definite whitecaps appeared, knocking the tugboat against its tow. Bumpers absorbed the shock, but Corman heard the tug's engines roar more loudly.

He pulled the cell phone out from under his slicker, thinking about calling the captain.

The barge rocked, the gondolas swaying side to side. The tug was now clearly backing away, and Corman couldn't tell if it was paying out line or had simply cast free.

At the shed, the VP had stopped his arm waving. All four men stared at the drama unfolding a quarter mile offshore.

Rising waves sent the barge up, then down, then up again, even farther. The blow was modest by the standards of an open sea, but bad for an enclosed harbor. The top-heavy railcars worsened the rocking. Smoke poured from the tug's stack as it reversed away as fast as it could.

A wave broke over the barge's side as it dipped into a trough. One of the gondolas lurched, and Corman thought he saw a cable snap and whip across the deck.

The cell phone was still in his hand, but he cleared the captain's number and dialed a different one.

It rang once, twice, three times.

"Yeah?"

"Hey," Corman said over the wind. "I've been thinking it over."

"Come to a decision?"

The barge's stern suddenly rose, ten or fifteen feet in the air, as the rear gondola came loose and tipped off its track. For a moment, it hung, suspended on half its wheels like a circus performer.

Then it fell sideways, skidded briefly, and fell off the side.

It was gone in an instant, nothing but a plume of spray and the barge heeling the other way. Two other cars broke free, sliding crazily on the deck, crashing into the third. The barge held together a moment longer, then turned all the way over.

It was upside down, all four cars gone. Five seconds, total loss. Even Corman, who'd expected disaster, felt briefly stunned by how fast it happened.

"Yes," he said finally. "This seems like a good time to move on."

"Hello?"

"Hi, Jake."

"Hey, Finn. What's up?"

"Wanted to let you know—he'll be joining us."

"Corman?"

"Yup."

"Awesome."

"He's in the area, too. Convenient."

"Fate."

"Coincidence."

"Whatever." Jake paused to spit, and Finn wondered where he was. He hadn't noticed any spittoons in the shop.

"Here's the thing. We need a driller, too."

"I figured."

"So maybe, Asher."

"Sure, he's good." Jake stopped. "No, wait a minute."

"He's not good. He's the best."

"No, no." Jake made a coughing sound that Finn deciphered as a laugh. "Corman and Asher? Work together? You might as well put Peyton Manning and Tom Brady on the same team. They won't last five minutes."

"They managed to get along in New Mexico."

"They ended up in the same prison, did you know that?"

"Uh, no."

"Prosecutors tried to split us all up, but I guess the state didn't have enough pens. So Corman and Asher did their three-to-fives in the same place."

"Hmm."

"Different floors, different blocks, but you know. Apparently, it didn't help that Corman got out early and Asher did every damn day of his sentence."

"Mouthed off, did he?" Finn had brought Asher into three jobs, and he'd been pain in the ass every time.

"Of course. They probably would have extended his time, but by the end, everyone hated him too much."

"All right."

"But you're right—he really is the best driller out there. And he probably needs the work."

"You're in touch?" Finn was surprised.

"No, no, I just mean, who else would hire him? Right side of the law or not? The only way to make Asher employable is to duct-tape his mouth shut."

"Okay, I take the point. But we need him anyway."

"If he's even interested."

CHAPTER THIRTEEN

Asher rolled the tanker across the broad dirt patch next to Kiowa Oil's temporary field office and parked right out front. He left the diesel running, because it was twenty-two degrees and he liked the cab warm and it wasn't his tab anyway. Half-frozen slush crunched under his boots. First snow had fallen back in September, early for North Dakota, but storms had alternated with unusual warm spells since then. Now the roads were ruts of ice and muck.

The office was a half-wide trailer set on unmortared cinder-block footings. The electrical connection looked dangerously jerry-rigged to Asher, and an oil tank provided fuel for the heater inside. After the porta-potty kept freezing, the Kiowa foreman had it moved up snug against the trailer, hoping to bleed some warmth through the wall.

The foreman's Ram was the only other truck parked nearby. A quarter mile down the road, a row of plastic Quonset huts huddled against arctic winds blasting across the prairie. Asher had a room in the man camp—a bunk, actually, in a four-man unit. After twelve hours hauling frack water, he was bone tired, so tired that even sleeping in what was basically a shipping container was mighty attractive. All the more so now that he was the only one left in his unit.

The boom felt like it was ending. Kiowa wasn't laying off, but suddenly, the pay wasn't quite so good, and guys had started wondering what the hell they were doing in the middle of freezing fucking nowhere. Some drifted back south, following rumors of recovery in warmer states. Others looked for jobs closer to Minot or even Williston. Especially with another winter closing in, anyone with a little cash saved up had to be thinking about opportunities elsewhere.

"You're late." The foreman wasn't much older than Asher, and he'd started out as a rigger, as dumb and tough as any of them. But the transition to management, such as it was, had erased all class sympathy. "Did you dump that last load of lease water?"

"Didn't have time." Asher shrugged. "They broke a stopcock on the holding tank, and it took an hour to get it working again. I had to wait."

The man frowned. "So where's the truck?"

Asher jerked a thumb over his shoulder. "Get someone else to drive it to the disposal. I've been on the clock since five a.m."

"Get the fuck back out there! It'll start to freeze, sitting out overnight."

"No."

"What?"

"DOT regulations. I've timed out. Fuck off."

A long glare, face reddening. "I told you to get out there. Finish your shift."

"Haul it yourself. I'm done for the day."

"I'll write you up."

"Yeah? Do your boss a favor—when you're done, take the report and shove it up your ass."

The man slapped his desk, hard enough to rattle the entire trailer. "All right, I've had enough. You're fired."

"Fine." Asher suddenly felt better. "That's great."

"Get off the property. I'll call the camp and tell them you've got an hour to clear your shit out."

Some extra clothing, all of it heavily insulated and permanently grimed. A broken Xbox. The bottle of Old Fitzgerald he was always too tired to drink. Asher could pack in about thirty seconds. "Fine by me. Just hand over my paycheck and you'll never see me again."

A pause, and then the man kind of smiled. "Paycheck? What paycheck would that be?"

Payday was Friday, the following afternoon. "You owe me for five days. Sixty-one, sixty-two hours, something like that." Asher's good feeling departed as fast as it had arrived.

"You're being terminated for cause. Walk out or I call the police."

An empty threat. They were in unincorporated territory, far from any local jurisdiction, and the highway patrol couldn't be bothered. But Asher didn't have much to bargain with, either.

"You owe me my fucking pay." Asher felt himself begin to snarl and cut it off. "And you better make it cash, now that I think about it."

The argument went nowhere. The foreman even started to grin, now that he could fuck Asher over.

"Kiowa's going to blackball you, too," he said. "Attitude like yours. You'll never work in the industry again."

Another empty threat—wildcatters didn't give a shit and the majors were too disorganized—but Asher focused on the core issue.

"Open the goddamned safe," he said through clenched teeth, "and hand over my fucking *money*."

Maybe the foreman finally realized the territory their conversation was entering, because he raised his hands. "Okay, okay, don't be an asshole. Hang on." He put his back to Asher, warily, and bent to the black AMSEC on the floor. A half minute of dial spinning, a ratcheting click, a few seconds of paper rustling, then he slammed the safe shut again and turned back.

"Four hundred and eighty," he said, unable to suppress a smile. "Poor performance, insubordination, failure to follow regulations, and generally being a shithead—I've reduced your rate to minimum wage. Normally, you'd be able to work your way back up the scale, if you cleaned up your act and kissed my ass enough, but since you just got fired, oh well." He proffered the thin wad of bills.

Asher stood, boiling, for a long moment. When he abruptly stepped forward, hand swinging out, the foreman shoved his chair backward and fumbled in the desk drawer. A moment later, he had a pistol in his other hand, dead center and unwavering on Asher's chest.

"Don't fuck with me," he said.

Asher, who'd been on the wrong side of a gun a few times, didn't move.

"No need for that," he said.

The foreman leaned forward to drop the money on the desk, then backed up again.

"Take it and leave."

Outside the trailer, Asher slammed the cheap-shit aluminum door and shoved the cash into his pocket. It was dark already, the winter night falling early, and a cold wind whistled across the empty lot. He stood for a few seconds, glaring at the tanker in front of him. It was still puffing exhaust, gleaming a bit in the trailer's security light.

The foreman wouldn't emerge until he heard Asher drive away. He was probably still holding the handgun at ready, prepared to shoot if the door opened again. Asher grunted and shook his head.

Then he studied the foreman's trailer.

It was a standard mobile office—boxy and flimsy, the rental company's logo peeling off the side. Wires drooped haphazardly from a junction box at one end, with the oil tank and its fitting at the other. An unused plumbing connection projected at floor level next to the oil hose.

Asher looked more closely at the pipe end. Out here on the prairie, there was no water supply to connect to—hence the porta-potty. The connection was a standard three-inch sewer pipe, reasonably clean because it had never been used.

If required by local code, and the budget could afford it, Kiowa might have hooked up a sink and toilet, maybe even a shower. As it was, the pipe terminated just on the other side of the wall. Probably not even capped. Why bother?

Asher looked at the fitting, then he looked at the tanker.

The frack water came out a three-inch hose, too.

Asher grinned.

Five minutes later, he stood by the tanker's control board, hand on the lever, and savored the moment. He had run the hose out as silently as possible, working carefully at the connection so the trailer didn't thump—though steady gusts of wind covered up any vibration he might have caused. The tank was full, thirty-six hundred gallons of theoretically decontaminated but still filthy water that had been pumped into the shale beds and forced back out endless times. It was nasty stuff, contaminated with benzene, toluene, and more, and Asher never let it splash on his arms.

He pulled the lever all the way open.

A sudden noise from the trailer—a high-pressure gush, not stopping, and yells from the foreman. The trailer rocked slightly. Banging sounds. The rush of water seemed to increase in volume.

The door slammed open, a cascade of water sheeting out and over the ramp. The foreman stood backlit in the doorway.

"Ashhhherrrrr!" he yelled, then he lost his footing in the torrent and tumbled down the steps, yelling the whole way.

Asher stood one more moment, etching the satisfying panorama into memory, then turned and jogged away.

His own truck was parked outside his housing unit, four hundred yards down the road. A half minute to grab his phone charger and some underwear, and he'd be on his way. He had a pocketful of twenties, a tank full of gas, and a story that was sure to be good for a few free rounds in Williston.

After that, who knew? He'd find something else. The world was full of opportunity for an enterprising man.

CHAPTER FOURTEEN

The rock gym was in a glazed-brick building at the edge of the East Village. Apartment block on one side, pizza shops and a Duane Reade across the avenue. Several bikes were chained to a rack out front, single-speeds and retro cruisers. Finn wasn't sure what to expect inside—a fake concrete cliff? But it was a pleasant, well-lit space with looming synthetic walls and a rainbow of handholds bolted everywhere.

"I go there most lunchtimes," Emily had said. "Unless Wes has some last-minute crisis. So, like twice a week."

"How about I take you somewhere to eat instead?"

"I never have lunch. That's a waste of time."

She'd called him in the morning. Something she didn't want to talk about on the phone, or maybe from her desk at the Heart Pine offices. So Finn had agreed to meet her here.

A haze of dust in the air. A few dozen climbers, on the walls, on the mats, belaying, sitting around. All had chalk bags at their waists or sitting nearby.

He found Emily quick enough, near the top of a steep overhang fifteen feet up. Black tights and a sleeveless top. She was midmove, swinging gently back then launching up and left. Her hand caught the hold, but momentum carried her too far and she slipped off. She hit the mat on her back.

"Damn."

Finn stepped forward and offered a hand. She was already rolling to her feet but took it anyway.

"The other climbers," he said, gesturing to a higher wall, "use safety gear. So they don't fall like that."

"No ropes for bouldering." Emily walked off the mat. "Any trouble getting in?"

"They seem to know you pretty well."

"It's low-key here. Not crazy like at Chelsea Piers."

Her shoulder and arm muscles were seriously cut, veins standing out from the exertion. Finn was impressed. "You have business meetings here often?"

"Never."

They sat at a bench near a row of open cubbies, most spilling jackets and backpacks and harnesses. Emily had a steel water bottle and an energy bar wrapped in wax paper. She held it out to him.

"Want some? I make them at home."

"Really?"

"Oats, almond butter, and flax meal."

He broke off a corner. "That's . . . healthy."

A guy walked by carrying a ladder and a rechargeable drill. Like three-fourths of the other men there, he had a beard, a wool cap, and very dusty pants. He nodded to Emily.

"You'll send that dyno next time for sure," he said.

"Sooner or later." When he'd disappeared to the back wall, she said to Finn, "He sets the cleverest routes."

They watched the other climbers while Emily finished her bar. Music played, a constant background of techno and mid-'80s nostalgia.

"So," Finn said.

"Okay." She flattened the wax paper, folded it up, and tucked it into a haversack with the water bottle. "Molybdenum. I've been thinking about your escapade."

"Yeah?"

"The London Metal Exchange introduced futures in 2010. But before that, the big traders were still hedging with direct contracts." She caught his frown. "Buying and selling in advance of delivery, that's all. Like a promise—I pay you now, but you don't have to give me the stuff until next July. See?"

"I guess."

"The point is, there was a market. Opaque but fairly liquid—annual trading volume in the billions of dollars."

"Well, sure. That's why we could sell the ore."

"How much was Wes's share?"

"He would have gotten two hundred thousand. One-third. He put up all the front money, which was about thirty."

"Not a bad return."

"It was safe money," Finn said. "But once we went down, he got zip."

Emily stretched, rolling her shoulders and pressing her hands to loosen the forearm muscles.

"Without a lot of research, digging up deals and prices, this is half guesswork. But here's how it might have gone: When news of the theft broke, prices would have fallen. Steep and sharp."

"Why?"

She shrugged. "It's what you see. Disruptions in supply generally push the price up. But when something screwy happens, especially when lawbreaking is involved, a lot of players' first reaction is to sell. Get out before something bad happens to *them*. I don't know how speculative the molybdenum market was back then, but 2007, 2008, people were doing crazy stupid shit. It was news, right?"

"What was?"

"You being caught."

"Oh, yeah." Front pages, television, internet news—they were media celebrities for days. "It was everywhere."

"So the price plummeted. If Wes was holding a bunch of short contracts, he could have made out like a bandit."

"Huh? You said the price went *down*."

"And if you're short, the more it falls, the more you make." Emily seemed amused. "Wall Street smoke and mirrors, yeah, but that's how things work."

She took a few minutes, explaining the maneuvers, and Finn kind of got it eventually.

"So how much could Wes have made?" he asked.

"I don't know. Too many variables—contract sizes, what the price actually did, how much he committed. But a sure thing like that? I bet 10x wouldn't be out of reach."

"'10x'?"

"Ten times his investment. Say he puts in a hundred grand, he takes out a million."

"Son of a *bitch*."

Emily put up a hand. "Hold on now. I looked, but the financial records from back then are all locked away in off-site storage. I'm just speculating."

"It's good enough for me."

"No. I mean, sure, Wes could have done it." She hesitated. "Be honest, I thought it was kind of odd he'd get involved for a low-six-figures payoff. This makes more sense."

"Yes." Grim.

"But so could anyone else—anyone who knew your plan ahead of time."

"Jake? Corman? *Asher?*" Finn almost growled. "Jake might barely understand what you're saying. Asher's probably never had a bank account in his life. But more than that, if any of them had a hundred grand lying around, they wouldn't have done the job at *all*."

"They could have told someone else." She waited a moment. "Some other investor. These hedge funds are always looking for an edge, trying to uncover that little nugget of inside information. I'm not saying they're *all* like Wes—"

Finn's certainty slipped into angry frustration. "We're back where we started. Any of them could have done it."

"Not quite." Emily stood up. "Now you know why."

Finn waited while Emily changed—fewer than five minutes in the locker room. She emerged in business clothes, well-cut dark wool and a subtle green silk scarf.

It matched her eyes.

Outside, Finn zipped his jacket against the November wind and shoved his hands into the pockets. Too damn cold up here. Down the block, a police cruiser was at the curb, lights flashing but no officers visible. He turned his back to it. Emily tapped her phone.

"I've got an Uber coming," she said. "Drop you somewhere?"

"No." He'd parked a few blocks away. "I have to ask you something."

"Okay."

He'd been thinking about the question for a while. A lot depended on her answer—including his willingness to continue with the entire project.

"Why are you doing this?"

"'This'?"

"Helping us out. Helping *me* out. We're not talking, I don't know, selling a few dubious stocks. This is a Class B felony."

A pair of climbers came out, pulling on their layers of fleece. Thin sunlight glinted from a passing windshield.

"You don't know what I do for Wes normally," Emily said.

"Jesus, what *else* is he into? Knocking over armored cars?"

She smiled. "You don't think you're the only source he's gone to for, ah, unconventional asset management?"

"I never really thought about it."

"Inside information, like I said. The only real way to beat the market. Digging out secrets means, well, sometimes you have to digger deeper than the boring old rules say you're allowed."

"Breaking into offices, spying on competitors, that sort of thing?"

She shrugged.

"That's him," Finn said. "I'm wondering about you."

Emily took her time, pulling out a pair of sunglasses, checking her phone again.

"Money," she said. "Wes truly fucked up, buying all that rhodium. If it collapses, I lose my job, I lose my bonus, *and* no one will ever hire me again."

"Okay."

"Save the deal, you save him—and that saves me."

"I guess that works," he said.

"It better." Emily checked her phone again.

That was all she seemed willing to say. Fair enough. Finn had similar motivations, in part.

"Speaking of money," he said. "If we're going to get this off the ground, Wes needs to pony up. We've got six weeks, and the expenses are going to build fast."

"How much?"

"Ballpark? Fifty, sixty thousand."

He said it wondering how Emily would respond. The figure was a little high, though not much more than a 10-percent overrun allowance. Lots of people seemed to figure, you're a criminal, you're gonna steal the fucking money, what do you need *more* for?

She smiled, crooked. "I'll tell him."

"Soon, eh?"

"You do your job and I'll do mine." A light blue Prius came silently down the street and pulled over when Emily waved to it. She looked back at Finn. "We're all in this together."

CHAPTER FIFTEEN

When Asher finally showed up, the others had been waiting nearly an hour.

"I got lost." First words, shoving the motel room door closed behind him. "Who picked this dump?"

They were inside room 15 of the Glenville Motor Court, nine o'clock at night. Finn had paid cash earlier in the day, returned after dark, and sat in his truck until Jake and Corman appeared. The place had seen better days—in about 1964. Threadbare quilts, a twelve-inch cathode-ray television with cracked knobs.

"The Hilton was booked," Jake said. "Wipe your boots off, for fuck's sake."

Corman stood by the wall holding a plastic bag of baby carrots, almost empty. He held out the last few to Asher, who gave him an incredulous look and dropped into the room's only chair. Jake sat on the bed with a half-eaten, paper-wrapped Italian sub in one hand, the smell of salami and pepperoncini strong.

Finn kept station at the door. The last he'd seen Asher, he was being hauled into a New Mexico State Patrol Humvee, bruised and bloody after not cooperating fast enough to suit the troopers. Corman—the same, though he'd been sufficiently docile, despite his size, to avoid a beating.

Seven years. Hard years, someone comparing before and after might think. Asher in particular, the beard still cut to a point but scraggly, the rest of him even more gnarly.

Corman had gone completely bald, though his massive pro-wrestler's build seemed undiminished. Only Jake was edging gracefully into middle age, still handsome, even dignified.

"All right," Finn said. "Jake and I have been studying on this for a week."

He unrolled a property map. Corman leaned forward, attention immediately drawn by the distinctive network of rail yard rights-of-way. Finn pointed. "There," he said. "A hundred yards from the street."

"Trains?" Asher, in disbelief. "We're robbing a fucking train *again*?"

Jake laughed. "Not quite."

Finn ran through it. He described the vault, what they'd seen. The high-tech security. Jake pitched in now and then. It didn't take long.

He stopped and waited. Jake finished his sandwich, crumpled the paper, and tossed it vaguely toward the bathroom door. Corman stood impassive, looking at the map.

"So . . ." said Asher, "some rich guy wants us to rip off his pal's gold supply."

"Rhodium," Finn said.

"And we're not supposed to take anything ourselves. All that trouble—"

"Four hundred fifty large," Jake said.

Asher shrugged. "A hundred each? Nice, but whatever; I could earn that in the oilfields."

"Tax free?"

Snort. "You're reaching."

Finn nodded. "Once we're inside, it might be kind of stupid not to take the metal after all. For ourselves."

"Fuck yes!" Asher didn't hesitate. "That's more like it!"

Corman's raspy voice was more measured. "I never dealt with rhodium before."

"It ain't radio*active*." Asher, suddenly an expert.

"Not what I meant." Corman looked at Finn. "You?"

"No." He thought he knew where the big man was headed.

"What's the market?"

"What'd you say, two thousand dollars an *ounce*?" Asher said. "People paying that kind of money, it won't be any problem finding buyers."

"No," Finn said. "Corman makes a reasonable point. Gold, silver, sure, we could fence it anywhere. But rhodium—I don't know who buys it, who uses it, how willing the buyers are to consider, ah . . . alternative sourcing. Hell, I don't even know what it's used *for*."

"So what do you think we can get? Twenty percent?"

"In there."

"Fifteen? Twenty-five?" Corman moved his massive hands slightly, a small *so-what* gesture.

"I hear you." Jake joined the thread. "The payoff's not as good. Finn's guy is willing to pay us clean. Versus having to haul out God knows how much metal, plus the trouble—and risk—of selling it."

"Seventy pounds." Finn had done the math already.

"What?"

"Seventy pounds of rhodium, nineteen hundred an ounce, at an eighty percent markdown. That's all it takes to net us the same as Wes is offering."

"Seventy pounds?"

"About."

"That's *all*?" Asher didn't need to hear anything more. "I could carry it out my*self*."

"And," Jake said, "it appears to me there's no reason to stop there."

"Right." Corman seemed almost to smile.

"How much is in there?" Asher said. "Total?"

"Minimum seven hundred fifty kilograms." Finn let them start to figure the arithmetic themselves.

"Mother*fucker*."

Grunt—an impressed one.

"Of course, some of it's fake," Finn said. "But our client is convinced his neighbor in the vault has at least enough to make up the difference."

That's all it took. Even Corman.

"Need a heavy truck to get that out, though," he said.

"We're not going to drive in."

"Then what?" Asher frowned, his dream of easy riches suddenly balked. "No way we can tunnel, they'll have motion sensors every two feet around the walls and floor."

"No." Jake leaned forward to point at the plan. "It's inside a *rail* yard. A hundred trains a day go in and out of there. Big, heavy, long trains . . ."

"Hah." Corman made a surprised sort of laugh.

"Right," said Finn. "Rumbling the ground around the clock. Vibration sensors would be useless."

"I'll be fucked." Asher looked more closely at the plan. "What's the scale?"

"Three-sixteenths."

"A hundred twenty-five meters from the warehouse to the vault," Jake said.

"The road," Corman said. "And two sidings. In between."

"That's right. The tunnel would run under all of them."

"A long-haul locomotive weighs two hundred tons."

Jake leaned back again, hands behind his head. "We'll shore it. Heavy timbers, maybe concrete pipe. We can manage."

More questions, most still unanswerable. Corman said little.

Finn wound it up. "We won't do it if it's not possible. Like always."

"No motion sensors," Jake said. "Other monitoring equipment, though. We need to find out exactly what's in there."

"Sure." Finn nodded. "But, again, like always, cameras and computers and whatever else are only as good as the people watching them."

"Yeah."

"They're humans, and humans make mistakes."

"We're humans, too, you know," Jake said.

"Not us," Finn said. "We never make mistakes."

CHAPTER SIXTEEN

S omeone made a mistake? Is that what you're telling me?" David met Sean outside the vault's truck entrance. Sean's cruiser was parked crossways to the ramp, lightbar strobing. It was dark at four thirty in the afternoon. The heavy sky smelled of snow. Sean had called him right before shift end, and he'd driven over directly from the dispatching center two minutes earlier.

"Not some*one*, no." Sean wasn't wearing a coat or hat or gloves but didn't seem to mind the cold. "Let's go talk with Pete."

They walked down the sloping truck ramp. Deliveries in and out of the vault were made underground, out of sight, in a white-painted concrete space more brightly lit than a normal truck bay. Next to a simple loading dock, a bullet-resistant glass window overlooked the entire space. Sean gestured to the guard inside, who stood to open a heavy metal door then relocked it behind them.

"What's up, Pete?" David's knee pinged and he tried to ignore it.

"He's inside." The guard hooked a thumb over his shoulder. "Clerk's office."

"New guy?"

"No. Been assigned here, oh, four or five weeks at least. His name's Teller."

"Okay." David took a moment to examine the bank of monitor screens above the guard's desk. They showed the familiar interior of the vault: hallway, wire enclosures, lockbox racks, a fisheye of the main room. No one was visible inside. "Tell me what happened."

"It's been a normal day. A few deliveries, the usual orders to move freight around inside." Some customers moved items in and out; other transactions were between parties who both rented space in the vault or handlers who would simply shift material from one owner's locked rack to another's. "The day guys left a half hour ago, and Teller went in for a walkaround. He's in there ten seconds, and the alarm goes off. The computer flagged him as a threat."

David looked at Sean. "Threat?"

"It didn't recognize him. Facial recognition. Remember? We put in the upgrade last year."

Security in the vault was ultimately David's responsibility, but corporate bean counters had insisted on contracting out his personnel. They made it sound like a standard precaution—don't let anyone get too cozy, avoid the risk of inside jobs—but he figured it was more about replacing his fully salaried employees with cheaper temps. In any event, the result was a constantly changing cast of guards, delivered from Stormwall Security Solutions, who were also responsible for all the monitoring.

"Facial recognition?"

"Stormwall's techs scan everyone into the database who's authorized to be inside. When the cameras see someone not in the database, they send up a rocket." Sean shrugged apologetically. "I had to follow procedures."

"I know." David looked again at the video screens, which remained completely uninteresting. "But you said this guy, ah, Teller, he's been here for a month already. Sounds like a simple mistake to me."

"You should see for yourself."

Sean opened the clerk's door and they stepped in, leaving Pete at his station. Inside, a large man sat by a desk, wearing Stormwall's usual blue uniform—the jumpsuit version used inside the vault. He turned when they entered, and David suppressed a start of surprise. The man's face was heavily bruised with a bandage over his left cheekbone and swelling around the eye.

"David Keegan. I'm the railroad's chief of security."

"Teller." The guy's voice was harsh and raspy, and David saw further contusions on his neck. "Sorry about all this."

"So . . . what, you ran into a door?"

"Had a match last night."

"Mixed martial arts," Sean said. "Right?"

"Stormwall pays minimum wage." The man raised one hand, like, *What can you do?* "Gotta make the rent somehow."

"How'd it go?" David wasn't exactly a fan, but he'd watched some pay-per-view with his grandson.

"Out in a guillotine choke. But that's all right, I still got my share of the purse. Two hundred bucks."

"That's good, then." David looked at Sean. "I'm missing something here."

"The facial recognition software." Sean seemed amused. "It's actually pretty good—grow a mustache, put cotton in your cheeks, add a pair of eyeglasses, it sees right through all that. That's because it relies on a set of measurements you shouldn't be able to modify, like distance between eyeballs and nose height, and, oh, I don't know. But Teller here"—he gestured politely—"getting smashed in the face created swelling. Along with the bandage tape, it was apparently enough to push the confidence factor below acceptable."

Which set off an internal alarm. Pete, sitting right outside, would have known not to escalate. He'd buzzed Teller into the vault a few minutes earlier, of course, bruises and all. But Stormwall did its monitoring remotely, at some consolidated office, and when the employee there got the alert, he checked the feed, and when he saw a big, battered man inside with the computer beeping "NOT RECOGNIZED," he followed his own procedures and hit the air-raid button.

"Thank God for computers," said David. "They make our lives so much easier."

"Can I go back to work?"

"What?"

"Because, like, I don't want to lose the pay."

David glanced at Sean. "Did you clock him out?"

"Sorry. Rules. I know you don't write them, but . . ."

The central office accountants again. David grimaced. "Yeah, of course. Put him back on, and voucher the missed time."

"Thanks, boss." Teller stood up. "I'm back in now?"

"I don't know. Are we going to go through this again as soon as you walk under a camera?"

"I got hold of Stormwall's manager just before you arrived," Sean said. "He promised to take care of it."

"All the same." David opened the office door. "Give them a little more time to make sure—have some coffee with Pete or something."

Back in the bay, David took a moment to look around. It was empty, doors to the vault closed, the only disorder a cluster of low carts pushed together at the side of the dock. A cold draft came down the ramp. Blue light from Sean's flashers blinked on the walls near the entrance.

"This reminds me," David said. "We probably need a few more Stormwall temps here on New Year's Eve."

"I already let them know."

"Yeah?" If David were further from retirement, he might be threatened by so competent a lieutenant.

"They're happy to send as many as we want. I talked to a VP who pitched their new special reaction force, too."

"Oh, no." David had an image of heavily armed mercenaries flooding his yard. "Absolutely not."

"Of course. Be kind of awesome, though, wouldn't it?"

"Don't mention it to Boggs. He'd order up a brigade."

Sean laughed. "No need for that."

"Nope." David started to walk up the ramp. "No need for that at all."

CHAPTER SEVENTEEN

"Computers." Finn capped off another five-gallon container. "That's the problem. All this technology."

"They're just tools." Jake kept his eye on the outflow valve, alert for drips and spatter.

"No. A hammer is a tool. An excavator is a tool. But computers are just one big pain in the ass."

"You having trouble with your phone again?"

They were in the galvanizing shop: a vast interior, sixty feet high, a single open floor. Finn slid another canister under the valve. He and Jake were crouched at the end of the shorter pickling tank—seventy-five hundred gallons of hydrochloric acid, enough to descale steel work twenty feet long. The shop's owner had shut the line down for the day, leaving them to it, but the acid still seemed in slow, constant motion. Nearby, molten zinc burbled quietly in its tank. The faint swashing sounds made Finn nervous.

"Hey, careful there!" he said. Jake had reopened the valve too quickly, and a small amount of acid splashed onto the floor. "Damn, I hate this stuff."

"You got gloves on, right?" Jake didn't seem concerned. "You got goggles on. You even got that fancy-pants apron. Don't worry about it."

True enough. Finn adjusted the shopworker's leather apron he'd borrowed and watched the gas can fill up. Jake stopped the flow at the right point, no rush.

"The scar on my leg is still dead white," Finn said. "From fifteen years ago. Remember that?"

Jake laughed. "Have to admit, we weren't so smart back then." They'd stolen a tanker out of the lot of a chemical distributor in Woodbridge, not sure exactly what was inside but confident that a Class 8 hazmat placard meant something valuable. It wasn't so different from hawking shoplifted steaks at restaurant alley doors: a hundred miles away, at the back entrance of another, less scrupulous company, Finn offered the foreman the entire vehicle for dirt cheap. The guy insisted on checking volume, reasonably enough, but when they opened the line, a sudden pressure release sprayed hydrogen fluoride everywhere. Finn, in front, got the worst of it.

"One more and we're done," he said now. Eleven of the plastic gas cans, red and yellow, innocuous enough. "You've got a closet for them, right?"

"What?"

"To store the cans."

"These aren't going in *my* shop." Jake looked offended. "Come on, the fumes. I don't have ventilation like they got here."

"Where did you think we were going to put them?" Finn tightened the second-to-last cap. "We don't have the warehouse yet, and I'm sleeping at a motel. Maid service won't like finding a superfund site in the room."

"Uh-uh." Jake shook his head. "Too dangerous."

"Too dangerous for you, so you want them next to my *bed*?"

They argued it out while the last can filled. In the end, all eleven went into the back of Jake's truck.

"What do we owe your buddy?" Finn asked.

"Nothing."

"Really?"

"He told me they go through hundreds of gallons of this stuff every month. Recyclers come by for pickle sludge and refill the entire tank. What we took is a drop in the bucket."

The air was clean and cold outside—at first pleasant, after the chemical sting inside the galvanizing shop, then a little too cold. Finn felt a shiver and glanced at the sky.

"Might rain again. Or snow."

"They'll be fine." Jake gestured at the array of canisters.

"All the same. You have a cover or something? Someone notices, it might be a little hard to explain."

"Sure."

Finn drove the truck fifty feet to park in front of Perricona. Jake went inside and came out a minute later with a blue plastic tarp. It was stained and frayed at the edges, bundled into a loose roll.

They flipped it over the truck bed and Finn began tying down the eyelets. Snow was in the air.

"So anyway," he said. "The computers, the cameras, the sensors. We'll need to bypass all that crap, and I'm way out of date."

"Breaking into systems, cracking security—it ain't so easy as in the movies."

"Maybe we can hire some geek teenager."

"I might know someone."

"Is he reliable?"

"She was on a job with one of my customers. Alarms, remote monitoring, hardwired sensing in the walls—kinda like this one, actually. Sounded impossible to me. But he said she broke it as easy as taking a piss."

Finn lashed the final eyelet to a bolt in the truck bed, tying it off with a taut-line hitch. "She?"

"Girls go to MIT, too, nowadays, I hear."

"She's from MIT?"

"I don't know." Jake shrugged. "I'm just saying. Cody liked her."

"Not sure I know Cody."

"He's a good guy. Kind of a fuckup though. He just started ten-to-thirteen at Rahway."

Finn tossed the rope end into the truck and straightened up. "That's some recommendation."

"It wasn't *her* fault. Cody was a little too easy with the money afterward. Went to the bars and started talking. Dumb, considering a reward was out."

"I'm not impressed."

"Well, he went to jail and she didn't."

Finn sighed. "We can't do it without a hacker."

"Nancy, Nicki—something like that. Want me to call her?"

The first snowflakes began to fall. Finn pulled on his gloves. "Get me the number, okay?" he said. "I'll sound her out."

CHAPTER EIGHTEEN

A t the first meeting, when Nicola Juravik was selling the project, she had way overshot the dress code: a fitted suit in dark gray, her most professional outfit. The CFO had shown up in khakis and a half-tucked polo shirt. One of his underlings actually wore flip-flops. So today, for the final presentation, it was motorcycle boots, a purple blazer, and a Rolex Daytona heavy enough to punch a guy out.

Naturally, the CFO strode into the conference room in chalk stripe and wingtips. A gold company pin gleamed in his lapel.

Nicola sighed.

"You're late." His name was Mark Kells, and he had thirteen inches and seventy pounds on her, all of it muscle. Last December, he'd broken an opposing player's cheekbone in a charity hockey match. "The board meeting's already started."

"Someone forgot to give my name to security." Nicola had spent ten minutes in the tower's lobby, waiting for visitor-badge authorization.

"Never mind that." Kells looked at his smartphone. "We have to go straight in. You good?"

"Um." Nicola, who'd just sat down, stood up. But her laptop case snagged, nearly tipping the chair over. She grabbed for it, and the laptop bag swung on its strap, knocking a folder off the table. Documents spilled.

"Damn. Sorry about that."

Kells looked at the papers, then at her. "Never mind."

Nicola felt her confidence start to wither. It didn't help that Kells looked like a *Men's Health* model. Other girls could have done the sexy-kitten thing, but Nicola had inherited her East European peasant genes undiluted. She was short and wide, and though endless hours in the gym kept her waistline more or less in check, she was also about as graceful as a wildebeest.

Fuck him. She ignored the mess on the floor. "Did you read the report?"

"Yeah, sure." He shrugged. "The main servers are secure, right? The network's fully patched and armored? All the procedures documented and ISO compliant?"

"Yes, but—"

"So everything's fine. Just what I expected." Kells made an impatient gesture. "Come on."

"That was just the first paragraph of my executive summary." Nicola suspected he'd read no further, even though she'd emailed him the final copy a week earlier. "There's more than just hardware policy—"

He cut her off again. "Yeah, yeah, I know. The board might have questions, but I'll handle all that. My IT guys gave me a prep packet this morning."

"I really think you ought—"

"We have to go." He opened the door and steered Nicola through. "Tell the board what they want to hear. You're only one of six items on the agenda, we've got plenty more to do today."

Which was certainly true. Gladco Enterprises had retail operations in fifty countries, and according to a tsunami of investigative reporting a month earlier, they had bribed officials, subverted justice, hired thugs, and generally taken illegal shortcuts in every single one of them. Weak, fumbled apologies from the chairman hadn't helped. Senators were calling for hearings.

Nicola's contract, to test and verify that the firm's computer operations were properly secured against hacking, was part of the board's response. She didn't know whether they wanted to stop the leaks, find the leakers, simply prove to the world that they were taking responsible action, or all of the above. And she didn't care. Her job was to see if she could break in, and if so, to explain how.

Today, she was a white hat.

They were on the executive floor, thirty stories up, all sounds hushed. Through broad windows in rooms they passed, Nicola could see sunlight reflecting off the US Bank Tower, its glare cut by polarized glass. Her boots clumped and slid on the glass-smooth hardwood floor.

She tried again. "Mark, the VPNs were properly passworded but I found—"

"Good." He slowed to take a sheaf of paper from a young man who appeared beside them—another hockey player, probably, with short hair, an athlete's build, and a suit almost as nice as his boss's. "What's this?"

"Q1 income statement." The guy glanced at Nicola, not bothering to hide his disdain. "Gross is down two percent, net up five."

"Excellent." Kells didn't seem cheered, though. "Come on in. Something comes up, you can answer the details." He pushed through a pair of dark wood doors, leading Nicola and the hockey player into the boardroom.

The entire rear wall was glass, looking out over Los Angeles. An oval table gleamed, twenty feet of polished granite already cluttered with papers, binders, and blue-glass tumblers of water. High-back leather chairs on chrome rollers. And fifteen men, all white, all over fifty, all wearing suits of dark blue or gray.

All staring at her.

Right. Nicola deliberately squared her shoulders in the garish blazer and smiled blandly back at them. It almost worked, until the laptop strap slipped and she had to grab awkwardly to keep the bag from falling again.

"Sorry we're late." Kells dropped into a chair. A six-foot flatscreen on the wall behind him displayed the Gladco logo. "Had to wait for her to get here."

"Let's keep it moving." The chairman, whose scowling and tight-lipped face had been all over the business media for weeks, leaned on his arms at the head of the table. "Who's this?"

"We contracted a stem-to-stern security audit," Kells said. "Part of it was full-scale penetration testing—"

"I know. It wasn't cheap. And they send us the intern?"

Nice. Nicola fought a sudden urge to laugh. "Gentlemen." She walked to the end of the table, opposite the chairman, and dropped her laptop bag to the polished surface. "I'm the principal, Nicola Juravik."

"Principle penetration tester?" One of the men seemed to think this was funny.

"Yes." She removed and opened her laptop without looking down.

"What do you penetrate?"

"Hardened firewalls." Nicola glanced at him. "Got any?"

A rustle of laughter down the table. Kells coughed.

"Nicola threw a four-thousand-node botnet against our network," he said. "Didn't make a scratch."

"Of course not." The chairman shook his head. "Booz Allen rebuilt our systems last year. They guaranteed we're secure."

She knew what they were thinking: *Where's the computer geek? She looks like my housekeeper, for Christ's sake. How can a girl do this stuff?*

"Who are you worried about?" Nicola, tapping at her keyboard, looked up long enough to see the chairman's frown. "Competitors? The Chinese? Anonymous? It matters—they all have different styles."

"Fuck all of them."

"Okay, fair enough."

A man to her left, with gray hair buzzed down to stubble, spoke up. "Is this even necessary? You said our computers are locked up tight. Why are we wasting time?"

"That's not—"

"Covering the bases." Kells smoothly overrode her answer. "We've had enough challenges in the media lately, right? We should be absolutely certain we have control over our own information flow."

"And do we?" The chairman seemed impatient.

Kells turned to Nicola. "Let's go through it. Any weaknesses in the network?"

"None that I was able to exploit." She hit one final command, then straightened up. "Some unsecured data on the point-of-sale network, but it was isolated to a few batch transfers—a careless store manager in Idaho, nothing to worry about."

"Remote access?"

"The VPN is bulletproof, and randomized password testing passed—a fifth-order dictionary attack couldn't shake anything loose." As she talked, back in the one realm she'd really mastered, her confidence trickled back.

"Physical security?"

Nicola hesitated. "That's not my domain. If someone loses a phone or a computer, you could have a problem. For what it's worth, I checked one laptop and didn't find any obvious weaknesses—disk encryption and overlay passwords were solid."

"Excellent." Kells paused. "Whose laptop was it? I don't remember authorizing a loaner."

It had been Kells's own, in fact, but Nicola just smiled. "It was in a conference room where I was waiting."

"Fine." He nodded and leaned back, looking toward the chairman. "I think that's it. Seems unnecessarily redundant, but the reorg put IT under my department only four months ago, and I wanted to be absolutely sure we're running a first-class operation." A nod to Nicola. "Which it seems we are."

"Good."

Most of the men at the table were still watching Nicola. An HVAC breeze blew steadily, cooling her under the purple jacket.

"We're not quite done," she said.

"Don't worry, your check's in the mail." Kells laughed.

Nicola hit a key on her laptop, and the screen at the front of the room lit up.

A file appeared—a spreadsheet list, abbreviations and numbers, a column of dates. She breathed out, releasing some tension she hadn't know was there.

The board members swung around, one after another, the chairman last of all as he realized they were staring at something behind him.

"What's *that*?" He squinted at the display. "Wait—how did you put it *up* there?"

"Check out the dates," Nicola said. "And the dollar figures. Look—I subtotaled some of them on the right." She flicked her trackpad, and the screen scrolled. "It took some work, but I was able to match them to news reports."

Muttering from the table, but the chairman got it first. "Holy shit!"

"Someone," Nicola said, "*someone* was evidently dumb enough to keep track of all those facilitation payments that have been in the news. In a nice, clear Excel file."

She was being polite. *Facilitation payments*—that meant bribes, generally in the six-figures-and-up range, and not just in countries like Romania and Paraguay. Tax authorities around the globe would be very interested in this data.

Very, very interested.

The chairman stood up. "Shut that off."

"As you wish." Nicola tapped a key and the display went dark.

"Whose file was that? How many copies are there? Where did it go?" Not panicky, because C-level executives never showed panic. But loud, and fast, and angry.

"I don't really do forensics. You'll have to put your own people on the backtrail."

"Surely you can tell us where you found it." His voice took on a dangerous edge.

"On the laptop I mentioned."

"And whose—"

"Tell you what." Nicola bent to her laptop. "Give me a few seconds here. I'll show you the obvious clues."

The room was absolutely silent but for the light clicking of her keyboard. Even the airflow had shut down. The men at the table seemed frozen in place.

"While we're waiting," said the chairman, "tell me one thing. Has it leaked? Anywhere outside the company? Anywhere at *all*?"

"I think you'd have heard if it had." Nicola paused, watched a file open, then nodded. "Here we go." She hit one more command, and the room's display brightened again.

"File metadata," she said. "Straight from the spreadsheet I found."

```
workgroup: acctg
log: ac234454n.bak
author: mkells
```

It only took a moment. Muttering rose as all eyes turned to Kells.

"Mark?" The chairman's icy gaze was unblinking. "Is this yours?"

Blustering and denial, but in seconds, the entire room had turned its collective blame on the CFO. Nicola shut down the display again, closed her laptop, and packed up. It took less than a minute. She traveled light.

"Excuse me?" she said. "The check that was mentioned."

"Don't worry." The chairman glared at her.

"Certified, drawn on a major bank. I'll pick it up on my way out. In, say"—Nicola looked at the Rolex—"four minutes."

"I don't know—"

"Four minutes." She smiled at the table. "A pleasure, gentlemen. May I be in touch about a recommendation? Well, we can discuss that later."

Outside, she found her own way back to reception, where the woman on the phone held up one finger, then put her hand over the mouthpiece. "One sec, okay, hon?"

"Sure." While Nicola waited, she dug her phone from bag. A cable got tangled up with it and fell, trailing to the floor. She quickly packed it back in and studied the phone.

"Because the chairman *said* so. Yes, that's right. Immediately . . . Get it up here. To me." The receptionist paused. "Oh, really? You want me to tell him that or shall I put you through directly? No?"

A minute later she hung up. "Sorry, it's going to be a few minutes."

"Not a problem. Thanks for your help."

"Perhaps I shouldn't ask, but . . . what were you doing in there?"

"Exactly what they hired me for, as it happens." Nicola shook her head. "Sometimes they're surprised."

"That's not the word I'd use."

When the check finally arrived, delivered by a young man somewhat out of breath, Nicola tucked it into her pocket and nodded thanks.

"Must be an exciting job you have," the receptionist said.

"Every assignment is different. Most are pretty dull."

"What are you doing next?"

"I'm not sure." Nicola looked at her phone again. "But this one has some potential."

CHAPTER NINETEEN

Six weeks was far too tight a schedule, but Finn still shouldn't have scheduled meetings with Nicola, Emily, and the real estate broker all the same morning.

The warehouse was much as he had assumed: concrete floor, plain metal walls, dusty and dim. A little light filtered through the bay-door windows, more from the clerestory overhead. The ground shook occasionally as trains rumbled past on the mainline just across the street. The broker was distracted the entire time, thumbing his phone and looking at his watch. Finn had a story all made up—expanding operations, Christmas season overflow, they needed a short-term solution for rail-to-port transshipment—but the broker was barely interested.

"What do you think?"

"I'll confirm it with corporate, and we should be good to go this week," Finn said. "Maybe as soon as tomorrow."

That got a moment's full attention. "Two months' advance, right?"

"I'll have a check in hand."

The broker grinned and even pocketed his phone long enough to shake hands. "Welcome to the neighborhood."

Nicola was next. Finn had barely seen the broker off when she drove up. He stood by his truck, giving a small wave to let her know she was at the right place. The weather had warmed but not much. Shifting winds carried diesel and oil fumes from the train yard across the avenue.

"Nicola?"

"Nice to meet you, Finn." She slammed the door of her silver econobox, presumably a rental, while he looked her over.

Heavy boots and a watch cap. Her handshake was hard. Short but blocky, like she'd be more at home swinging a shovel than sitting at a keyboard. Not pretty, and that was probably all to the good. He imagined her sitting between Asher and Corman, and it almost worked.

"Thanks for coming."

"It was a lot warmer in California."

Some who-do-you-know? and have-you-heard-from? confirmed bona fides. Jake had asked around, and though the guy in jail might not be reliable on his own, several other contacts had confirmed her ability and discretion. Finn assumed she'd done the same on him.

"So that's the target over there." He explained the project in broad terms.

"Uh-huh . . . Got it . . . That's interesting." She paid attention, asked a few questions.

"What do you think?"

Nicola smiled. "It's freezing. Can we talk inside somewhere?"

"Sure."

They ended up at Karl's Lunch, a few blocks away. Typical workingman's diner—Formica tables and a luncheonette bar, ESPN on the screen and a counterman by the fryolator. They took a booth in the back, alongside a wall-mounted heater that seemed to be running at max. It was plenty warm inside, and the heater's buzzy hum made their conversation private.

"Deniability," said Nicola, holding her coffee cup in two hands but not drinking. "You want to know what's most important to me on a job, that's it. I operate from cover."

"How does that work?"

"We figure out what needs to be done, coordinate schedules, draw up a plan. Then we split up. You go do your thing. I take care of my end on my own."

"Fair enough."

The waitress brought over their order. "Ham, eggs, and biscuits must be for you," she said to Finn, setting the large platter down too quickly for him to correct her. Nicola got a half grapefruit. When the waitress had gone, they switched plates.

"I already had breakfast," Finn said.

"Me, too." Nicola shook hot sauce over her entire dish. "Doesn't mean I'm not hungry again."

Finn watched her eat with some admiration.

"Here's my problem," he said. "I've worked just about all the trades, one time or another. Heavy equipment, electrical, carpentry, whatever. I started in the mills, back before they all closed, and I've probably still got seniority with the pipefitters, somewhere."

"Uh-huh."

"So when I'm running a job, anything I tell someone to do, I know how to do it myself, right? What's possible, what isn't. How long it's going to take. What to do when the compressor breaks, how many Sawzall blades we'll need to go through a wall. I've done it all."

"Yup." Nicola had already finished all the ham and most of the eggs. "But computers, they're a big mystery, right? You kind of know what needs to happen, but it might as well be wizards and vampires."

"Yes."

"So you're not sure about me."

Finn nodded. "I can't even ask the right questions. Have to just take it all on faith, basically."

"You've got a single-point-of-failure problem, too. Say we're at zero hour, and I get hit by a bus. You're fucked."

"Exactly right." Finn sipped his coffee. "Is this how you sell all your jobs?"

Nicola grinned. "Let me ask you something. Way back at the dawn of time, when you got your first paying employment—"

"It wasn't *that* long ago."

"I know, the big comet had already killed all the lizards. Anyway. I'd guess what you mostly did was, there's a big pile of shit *here* that needs to be over *there*. And here's a shovel."

"Well . . . that's pretty close."

"But after a while, you got good with the shovel, so they let you pick up a pipe wrench now and then. Maybe the hammer drill. Even drive the truck on occasion—go get cigarettes or a load of two-by-fours."

Finn looked at her. "Hammer drill?"

"Nothing I'd ever use." Nicola scraped her last biscuit across the plate, scouring it clean. "But see, that's exactly the point. I did the same damn thing. Started out fixing computers for the Geek Squad. Remember them? Stupid fucking cars, clip-on ties? They didn't think I was legally employable, I had to bring in a birth certificate."

"Really?"

"I didn't go to college to learn this stuff," Nicola said. "I taught myself. Mostly by fucking things up and then having to fix it while everyone yelled at me. But just like you, I've done it all. I've coded injection scripts in fucking assembler, which is about as mind-numbing as you can imagine. I've gone to war with Belorussian gangs launching DDOS takedowns from a quarter-million-node botnet. For five days, I *owned* a Dutch certificate authority—I heard Google called the NSA in on that one. You can imagine."

"Actually, no," Finn said, "I can't imagine. I didn't understand a word of that."

She shrugged. "Let's see. Do you know Jonesy Malloy?"

"No."

"Bull Hauer? Tim Creed?" Nicola grimaced as Finn kept shaking his head. "How about Mick Tresfort?"

"Okay, sure."

"Well enough to call him up?"

"Probably. He still owes me two hundred bucks on a Steelers game." Back before Finn had gone to jail, that was.

"Right. So when you're talking, ask him about Alderville. Three years ago. He brought me on for alarm bypass while his guys went into a pharma warehouse. Eight million dollars of hospital narcotics—a good payday, even at black market discounting."

"And what will Mick tell me?"

"The fact he's not in prison is all you really need to know. I had the security systems totally under control, but, you know, bad luck—some neighborhood watch asshole noticed the truck back in at three a.m. and called the police."

"High-end pharmaceuticals," Finn said. "Real money there, I've heard. What did you do?"

"The warehouse cameras were monitored by a central office a hundred miles away—a contract agency, and they had dozens of other facilities on watch. Of course, I've got local 911 and the emergency frequencies on the scanner, just in case. When I hear the call, I know we have like three minutes." She raised her eyebrows. "In two minutes and seventeen seconds, I trip every single circuit the monitoring company has open. Screaming alarms at three dozen companies all over the Atlanta metro area."

"Nice."

"It was chaos, of course. Mick got away in the confusion."

Finn decided to be impressed. He'd check the story, but what the hell, he liked her.

"Good," he said. "What's your availability in the next month or so?"

"Oh, I'm free." Nicola frowned. "But that's not much time."

"Really? Weren't you just telling me something about two minutes and seventeen seconds?"

"Ha ha." Nicola drained her coffee. "It's not like the movies. What you're talking about isn't just the alarms. I'm going to have research the systems the railroad uses—proprietary, probably, but even if not, I've never dealt with this industry. There's a learning curve. The software is the *easy* part. Figuring out what to attack, and how, that's what you're paying me for."

"Hmm." Finn studied her face. "Did we just start negotiating?"

Nicola laughed. "I'm not trying to jack you. I get the same as everyone else, right?"

"Sure."

"Sometimes—what do the firefighters call it when they can't just point the hoses from outside, and they have to go into the building?"

"Inside attack."

"That's right. Sometimes, jobs like we're talking about, the guys doing inside attack figure they should earn more than the girl sitting in a comfy chair outside."

"Nope." Finn leaned back in the booth, more and more comfortable with her. "We're like pirates here—everyone gets an equal share."

"Good." Nicola pushed her plates aside. "Okay. Let's talk about some details. Do you know who's in—"

A ringtone sounded from her jacket pocket. She pulled out her phone and glanced at the screen, then swiped it a couple times.

"Sorry," she said, tapping the screen, then again, with increasing annoyance. "The damn thing just ran out of battery." She looked up. "Hey, do you think . . . ?"

"What?"

"Could I borrow your phone? Just for a sec? Terribly rude, I know, there's this call I was waiting for."

"Sure." Finn handed over his. There was nothing on it he had to worry about—no contact list, no emails, no website shortcuts. He used it for phone calls and nothing else.

"Thanks." Nicola took a moment to familiarize herself with the screen, tapped a few times, and dialed. She held it to her ear. "And . . . no answer. Shit. Sorry about that."

She handed back the phone. As Finn was putting it away, someone stepped up to their booth—not the waitress and coming in on his blind side, surprising him. For a moment, he went into reaction mode, swinging around fast.

"Hi, Finn." Emily, smiling at him, but cautious, seeing Nicola. She was carrying a laptop case over one shoulder, a scarf still wrapped around her neck and chin.

"Em— Uh, hey." He looked from one to the other. "Didn't we say eleven?"

"Not as much traffic as I expected."

Well, it wasn't like she was unaware of what Finn was up to. He gestured an introduction. "This is . . . ah—"

"Nicola." She stood, accidentally knocking the table with her hip. Plates and cutlery rattled. She glanced down but ignored it and held out her hand.

If she was intimidated by Emily—taller, beautiful, immaculate—it didn't show.

"Emily." No last names. "Sorry, didn't mean to interrupt."

"No problem." Finn pushed his finished grapefruit aside. "Nicola, can we take a break? You could get another coffee. Emily and I have some, ah . . . paperwork to go over."

"Sure." Nicola leaned over to pick up her coat. "Take your time."

Emily watched her walk to the counter and sit down, politely choosing a stool with her back to them.

"Sorry," she said again. "Weren't we going to meet at the warehouse?"

"Never mind." Finn gestured to Nicola's side of the booth. "Have a seat. It's a lot more comfortable inside."

The waitress came by and cleared the plates. Emily ordered tea. The heater cycled off, then on again. Condensation had slowly built up on the plateglass windows along the front, diffusing the day's light.

"There's a problem," Emily said.

Uh-oh.

Finn sighed. "What's going on?"

"Heart Pine is being flooded by redemption requests. Rumors, bad luck, I don't know."

"Redemption?"

"Investors want their money back. Right this second. And the way the agreements are written, Wes doesn't have much choice."

Over the years, Finn had organized a dozen major operations—big jobs, the ones that took months of setup, many people involved. In only two cases did the work go more or less as planned.

Things happened. You dealt with it.

"He told me he was golden," Finn said. "You were there, too. He was worried that news of the counterfeit ingots *might* get out—not that it already had."

"I don't think it's that. I've asked some of the investors myself, when they call in, and I've been following the news. It has more to do with the market generally. China's caught cold, commodities everywhere are slumping, and people figure Wes is simply overexposed. It's a herd mentality. Once a few loudmouths make up their mind, everyone else falls all over himself doing the same thing."

"That sounds stupid."

"Not really. Everybody's measured against benchmarks nowadays. Make money, lose money, it doesn't matter so long as you're no worse than average. The wrongest thing you can do is something different from everyone else—because that's how you miss the target."

"And . . . Wes is in the doghouse."

"Well, his funds are."

"So the job's off."

"No, no, I didn't say that." Emily sat straighter in the booth. "If anything, Wes is even more keen that you go ahead. In fact, he said he's hoping to spin it into an insurance settlement, too. Solve the counterfeit problem but make a little profit on top."

Of course. "If all the lights are still green, what's the issue?"

Emily hesitated. "He doesn't have the working capital."

"Working capital?" It took Finn a moment. "What, you mean *our* money?"

"Yes."

The waitress dropped off Emily's tea. Lipton, in a bag. She squeezed it out and dumped in two sugars.

"So how much can he front us?" Finn asked.

Emily made an apologetic face. "Eighteen thousand. It's all he can scrape together."

"On top of the ten you already gave me?"

"No. Inclusive."

Finn sat back against the booth's vinyl. "We need five times that!"

"Let me quote: 'How expensive can it be to dig a fucking hole?'" Emily grinned. "'I'll buy the damn pickaxes myself,' he said."

"Jesus Christ."

They fell silent. Finn ran contingencies in his head, looking for a way through.

Emily reached over and touched his forearm.

"What I'm seeing?" she said. "Wes is going *down*."

"What do you mean?"

"It's always been a little rough and ready, the way he operates. Like we were talking about. He skates right along the edge."

"He hired me. Twice."

"There you go. Not, I mean—you know what I mean."

"Uh-huh. So he's, what, Heart Pine is falling apart?"

"It's not pretty."

Finn considered. "Does that mean that everything—the company, his funds, his future—everything depends on us doing this job?"

"I think you're the Hail Mary."

The waitress came by again, cleared the last dishes, and left a ticket. Approaching lunchtime, the diner was slowly filling. Finn looked over at Nicola, who had struck up a cheerful conversation with the counterman.

"And he can only scrape up eight grand?"

"I don't know. That's really nothing—literal pocket change for him." Emily shook her head slightly. "Crash and fucking burn."

"What's he doing with the metal?"

"Nothing. He can't sell it, because of the counterfeits."

"How long does he have?"

"The way things are going, I'd say the end of the year. No one wants a blowup right as they're closing their books. But come January, they're going to be at the door with pitchforks and torches."

"Then . . . our schedule still works."

"By the calendar, yes." She picked up the tab and glanced at the scrawled figures. "He's counting on you, Finn."

The money was a problem. Finn wasn't sure how they could do the job for nothing—for example, he had a day to come up with twenty-six thousand dollars for the broker. But if they could make it work somehow, once inside, they were already planning to grab everything for themselves. Wes fucking up, over in his expensive midtown offices, was basically irrelevant.

Finn looked at Emily for a long moment, wondering.

"What do you think we should do?" he asked, genuinely curious.

"Exactly what you've been planning." Her smile had a cold edge. "And then clean him the fuck out."

CHAPTER TWENTY

I'm telling you, this is what the internet is for." Asher slumped in the panel van's passenger seat, grousing. "Companies want to sell stuff, they put it online. Why the fuck are we driving all over New Jersey? We could Google it, make a few phone calls, finish in thirty minutes."

Corman grunted. They were in heavy traffic on the Garden State Parkway, vehicles stopping and starting, brake lights glowing in the dusk across all six lanes. He drove warily, one full car length of distance at all times, hands at two and ten o'clock.

"Or better yet, I bet there's probably a half dozen websites that are, like, specialized. *Used-excavators-cheap-dot-com*, some shit like that. Pictures and everything, you know?"

Some jackass abruptly tried to change lanes, causing panic stops all around. Corman hit the brakes, jolting the van hard. Horns blew.

"*Fuck* this." Asher had been thrown against the dash. "Can't you—"

"Put your seat belt on."

"I never wear them."

"Dumb."

"I never told you about that time I saw a guy roll his car off the highway? Must have been drunk or who knows what, sun shining and all. He wasn't strapped in, that's why he lived—went right out through the window, and the car slid into the river. He'd've drowned for sure if he'd been stuck inside."

"Yeah."

"That's what I'm saying. Saved his life."

"Yeah, you *told* me already."

They crawled on through the rush-hour mire. Corman was hungry, but he didn't say anything. No point in reminding Asher of something else to complain about.

"I liked the last one." Asher had his phone out, swiping at the screen. "Got a nice picture of it. That Chinese skid steer. Guy seemed willing to deal, too."

"They were all willing to deal," said Corman. "Not much demand for electric-motor excavators."

"No shit. It was me, I'd drive over the fucking cable all the time, probably electrocute myself." He looked up. "Aren't we there yet?"

"Almost." Corman had his signal on for the next exit. "You got maps on that thing?"

"I thought you knew where we were going!"

"Finn just told me the address."

Asher got the phone's GPS going. "Looks like . . . take a right off the ramp. Down there a ways."

It was an industrial zone—chain link and truck lots, metal-walled Butler buildings and piles of scrap. Corman followed Asher's directions, and they turned off the main road, bumping down a rutted way between rows of closely parked cargo trailers. Most carried dirty forty-foot containers, paint flaking and streaked with grime.

"I don't know why we couldn't just meet at the motel, same as we been doing," Asher said.

"Finn said the hacker girl didn't think it was safe."

"What the hell does *she* know?"

Corman shrugged. "More than me and you—about computers."

"You ask me, she's fucking with us."

"Didn't ask."

They rounded a corner, the long row of containers finally ending.

"Whoa!" Asher sat up. "Look at that."

A dozen school buses were parked on one side of an asphalt apron. Crammed in front of them were several airplane fuselages, from a little executive jet up to what looked like a 747. All were damaged—scorched by fire, wings torn off, tilted at bad angles on smashed landing gears.

"You know," said Asher, "I don't think the airlines want people to see *this* shit."

Behind the aircraft, a row of cranes pointed into the sky. Cherry pickers, tower cranes, hydraulic forklifts. It was going dark, and a few antiquated sodium lights cast more shadow than illumination.

Corman rolled the window down. He thought he smelled smoke—not the pleasant wood-fired kind, but oily and chemical laden.

"Weren't we, like, driving through suburbs a couple miles back?" Asher seemed impressed.

"I don't know." Corman closed his window. "Which way now?"

"Up ahead." Asher gestured. "Somewhere. Was this her idea?"

"What?"

"The hacker girl. Did she choose the place? Because, you know, this ain't exactly the Microsoft campus."

They drove past a lot full of delivery trucks, old ones, crusted with graffiti and dirt, all parked nose to tail and apparently abandoned.

"Tell you what," Corman said. "Maybe we can find an excavator right here."

Finn looked around. Uninsulated metal siding, some light fixtures way up at the roof, and a dirty concrete floor visible between vast heaps of junk. Broad roller doors looked out at even larger piles of scrap, pushed twenty feet high by the front loader still at work around the corner. Absolutely nothing natural visible anywhere, except for dirt—no trees, no grass, no creatures, no bugs even. Rats maybe, somewhere. But what would they eat?

Over engine noise and clanking from the front loader, Finn said, "Fuck it all. Maybe I can just get a job here."

Jake laughed. "Tinch sits in the office all day. Nicer in there."

Tinch was Jake's contact. Happy to let them use the warehouse after hours, equally happy to take the two bills Jake had offered.

The front loader's engine faded, then cut out completely, coughing into silence. Darkness was falling fast. Jake found a wall panel and threw the breaker, switching on three overhead bulbs just as the equipment operator looked in the door.

"Going now," the man said. He had a helmet in one hand, heavy gloves in the other, a thick coating of grime and dirt over his boots and coveralls. "Tinch says you can close up. Main thing, be sure you close the padlocks on the gate."

"Appreciate it."

"Don't go wandering around other side of the fence. Tinch mentioned, right? They got Dobermans over there."

"You don't?" Jake said.

"Who'd steal this shit?" The man half waved and disappeared.

Finn looked at a ten-foot jumble of plumbing scrap next to him: brass pipe, fixtures and fittings, the pipes bent and broken, everything tarnished, old.

"Someone already did," he said. "Stripped it from abandoned buildings."

"Yeah."

"Maybe not abandoned, some of them."

Jake shrugged. "Could be contractors. Tear-outs. Someone shows up with a pickup truck full, I don't think Tinch is gonna ask about provenance."

Corman and Asher arrived, bickering.

"Trouble finding your way?" Finn said.

"No."

Grunt.

"I *knew* where we were going, all you had to do was—"

Jake found some mismatched crates along the wall, pulled them out to sit on. The incandescents overhead cast dim and inadequate light. Finn walked around a bit, checking visibility, but even through the open doors, mountains of scrap outside blocked anyone from seeing them.

"Hey, guys." Nicola strode in, gray courier bag over one shoulder, gray jacket, gray pants, gray hat. "Hi, Finn. How's it going?"

Conversation stopped dead.

"Glad you could make it, Nicola." Finn pointed. "Corman, Asher, Jake."

"Nice to meet you." She kind of waved, looked around, and chose the closest crate. It creaked as she thumped her butt down onto it. "Love the setting."

"Really?"

"This is *exactly* where you should be planning the heist of the century."

Corman grunted. Finn thought amusement might have been in there somewhere, but it was hard to tell.

"This is a dump," Asher said. "Literally. A fucking junkyard. What was wrong with the hotel room?"

"Hang on." Nicola stared at her cell phone, then raised it in the air and moved it left and right. Seconds passed.

"No signal?" Jake asked politely.

Another few moments, and Nicola put the phone down, looked at everyone. "Just a quick check," she said. "Clean. If someone's got a wire in here, they're using oddball frequencies. Seems unlikely."

"Uh-huh," Jake said. "That's like, what, you got some kind of special app on that?"

"Modified hardware." Nicola unfolded a thick metallic bag and unsnapped it. "Okay, everyone, time to hand over your phones. In here."

No one moved. In the silence, Finn could hear a truck grinding into gear nearby. The air smelled of grease and metal.

"How about I just take the battery out?" Jake, smiling, tried to charm away the tension. "That's what they do on TV."

Nicola shook her head. "Not good enough."

"No." Asher crossed his arms. "Who's running this fucking show? We don't even know you. I'm not handing over anything."

A snort from Corman, which could have meant anything. But no one reached for his phone.

"Finn?" She looked his way.

"You're the expert," he said. "But . . ."

"Okay." Nicola set the Faraday bag aside and found her own phone again. "We need the dog and the pony, that's fine. Give me a minute here."

They watched her run a cable to another device, half visible in the courier bag—small, black, anonymous. No blinking lights. She tapped at the screen.

Tinny sounds, too faint to understand.

"Can't hear it," Finn said.

"Sorry." She tapped again. A scratchy voice blared out:

"—OUGHT YOU KNEW WHERE WE WERE GOING."

"FINN JUST TOLD ME THE ADDRESS."

"LOOKS LIKE . . . TAKE A RIGHT OFF THE RAMP."

Asher suddenly leaned forward, hands on his knees. "What the fuck? Is that—?"

Jake looked puzzled. Corman raised an eyebrow. Finn kept a poker face, not sure what Nicola was doing. A clanging in the yard nearby obscured the playback for a moment.

"—THIS HER IDEA?"

"WHAT?"

"THE HACKER GIRL. DID SHE CHOOSE THE PLACE? BECAU—"

She tapped again, abruptly cutting the sound, and looked up with a bright smile. "Anybody recognize that?"

"That's impossible." Asher glared at Corman. "You're in on this, aren't you?"

Shrug.

"Know what? Not fucking funny."

Corman's voice was deep and slow. "Twenty minutes ago," he said. "Tops."

"What?"

He looked at Finn. "Me and the rockhead, talking in the truck on the way over. Not half an hour ago."

Asher squawked. Finn sighed. "Magic."

Nicola shook her head again. "No." All business now, sitting straight on the crate, playfulness gone. "I got your numbers from Finn's phone yesterday. He didn't notice. Last night, I phished each of you—remember the text you got? *Call me back its super important*?"

"Sure," Jake said. "Deleted it straightaway."

"Smart." Nicola inclined her head in his direction. "That's the right thing to do if you don't know who it is. Because there might be a payload, some bad code, a little bit of malware hidden in the link."

"Malware?"

"Oh, for instance, a root exploit with a process hack." She saw their incomprehension. "Look, that device in your hand, it's got a microphone, a computer, a cellular connection, and Wi-Fi. A *five-year-old* could turn it into a remote listening device."

Finn replayed his memory from the diner yesterday morning. He'd handed her the phone, she glanced at it, tapped the screen once or twice.

She'd memorized his entire call list, with no obvious break in the conversation, in less than ten seconds.

"Okay, I'm impressed." He turned at the others. "Are you impressed?"

Grumbling.

"Only one of you clicked through," Nicola said helpfully. "About average."

They all looked at Asher.

"What? What?"

Eventually, they passed over their devices. She dropped them in the metallized bag, folded the top over a Velcro strip, and set it on a vacant crate.

"Wait a minute," Asher said. "What about the batteries? You didn't even turn them off! What the—"

"Tinfoil. Mesh something." Corman looked at Nicola. "Right?"

"Exactly. Blocks everything."

They finally got down to business. The air was cold and getting colder, the crates not comfortable.

"Before we start," said Finn. "There's a decision to make."

Jake caught the tone and looked hard at him, which flagged Corman's attention.

"Long and short," Finn said, "Wes is pulling back."

Silence and frowns.

"What does that mean?" Jake asked slowly.

"Business is bad. He's losing cash. Customers are withdrawing their investments." Finn raised his hands, like, *Who knows?* "Everything is a lot tighter all of a sudden."

"So?"

"So, apparently, he's unable to front us for setup."

A long beat. Asher, who'd been focused on Nicola and her equipment, looked up, grimacing.

"That's bullshit." Jake, speaking for everyone.

"I agree."

"You can't do something like this for *free*. The boring rig alone is going to cost thirteen grand."

"Yup."

"And even if we dug our way in with shovels, how do we get paid if he's got no money?"

The complaints became general, except for Nicola, who frowned slightly and said nothing. Finn let them grouse awhile.

"Here's the thing," he said, when the muttering died down. "I got nothing else lined up. As you know."

"I quit my job and drove all the way across the country!" Asher, aggrieved.

Corman looked at him. "You *quit*?"

But Jake's expression eased. "Wait a minute. You've got an idea, don't you?"

"Oh, yes." Finn nodded.

"And?"

"We need front money. Takes money to make money, right? But Wes says he's not liquid."

"What?"

"Says he's broke. Happy to pay us all we want when we're done, once he gets over this cash-flow hump, but until then, we're on our own."

"Yeah . . ."

"So," Finn shrugged, "we're going to have to bootstrap."

"Uh-huh." Corman, unimpressed. "Bootstrap a hundred grand."

"Plus or minus."

"If we had that much, we might not need to do the damn job in the first place," said Asher, pointing out the obvious.

A siren in the distance, maybe out on the Garden State, silenced them for a minute. When it faded away, Nicola raised her hand like a student at her desk.

"Uh, yes, Nicola?"

"You don't seem to bothered by this development."

"Well—"

"You know how to get the money we need, don't you?"

"Maybe."

"Want to share?"

"Wes may not have any cash lying around." Finn felt a small smile. "But he likes cars."

"Cars?"

"Nice cars. Fast, expensive cars." Pause. "In fact, he collects them."

The mood changed.

"I like cars, too," she said. "*Especially* the fast, expensive kind."

"We'd have to work fast," Finn said. "Schedule's too damn tight already."

Only Asher was unmoved.

"You're talking about a whole second job," he said. "Doubles the work, practically. Where are all these shiny roadsters? I assume Wes lives in some huge mansion. Electric fences, alarms, guard service, dogs, God knows what."

"There are far too many to keep in the garage. He's got a warehouse in Windham County. Outside Hartford somewhere."

"Ah." He looked a little more happy. "But still—"

"This one is *easy*," Finn said. "What do you say? Want to do it?"

CHAPTER TWENTY-ONE

Their cash had gone, but the expenses weren't going to disappear. From here on out, they had to be creative. So, bright and early the next morning, sunshine on the streets and an arepa from a pushcart in one hand, Finn dialed the broker.

"Hey, I was just thinking about you. How's it going?"

"Couldn't be better."

"Corporate's on board?"

"They just want to get this done."

"Then we're all the same page." The broker laughed.

The streetlight changed, and a massive garbage hauler lurched into motion, engine roaring. Finn waited until the noise eased.

"I'm ready to sign the papers," he said. "But there's a hitch."

"Oh?"

"We're in the usual year-end cash-flow crunch."

"Yes . . . ?"

"On the other hand, prospects are looking even better than I thought. So I tell you what—forget the short term, we'll sign a five-year lease."

"Excellent!"

"However . . ."

A long beat. "Yes?"

"You'll have to abate the first quarter's rent."

Silence.

"But . . . I'm afraid . . . I don't think that's going to be possible."

"Hey, I'm not asking for a discount. Just roll it into the next three quarters. Hell, you want to balloon it all at the end, that's fine, too."

"Uh-huh."

"Like I said, this is just about cash flow." Finn took a bite of arepa and spoke around it. "Our order book is solid. But I can't talk anyone into paying in advance—you know how it goes."

The broker laughed again, less convincingly. "Yeah, but—"

"So, okay, I'm asking for some help over the hurdle, but I know you can't do this for free. Help me make this happen, and maybe I can help *you* out, okay? Throw a couple extra points in the back end, and I'll make sure we pay them down first."

"Uh . . ."

"We can get this done as soon as possible. That's got to be good for your quota, am I wrong?"

"Well, ah, we—"

"And if it'll help smooth the way, let's see . . . I could make the bonus three points." Finn paused, wondering if he was going to have to spell it out. "If necessary, on a *separate invoice*."

"Oh. Okay. Okay!" The broker came back strong, finally catching on. "Got you, right. No, I don't think we have to make the paperwork complicated."

"Good."

"In fact, we can probably handle that piece informally."

Finn smiled. "Indeed."

"On an accelerated schedule, though. To make things as expeditious as possible."

The arepa was only half gone, but Finn tossed it into a trash can at the corner. "When were you thinking?" he said.

"No need to waste time." The broker was back to his usual cheerful self. "How about this afternoon?"

Late in the day, David met Sean on the old bridge across the rails at the neck of the classification yard, where the incoming line branched into numerous parallel tracks, one after another. The span was ancient cast iron, as old as the yard itself, and Penn Southern maintained it out of nostalgia more than anything. The walkway had a few weathered milk crates and a heap of cigarette butts lying around—the switchies came up for breaks when the weather was good.

The sun was setting behind Newark, orange sky fading into dark purple. A few yard locomotives pushed cuts around below them, clanking here and there. Long rows of flatcars and tankers and gondolas stood silent, waiting their turns.

"I like it up here," David said, ignoring the pain in his knees from the climb. "You don't get nearly as good a view from the dispatch tower."

"All those cars." Sean leaned on the rail, looking over the acres of track and rolling stock. "Hard to imagine how they did it in the old days, keeping track of everything on paper and chalkboards."

"They were smarter back then. Computers make us dumb."

Sean looked at the phone in his hand, then put it away. "Sure thing, boss."

"You sound like my grandkids. *Right, Grandpa. Uh-huh, sure.*"

A fully assembled train eased its way out through the north portal, the long row of autoracks and containers rattling beneath them. David gave the engineer a half salute, and the locomotive's whistle sounded briefly.

"The shop is working on a flatbed for the excavator," Sean said. "Welding on some new supports, adding tie-down points. Shouldn't be a problem to shift it off the railcar."

"What were you doing in there?"

"Naw, I wasn't in the shop. I ran into the foreman in the cafeteria. He didn't seem worried about it."

"I'm sure they'll move it in and move it out, no problem." David gestured to the parking lot in front of the administration buildings. "The trouble's going to be over there."

"Yeah, I guess."

"They want to protest, where else can they go? The rest of the perimeter is just a big fence. The entrance is the logical gathering space."

"So what are we going to do about it?"

"If it were up to me? Absolutely nothing. So long as they're not throwing themselves across the tracks, I don't care. If we keep the doors and the yard gate locked, all they can do is stand around. We could have a few guys outside, offer them coffee."

"So is it up to you?"

"Of course not." David shrugged. "Boggs thinks the best response is to put a hundred paramilitaries in deep ranks with shields and beanbag shotguns. Maybe borrow that new sonic cannon the Newark police just got. You know, just to keep everyone calm."

Sean laughed. "He really does want a riot, doesn't he?"

The sun was low enough in the smoggy sky to clear the lowermost cloud cover, and its last rays illuminated the dispatch tower in a blaze of yellow light. David wished he had his camera.

"With any luck, it'll be ten degrees and sleeting," he said. "And everyone will go home after half an hour."

"Could happen."

"Boggs is going to be here himself, you know."

"Really?" Sean was surprised.

"Don't tell anybody."

"But if he's *here*, and something goes sideways . . ."

"I know. It's all on Boggs. He can't blame someone else." David nodded. "Which is maybe why the battalion of riot troops."

"Oh, man." Sean grinned. "This is gonna be great."

CHAPTER TWENTY-TWO

Finn picked Emily up down the street from the Heart Pine offices, stopping in front of a hydrant. It was after six, streetlights on, the block seeming darker because of plastic-wrapped scaffolding looming up a tower under renovation. She didn't see him or recognize the vehicle, so he got out and waved.

She walked up laughing.

"What *is* this thing? It's so cute!" The microtruck had a tiny two-person cab and an open bed. A blunt front and round headlights that gave it a toddler's toy-car look. It rode on tires much smaller than normal. The entire vehicle was barely over five feet tall, less than that wide, and about twelve feet long.

"It's a Kei truck," Finn said. "And we need it for the job. Hop in."

Inside, he sat hunched, his head brushing the roof, knees bent under the wheel. Emily got in the other side.

"Where did this come from? A carnival ride?"

"Bought it from a community college over in Jersey. Their maintenance guys were trading up."

"I thought you didn't have any money left."

"That was the last of it."

The cab was still littered with old papers, fast-food debris, and dirt. As Finn shoved the gearshift and moved back into traffic, something clattered around in the bed behind them.

"They didn't bother cleaning it up for you." Emily kept her bag in her lap.

"It was kind of an informal transaction."

"I hope you're not planning to drive on the interstate." The engine whined as Finn pushed it up to thirty-five. "Or even the parkways."

Finn looked over at her. "Would you rather walk home?"

"Oh, no. This is fun."

Crosstown rush hour was slow, pedestrian crowds dense at the corners. Finn kept to the smaller streets. Emily had her window open a few inches, and they drove past evening restaurant smells: smoke, fryer oil, a tang of spice. Illuminated signs glowed in the falling dusk.

"I checked the records," Emily said, getting down to business. "On his estate."

"Have to say I'm still surprised Wes keeps his personal book-keeping in the office."

"None of us actually work on it for him—he has an accountant come in."

"Hmm." Finn changed lanes, irritating a livery car driver. Horns blew. "What did you find out?"

"He's insured, barely. Burn down his mansion, he could build one maybe half as big."

"No need for that."

"And I didn't know he had a yacht."

"Oh?"

"Forty-seven feet long. Funny he never talks about it."

Finn glanced at her. "These files are out in the open? Not locked up? Any of you could flip through them whenever you want?"

"There are keys." She paused. "I need to know where they are, because I work with the auditors every year. Wes's private cabinet happens to be there, too."

"He didn't notice?"

"Don't worry about it. I went in early, before anyone else this morning."

Finn didn't want her getting caught. It would blow the plan, of course.

But he didn't want her getting in trouble, either.

"So the cars . . ." he said.

"His insurance rates will go up." Emily shrugged. "A lot, probably."

They drove into the Midtown Tunnel, inching along in the homeward tide. In the tube, it was dim and claustrophobic, the walls stained and damp.

"I'm not sure how to put this," Finn said, eyes on the endless taillights glowing ahead of them.

Emily waited. "Yes?"

"Have you switched sides?"

"Hmm."

"Before you were, I don't know, Wes's right-hand woman. Or something. Now . . ."

"I haven't switched sides." She turned to face him. "But when you come out of the vault with all that metal? Wes starts to circle much, much closer to the drain."

They'd been circling around the question themselves. Finn wanted it out in the open. "That insurance you mentioned isn't going to help, I take it."

She laughed. "Nope. And that's also the point when I bail out."

"Good."

"Wes is going down that drain by himself."

It eased Finn's worries. In fact, the more he thought about it, the better he felt.

"Exactly," he said.

They finally came out of the tunnel, into the scratchy night of Queens. Off the highway, the surface roads were no less crowded, taxis and commuters and the occasional bus jostling for lane space. Finn followed Emily's directions, alongside train tracks and then down Forty-Seventh Street for blocks and blocks.

He slowed and double-parked where she indicated, in front of a narrow three-story tenement with a tiny yard enclosed in chain link. Finn looked up at it.

"Not what I expected," he said.

"No?"

"A downtown loft? Tribeca penthouse? I don't know, I thought all you one-percenters needed twenty thousand square feet and a helipad."

"I'm an *employee*. If I had that kind of money . . . Fuck, I sure wouldn't be working for Wes."

Finn grimaced. "Me neither."

"Thanks for the ride." Emily's hand was on the door release, but she didn't open it.

"Sure." He glanced over. "How about I take you out to dinner?"

"Now?"

"Yeah. But, um, the fact is . . ." He frowned.

"What?"

"I don't have much money left. Buying this truck cleaned me out. So it'll have to be cheap."

Emily laughed. "I think I can cover it. This time."

Jimena's was small, bright, and cheerful. Yellow walls, dark wood. Finn eased his way into a narrow gap, jostling the table. That dislodged the candle in its center, a dim flame inside a sphere of red glass. The candle holder rolled off the table and Finn caught it just below the edge, one-handed.

"Nice," said Emily. The candle hadn't even gone out.

Finn settled it, and himself, back in place. "Lucky."

They didn't spend much time on the menu, which was scrawled on a chalkboard behind the counter. "I usually get *hilachas*," said Emily. "The *chuchitos* are good, too."

"Sounds fine to me."

The waiter appeared and agreed, taking their orders on a plain notepad, filling water glasses out of a plastic pitcher, and pointing out a list of beers they had in bottles. He wandered away, checked in with the two other occupied tables—half the room's seating—and disappeared into the kitchen. Latin pop drifted from a radio in the back, along with banging pans and the hum of a blower fan.

The waiter dropped off two SingleCut beers—no glasses, but at least they'd been opened—and Finn raised his to Emily. "Cheers."

"By the way," she said, "did you know your girl Nicola is a climber?"

"Really?"

"We got to talking a bit at the diner."

"Not about the job, I hope."

"Just climbing."

"She as strong as you?"

"Stronger, maybe. Not as good a climber." No false modesty for Emily. "Just spends time on the wall now and then."

"You looked really good." He let it hang a moment. "On the wall."

A brilliant smile. "Thanks."

The *chuchitos* were smaller than regular tamales, sprinkled with a hard, salty cheese. Finn took his time, appreciating the flavors. Emily worked on her shredded beef.

"If you're so broke you can't buy me dinner," she said, "how are you funding the, ah, project?"

"The cars, of course. We also got the warehouse for nothing—well, eighteen hundred bucks." He described his dealings with the broker. "Actually, that was a bit much, but I didn't want to argue with him."

"*Another* informal transaction."

"He gets some pocket money and a signed lease. We won't default until the next calendar year, which is forever in broker time. Seems like a win-win to me."

They both went for the *recado* sauce at the same time, bumping hands. He caught her eye, and the moment extended.

Emily broke it, returning to her meal and looking away with an amused expression Finn couldn't interpret. Another few customers came in. The server bustled about.

"How much does Wes know?" Finn asked.

A moment's confusion. "About us?"

Which, in turn, caught Finn off guard. He covered by shaking his head. "The job."

"Not much. He doesn't *want* to know."

"Did you tell him the date we're planning?"

She thought. "Early January. No more specific than that."

"Good. Let's leave it that way."

They finished the meal and ordered Atitlán coffee. The other tables were now full. Despite the restaurant's small size, the larger crowd increased their privacy, because the noise and multiple conversations covered up their own.

"How did you get into this?" Emily asked.

"Working for Wes?"

"What you do."

"Oh." He added the smallest amount of cream to his coffee. "The same way most people end up where they are—by accident. I grew up outside Pittsburgh, and when I got out of high school, the mill was still hiring. Then, a couple years later, they shut it down. After the layoffs, they hired me back to dismantle equipment—everything was being sold to Bangladesh or Vietnam or somewhere. I was nineteen and I had to cross a union line to do it." He fell silent, remembering the yelling, rocks in the air, guys swearing they'd stomp him later. All for fifty cents over minimum wage. "Didn't take long to realize I could do the exact same job in the middle of the night and sell the machinery myself. After that—" He lifted one shoulder briefly, like, *You know.*

"So you've been an outlaw your whole working life."

"'Outlaw.'" That was funny. "I guess so. How about you?"

"Bad choices, about the same age as you."

Finn waited. "'Bad choices?'"

"Harvard Business School."

"No. Really?" He peered at her. "And you ended up with Wes?"

"The ethics seminar didn't stick." Emily grinned. "The real problem was graduating into the teeth of the global financial meltdown. Not a lot of jobs on offer then. And after a few years, no one's hiring you to start over—not when they have a fresh crop of new MBAs to choose from, none of them burned out and cynical."

"Is that you? Burned out and cynical?"

"As hard-edged as they come, Finn." She raised her small porcelain cup in salute. "You have no idea."

Setting up the deal was surprisingly easy.

"You have a *shopping* list?" The man Corman introduced as Gil scratched his beard and squinted at the paper. It flapped in the cold breeze outside his garage.

"More or less." The evening before, Nicola had found a local newspaper clipping online, from two years earlier when Wes had displayed many of his cars at a Memorial Day vintage-car rally in Greenwich. Along with the insurance declaration provided by

Emily, Finn had been able to compile an inventory, which Nicola rapidly retyped and printed.

Nothing to identify the owner or location, of course.

"Huh."

They stood by the side of Gil's body shop in a light industrial zone south of Elizabeth. When Corman had hinted at their purpose, Gil had led them away from the shop mechanics, around the side of the building. The usual noises drifted from inside—air wrench, a compressor, late '70s classic rock on the boom box.

"You pick what you want," said Finn. "Lots more there than we can fit on a single car carrier."

"You're not gonna drive them away one by one?" Gil looked up, then back at the sheet.

"Don't have enough people for that."

"I guess the Lamborghini might be good. And the Bugatti. A Shelby Cobra! . . . Nice." He spent a few minutes marking the paper with pencil ticks and greasy fingerprints.

Corman stood in the background, arms crossed, looking around rather than focusing on their quiet discussion. Thin sunlight filtered through low gray clouds, not providing any noticeable warmth.

"Might be we can do business." Gil handed the sheets back.

"Up to a dozen cars will fit the autorack. 'Course we won't know exactly which ones we can get until we're inside." Finn looked up from the paper. "How about this? We ballpark some figures, get a range for the different cars. Then I'll call you when we're done, tell you what's loaded up."

Gil frowned. "I dunno—"

"We can use some dumb code if you want. Or we can buy a couple burner phones. The point is you need to know how much to have in the duffel bag when we meet up."

They worked it out. Gil lowballed them some, but not too bad. Finn didn't think they needed to worry about a hijack, because Gil wouldn't know where they were until they showed up at the rendezvous.

"When we get there with the merchandise," he said, "I don't expect any surprises. Right?"

"Of course not." Gil managed to look offended. "You don't cross family."

"What?"

"He didn't tell you?"

Finn looked over at Corman. "Tell me what?"

"We're cousins," said Gil. "Birthdays are just a week apart."

"Really?"

Corman made a dismissive sound. "Mother's side."

"You don't look it." Gil had to be two feet shorter and a hundred pounds weaker than his relative.

"Don't worry," Gil said. "Anyway, only a moron would fuck with Corman."

"Good point." Finn folded the paper and tucked into his jacket. "Oh, one other thing."

"Yeah?"

"We haven't lined up the car carrier yet." He grinned. "Maybe you could lend us one?"

CHAPTER TWENTY-THREE

A sher looked at the rows of red plastic cans they'd just unloaded from Jake's truck. They'd shut the warehouse doors, closing out not just the brisk, sleet-spattering wind but also the view to any curious passersby. The high interior lights were on, buzzing from the thirty-foot ceiling. Even with the clerestory windows, it was dim all the time.

Dust rose as Jake swept the empty concrete floor, pushing a well-used broom with no particular attention to thoroughness.

"How we gonna do this?" Asher said.

"Set the lines first, I think." Jake ran the broom all the way to one wall and leaned it there, abandoning the pile of dirt and small debris. He walked back and handed over the clip end of a chalk line. "Here."

They'd marked the corner points already: short pieces of blue masking tape at the vertices of a ten-by-fifteen rectangle, its far end close to the street-side wall. Once they started digging, it would block one of the bay doors.

Asher knelt and held down the end of the string. Jake scrolled it out of the metal holder, walking over to the next corner. He held down his end and snapped a dusty yellow line on the floor. They repeated the operation three more times.

"Finn says a one-foot grid." Jake cranked the line into its holder, rechalking the string.

"We got enough acid for that?"

"Hope so."

They measured end points and started laying down the checkerboard.

"Corman should be doing this," Asher said. "Why don't I get to drive the fancy cars?"

"Because." Jake moved to the next point, snapped another line.

"Because what?"

"Because look at your fucking truck. It's so dented up, you're lucky you don't get pulled over on general principles."

"So?"

They finished one set of lines and started on the perpendiculars. Jake shook the holder, chalk running low.

"Corman seem different to you?" Asher said.

"Different?"

"I dunno. He ain't hardly said ten words to me since we got here. Like he's pissed about something."

Jake laughed. "Corman doesn't get angry."

"Not at you, maybe."

"I guess that's the difference between us."

"Huh? You don't do a lot of yelling yourself."

"No, I mean—" Jake shook his head. "Never mind."

They finished the grid. Asher opened one of the jugs and sniffed.

"Jesus fuck." He put it down fast, eyes watering.

"Be careful there." Jake tossed him safety goggles and a pair of heavy rubber gloves. "Don't splash any of that on your pants."

Finn had rigged them a dispenser: a screw-on spout fit into a length of plastic tubing ending in a narrow funnel. It was held together with duct tape. Jake took the gas can Asher had opened and connected the cap, tightening it carefully.

"You carry the container," Jake said. "I'll guide the funnel. Keep the flow nice and steady. We don't need to flood the floor."

They tried it, starting at the far end of the grid.

"That's good." Jake walked backward along the line, pouring a steady dribble along the chalk. "Maybe a little more. No, a little faster, this will take all afternoon at—wait, that's too fast. Wait. Slow down! Stop! It's slopping everywh— Holy *shit*!"

Hydrochloric acid overflowed the connection with the funnel, spilling in a messy spray. Jake dropped it and jumped back. The concrete hissed where the drops fell. Along the chalk line, carbonates burbled in a white fizz.

"Nice." Asher held the canister one-handed, peering down at the action. "I could use this shit to clean my bathtub."

"Changed my mind," Jake said. "*I'll* carry the container."

They kept going, slowly emptying the first jugs. After finishing the entire grid, they started over and did it again.

Asher put down the funnel and stood, stretching his back.

"Fuck it," he said. "That's got to be good enough."

Jake looked at the jagged grooves they'd cut into the floor. "Concrete's probably eight inches thick, right? The whole point of this is to avoid jackhammers, keep everything quiet. We need to go as far through as possible."

"I don't mind a jackhammer. Ran one for days at a time when I was a kid."

"Yeah, and that's why you can't hear for shit."

"What?"

Another half hour and they were down to the last five gallons of hydrochloric. The air was thick with stinging fumes. Jake stood back to examine the floor, wiping at his eyes.

"Okay, good enough," he said.

"About fucking time." Asher carried the last empty over to the row of jugs and dropped it with the rest. "Still got some left here."

"That's okay. Might use it later if the excavator can't deal with this."

The excavator itself sat quietly at the back wall, opposite the hazmat dump of acid containers. They'd brought it in on a flatbed trailer attached to Jake's truck, because Asher's Tacoma was underpowered for the haul. The machine was a rental, one week in advance, small-bill cash, from a huge equipment supplier in Union. Jake had handled the negotiations, conducted in the shade of the vast metal shed, while Asher wandered among the rows of bore rigs.

He didn't think they were off the books completely, but he figured a good part of Jake's stack of fifties had gone into the other man's pocket. Easing the way.

"I still think Corman should have been on duty today," he said. "Don't figure how he even fits into one of those fucking Lamborghinis. Probably break the shocks when he gets in."

"What is it with you two?"

"What?"

"He does what he's supposed to and doesn't complain about it all the time. Is that a problem?"

Asher pulled off his gloves, then the goggles. "I told you: He's acting different."

"Yeah, you said. *Too* quiet."

"Exactly."

"Maybe he just doesn't have anything to say to you."

"Ah, fuck it." Asher set his safety gear on a cheap folding table they'd gotten off Craigslist along with a half dozen plastic chairs and some large plastic crates. "What time is it? Think they're on their way back yet?"

Jake looked at his watch. "Should just be getting started."

"None too soon." Asher sat in one of the chairs. It bent alarmingly, then a few seconds later collapsed, dumping him to the floor. "Yow!"

"Hey, don't break the furniture."

"Piece of shit." He got up, kicked the chair into a corner.

Jake placed his own gloves and goggles in a clean plastic bucket, along with the chalk line and measuring tape. He looked thoughtfully at the excavator. It was still on the trailer, strapped down.

"We should probably give that a test," he said.

Asher shrugged. "It worked at the rental yard."

"All he did was turn the motor on."

"Yeah, yeah, okay."

Electric or not, the thing was no toy. Full-size operator seat and controls under open roll bars, hydraulic arm with a five-meter radius, steel tracks. These last had caught Asher's attention.

"Gonna tear the hell out of the floor with those," he said.

Jake picked up the coiled power cable, grunting at its weight, and stepped off the trailer.

"Find an outlet," he said.

Asher took the plug end and dragged it across the floor. "Hard to believe this runs off standard one-twenty," he said. "Like plugging in a shop vac."

"It's not the volts that matter, it's the amps." Jake found the power receptacle on the rear of the operator's platform, snapped the cable into its holdfast, and looked over. "You good?"

"I guess." Asher had found a panel of outlets near the breaker box. "Don't know if it's live, though."

"We'll find out."

Jake clambered onto the operator's seat and took a moment to dry-shift the controls. Then he turned the key, pressed a button, and yanked the skid-steer handle. The motor spun into gear, no louder than a car engine, and Jake backed it off the trailer.

"Don't run over the cord," Asher said.

Jake gave him a look and moved to the grid. Hydraulics whined, more noisily, as he lifted the bucket arm, then swiveled right, left.

"Let's try it out," he said, and shoved the handle forward, slamming the bucket's toothed edge into the concrete floor.

CRACK!

A burst of white fire at the junction box, then a second explosion. Asher felt a burn spatter across his arm and dove for the floor. Every light went out at the same instant, plunging the building into darkness.

"What the *fuck*?"

Dead silence in the dark. The excavator was still, its outline barely visible in faint light from the clerestory.

"You okay?"

Asher felt his arm, wincing. "I think you *melted* the cocksucker." He saw shadows move—Jake, climbing off the machine.

"You know," Jake said, "this might be a problem."

CHAPTER TWENTY-FOUR

They drove through town a little under the speed limit—twenty-five, low enough to get a good look around. Not that there was much to see. One main street, two gas stations, various small and dilapidated businesses. Churches. A convenience store, brightly lit in the evening dark.

"There it is," said Finn. He pointed through the truck's windshield to a low concrete building surrounded by blacktop, a plain illuminated sign above the glass doors reading POLICE.

"Yup." Corman was at the wheel.

"Keep going. We'll find someplace to stop down the road."

Grunt.

"Shift change should be in . . . twenty minutes. Don't go far."

A few minutes later, the rig was parked behind a shuttered roadhouse, the engine ticking and grumbling to rest. Gil's loaner was at least two decades old, a sagging Kenworth tractor hitched to an enclosed trailer fifty feet long. The trailer's undercarriage sat low to the ground, much lower than a typical freight hauler, with a flip-out door and extra hydraulics at the end. With two interior levels, it could hold as many as ten cars, depending on their sizes. That was two fewer than an open autorack, but Gil's trailer kept the world from seeing what was inside.

"You might want to wait over there somewhere," Finn said. "Behind a tree. In case it's a bunch of redneck cops who come back here instead of me."

"Uh-huh." Corman nodded.

"Half hour ought to do it."

The night was cold, clear, and moonless. Finn walked along the left side of the road, squinting into the infrequent headlights of passing traffic, until the first intersection. After that, he kept one block south, parallel to the main road, passing small bungalow-type houses. Most had weedy yards and firewood stacked somewhere close to their doors.

Close to the police station, he stopped, standing by an SUV parked in front of a dark house. The vehicle's hood was halfway warm. He waited, absently patting his pocket to check that the papers were there.

A car pulled into the station's lot and went around back. It didn't reappear, and no one walked to the front, so Finn assumed the driver had entered the building through another door. A few minutes later, a cruiser bumped into the lot. An officer got out, stretched his back, and went inside.

The night air was cold.

Finn adjusted his insulated cap, pulling the brim low. He walked across the street—no oncoming traffic visible in either direction—up to the doors and straight through without stopping.

Pretty much what he'd expected: a counter, some cheap vinyl-covered chairs, a view into a larger room with metal desks and clutter and cabinets along the wall.

More important, no cameras that he could see.

The interview room probably had a video setup and maybe the holding pens. But nothing in the front. Most little towns, especially in live-free-or-die country, kept their law-enforcement agencies on short budgets. A spare dollar would more likely be spent on Tasers or bullets, not more tech equipment.

Staffing was bare bones for similar reasons. Maybe they'd have a civilian receptionist during the day, but for now, a woman with a headset sat behind a monitor in back of the counter.

"May we help you?" She was probably the dispatcher. Town this small, she might handle fire and EMS, too.

"I was hoping to talk with one of your officers?" Nonthreatening and polite.

"Could be." She twisted to look into the other bullpen. Finn could see one uniform and one guy in a sweatshirt and jeans talking to each other at the coffee machine. "What's it about?"

"A courtesy call." Finn pulled the envelope from his jacket. "Doing a repo in the county, just wanted to let you know first."

She called back, and the two men looked at her. "Go on around," she said to Finn.

The uniformed officer had his gun belt in one hand and a worn leather folder in the other, so Finn didn't offer to shake.

"George Hayduke," he said. "Line Drive Recovery, up from Bridgeport?"

"Yeah?"

"Order of attachment." He unfolded a set of papers from the envelope and held it out. "We're repoing some cars tonight."

The man glanced at the document. "ID?"

"Sure." Finn extracted another paper from his wallet, this one creased and worn at the edges. "State license. You want to see a bond certificate?"

"Nah." The man skimmed down. "*Nine* vehicles?"

"Yes." Finn grinned. "Nice, huh? Normally, I'd have to drive all over the state for that many. It's like a whole week's worth of work in one night."

"Hall's Pond Road."

"That storage place," said the other man, listening in. "You know, out past the Agway."

"That's right." Finn nodded. "Guy keeps them on ice there. Like a collection."

"'*Ex parte* order . . . property we have rights to, in a nonresidential facility secured by a lock susceptible to blah blah . . .'" He flipped to the end. "'Authorized by . . . Judge Willis'? When did you get to him?"

And that was the crux. Anyone could forge up legal documents nowadays. Nicola had found boilerplate language, along with color templates for the PI license, right on the Internet. The actual authorization, though—Finn was willing to try and dupe a couple of rural cops, but a state judge was a different matter. No way was he willing to walk into a court office under feloniously false pretenses. Conveniently, however, Connecticut had begun putting judicial opinions online as PDFs. With a little searching—Nicola again—and some careful copying, they'd forged a signature almost as authentic as the judge's own.

And at seven p.m., Finn hoped the policeman wouldn't actually try to call the judge to confirm it.

"This afternoon," he said. "After midday sessions."

"Nine vehicles." The officer whistled. "A Lamborghini. A Bugatti—jeez. What'd he do?"

"Dunno." Finn raised his hand, like, *Who knows?* "Get behind with somebody, though, they'll come after anything you got. Guy I know specializes in boats—collects them right out of the marinas. Being rich doesn't stop people from being stupid."

The man laughed. "Goes the other way, too."

"If that was true, I'd be driving a Lambo myself."

The cop going off duty lost interest. "Normally, we'd send a duty officer with you," he said, and looked at the other man. "Hank?"

"Been quiet tonight?"

"Usual."

"Well—no, I guess not. I got paperwork."

The first officer handed back Finn's papers. "Okay then. Know where you're going?"

"Yeah. We checked it out before we got the order."

"And the alarms. Hank, don't they have a silent?"

"Yup. We get a false call every couple months. Chipmunk runs past the electric eye or whatever."

The officer looked at Finn. "It rings, we have to drive out there. Write up a report."

"Yeah, I—"

"Which is at least an hour of plain wasted time."

"Don't worry about it." Finn tucked the papers away. "We got the panel code."

"Really?" He looked surprised.

"Research. Makes everything easier, you know?" In fact, Emily had seen the alarm company's reminder card, with the codes written right on it, in the same folder as the storage unit's insurance information. "It shouldn't go off, but if it does, you know it's us. No need for lights and sirens and guns."

"No."

Finn put his hat back on. "Thanks, guys, I appreciate it."

"There's any kind of a problem, you just turn around and leave, okay? We don't need more to do tonight. You can work it out in daylight."

"Absolutely." Finn smiled. "I'm sure there won't be any problems at all."

CHAPTER TWENTY-FIVE

D o you *know* what your lunatics are up to?"

Nicola was the first one Finn saw as he bumped the Kei truck through the bay door, and she seemed upset. He rolled down his window.

"Not exactly—"

"It's not like anyone here can file for workers' comp." Hands on her wide hips. "Not that they'd be filing anything anyway—they'd be dead."

Morning at the warehouse, a damp cold and gray light filtering from the windows high above. Finn parked the truck just inside the bay, got out, and pulled the door back down with a resounding crash. He looked past Nicola, who'd been working her laptop at the folding table.

"Hey, they got the excavator." He paused. "Why is it so dark in here?"

"There's no power." Nicola gestured at the wall, where a gray metal box hung wrecked, door sagging open, all shattered plastic and torn wire.

"Uh-oh." Finn squinted, picking out the cable running along the floor to the excavator. "Blew it out?"

"Of course. The problem is, they're fixing it."

Finn was still groggy, insufficiently caffeinated. Working off Gil's list, it had taken Corman and himself two hours to load the cars the night before, even though Emily had told them exactly where the key box was. On the way out, he'd reset the alarm and secured the fifteen-foot sliding doors with a duplicate ABUS padlock. The original had resisted Corman's plasma torch for nearly five minutes. There were scorch marks on the metal now, but he'd smudged them up. The new lock looked the same, just shinier.

With luck, whoever next showed up would merely assume that something was wrong with it, or that he had the wrong key.

After that, another two hours to Gil's transfer point, a truck stop on I-95. Well lit and busy, its tarmac filled with rigs hauling in and out of the city, the parking area was safe and discreet for both sides of the transaction. Like the entire job, it had gone smooth and easy.

"Why is it a problem if they're fixing it?" Finn said now, still trying to catch up. He held a black nylon duffel in each hand.

"Take a look." She flicked her head toward the back, where a second door led to the rear of the building. "I'm not going anywhere near them."

He dropped the bags by the table and walked out. Behind the warehouse, a fifteen-foot strip of old pavement filled in the property, up to the chain-link-and-razor-wire fence of the adjacent lot. Finn thought their neighbor did forwarding or something—trucks came and went irregularly. In the early morning, the lot was empty, the docks shuttered.

Jake was up a utility pole at the fence, working inside its drum transformer. The cowling was open, a heavy cable dangling. Below him, Asher looked up, hands shading his eyes.

"Uh, Jake?" Finn kept his voice quiet, not wanting to startle him in the slightest way.

"Oh, hey, Finn."

"What the fuck are you doing up there?"

"We need power. Got barely enough to run Nicola's computer, let alone the TBM."

Finn had done just enough electrical to know that he didn't want to be anywhere near a live transmission line. "Didn't know you had a linesman's rating, Jake."

"Nope. Helped a buddy out some though."

He was wearing safety goggles, a hard hat, and heavy black rubber gloves that went almost to his elbows. His jacket was fully zipped, tucked out of the way. He looked as professional as any other pole monkey Finn had worked with.

"What is it carrying?"

"We'll tap it for eighty amps. More than enough."

"Isn't the utility going to notice?"

"Fuck no. We could power half of Newark before they woke up over there."

"Uh-huh." Finn watched him work for a minute. Jake pulled the cable through a spare bushing on the drum while Asher fed him some slack and then began tying it off inside. "You sure about this?"

"It ain't rocket science." He tipped his head toward the neighboring warehouse. "My first thought was we could just tap it out of their junction box, but I didn't want to go climbing over that riot wire."

"No shit," Asher said, but he kept his eyes on Jake. The electricians' union had rules requiring two men for high-voltage work: the second there only to watch the first, helping avoid fatal errors. Asher was doing his job.

"Okay then." Finn nodded, more to himself. "I'll leave you all to it."

Inside, he found Nicola back at work on her laptop. She had a cup of take-out coffee, a Tip Top box open next to it. The table was crowded with other odds and ends as well: gloves, tools, a four-foot pry bar.

Now that he noticed, the air still smelled slightly of burnt plastic and ozone.

"They know what they're doing," Finn said. "And we do need the lights back on."

"If you say so."

"How's it going? Are you in Penn Southern's systems yet?"

She gave him a mouth-turned-down, exasperated look. "Of course. Took about two minutes. We're not hacking missile silos here."

Finn paused. "Nuclear missiles? How long does *that* take?"

"Depends. The USAF is easier than Britain."

"Are you serious?"

She looked up. "Don't worry. Occasionally, the missile crews have some basic internet, but it's always air-gapped from anything real. It's impossible to get near the launch sequence."

"That's . . . good to know, I guess."

Finn examined the acid-etched gridlines in the floor. The cuts were narrow and jagged but deep. He retrieved the pry bar, glanced over Nicola's shoulder, saw her screen deep with code, and walked back. The concrete resisted, then broke a little, the foot-square block shifting in place. Rocking the bar back and forth, he was able to loosen it up.

Good enough. The excavator would have little difficulty. He dropped the bar on the floor.

Ten minutes later, Jake came in, pulling off the high-voltage gloves.

"Done," he said. "Asher's going to bring the line in."

"Those breakers are beyond salvage, aren't they?"

Jake looked at the wreckage on the wall. "You think?"

"I really hope you're not planning to end it off right in the middle of the floor."

"I got a new box in the truck. We'll hook it up."

Jake hollered back at Asher, who responded with some muffled swearing, and started yanking the cable through the same supply conduit. Nicola frowned at them, then went back to work. The room fell quiet, apart from the frequent, steady rumble of trains nearby and Asher's nonstop mutter of complaint.

Finn added *Radio* to his mental to-do list.

What else? He looked around. Plywood, two-by-fours, and framing screws for the curtain wall. Power drills. The skate-wheel conveyor—forty segments, each ten feet long. They might need two trucks. Battery lanterns. Welding kit and bar stock to refit the Kei truck.

Water, oranges, chips. Jake liked granola bars. Asher needed beer. A lot to remember.

Finn was measuring the Kei truck's chassis when Corman came in. He'd slept and changed, it looked like. He identified the doughnut box immediately.

"Morning, big guy." Nicola was about half Corman's mass, a difference all the more obvious when he stood over her at the table, but she didn't seem to notice. "Try the strawberry cream. I like those."

"Yo." Finn waved Jake and Asher over. "Team meeting."

They stood around. Nicola clicked some keys and her screen went blank. She leaned back in the chair.

"It's December third," Finn said. "That means we have exactly four weeks. There's a lot to do. I think the plan is sound, but you know how it goes—we're going to hit snags. Problems will occur. If anything happens, anything that increases the chances of getting caught, we drop it and walk away."

He looked around. "I've said this to each of you, and I want to say it once more. I just got out of jail. I did not enjoy my time inside. And I'm not going back."

Asher nodded, like, *Yeah, yeah.* Nicola had a small smile. Corman and Jake just watched.

"With that in mind"—Finn reached down and retrieved one of the two black duffels—"let's take a look at this."

He unzipped the bag with a somewhat self-consciously dramatic flourish.

Nicola leaned forward to look inside. "What?"

"Oops, wrong one." Finn dropped it on the cluttered tabletop. "That's the laser. I meant this one." He grabbed the other duffel, no ceremony this time, and opened it up.

A respectful silence. They all stared at the money.

"Two hundred forty thousand dollars," Finn said. "Hundreds and fifties, which seems to be how Gil does business."

"He liked the cars," said Nicola.

"And paid what we agreed." Finn nodded. "Always nice to find a man who keeps his word."

"That's great," said Jake. "Now we don't have to steal everything else, too."

"It should more than cover the entire budget."

"Awesome." Asher reached out, drawn like a magnet to the cash. "So how about we get a decent dinner tonight? At least once?"

Only Corman didn't say anything, but he caught Finn's eye with a questioning look.

"Right." Finn zipped the duffel shut again, nearly catching Asher's fingers. "Almost a quarter mil. We can spend it all on this project . . . or we could divide it up now and go our separate ways. That's forty-five, fifty each, right? Risk free. Right here."

"That's almost half what Wes is paying us," said Nicola.

"Yes."

"But what about the rhodium?" Jake said. "I thought we were going for the haul. That's *nothing*, there." He flicked one hand at the bag. "We go in and get the metal, we make twenty times that."

"Against the risk of getting caught." Finn put his hands in his pockets. "I know I'm a broken record here, but you have to be sure. Are we committed to the job?"

"Wes thinks you're just going in to make a mess and pull the alarm," said Nicola. "Doesn't he? Have you told him the plan's a little bigger now?"

"Not necessary," Finn said.

"He's paying us to rob him?" Asher grinned. "Man might be a little upset about that."

"Could be."

"Well, fuck yeah, I'm committed. I'm in. I want a million dollars!"

"Me, too," said Nicola. Jake nodded and Corman grunted.

"Excellent."

They started talking details. Where to get the jacking pipe, how to move the metal through it, timing.

"What about noise?" Nicola asked.

"It's underground." Asher was dismissive. "Nobody'll hear anything."

"I looked it up online. There's video. Didn't seem that quiet to me."

"It shouldn't be a problem until we get close," Finn said. "And at that point, we can stop and start, save the noisiest periods for when a train is passing."

"We need semtex." Asher, coming in from left field.

"What?" Nicola said.

"Plastic explosive."

"I know what it *is*—"

"Just in case."

"In case what?"

"It's like duct tape. A million uses."

An argument started. Finn let it run a minute then shut them down. "No explosives," he said firmly. "We're digging our way in. This isn't Hollywood. We're not blowing shit up just for fun."

Asher took the last doughnut. Nicola flicked on her screen. Jake went back to the breaker box, which he and Asher had mounted on the wall and were now wiring up.

Finn handed the duffel to Corman. "When Jake's done," he said, "how about you two go rent us a tunnel-boring machine?"

An hour later, the door closed behind Corman and Jake. Nicola continued to mutter at her laptop. Finn and Asher were studying the Kei truck's undercarriage, lying on the floor underneath it, discussing how to reinforce the suspension.

"Gonna need solid tires, too," Asher said. "If you want to drive faster than two miles an hour."

"I thought we could just let out some air. So the extra weight doesn't pop them."

"No, the heavier it is, the *more* pressure you need. But these are too small for that."

"Hmm."

"Big trucks, big tires."

"Uh-huh." Finn thought about the massive wheels on the equipment in, say, open pit mines. "If that's true, why doesn't everyone use solid rubber? Never get a flat tire for *any* reason that way."

"They overheat too fast. Melt right off the rims. But we can probably find a specialty wheel somewhere." Asher patted the truck. "Might look funny, but on this vehicle, who'll notice?"

Finn stood and stretched. Asher dusted his pants and headed for the bathroom in the building's rear. With the lights on, and the day lightening in late morning, the warehouse interior was now almost brightly illuminated. Dirt and clutter were much more apparent. Finn added a trash barrel and a second broom to the list.

A well-kept worksite encouraged conscientious work.

"Finn." Nicola called him over.

"Yeah?"

"I'm finding . . . something. In the traffic over there." She spoke quietly, not obviously keeping secrets from Asher but not shouting, either.

"The rail traffic?" He didn't know what she meant.

"No. Comms traffic. The dispatchers have an internal messaging system. It's hard to follow, because I don't understand most of the abbreviations. I think they're talking on the radio and the phones, too, and I can't hear that, so I only get pieces of the conversations." She shook her head. "Anyway."

"So what are you seeing?"

"I'm not sure. Some kind of special project or something. One guy started complaining about how it's completely screwing up his schedule. Someone else is going on about how the yards as far away as Pittsburgh will be affected. Bunch of other comments like that in between what looks like more routine business."

"Okay," Finn said. "But that's not unusual, is it? Run a big complicated railroad, thousands of cars and hundreds of trains, stuff probably comes up all the time."

"Maybe, though this seems out of the ordinary." She shrugged. "Not that I have any idea. But the reason we might want to pay attention is the date."

Finn sighed. "Don't tell me."

"Yes." She pointed at the screen. "December thirty-first, middle of the night."

Of course.

"Well," said Finn. "It's going to be busy night, isn't it?"

CHAPTER TWENTY-SIX

W alking through the park gate, Finn paused to let a young mother on her way out pass through. She was pushing a Euro-styled baby carriage, the kind with three wheels on a shaped titanium frame and a vibrant green-and-blue nylon dome.

"—cold as shit," the woman was saying into her cell phone. "'Get the baby fresh air,' they're always telling me, but this isn't a park, it's a fucking prison yard."

Okay, a babysitter then. He nodded as she passed, was ignored in return, and continued in.

Needless to say, it sure didn't feel like a prison yard to Finn. Too much concrete and brick, yes, with scant patches of dirt behind asphalt curbs. Barren, the few trees leafless and stark against the dull gray of encroaching apartment blocks. And the benches he could see were missing slats—even though the wooden planks were probably two-by-threes, held in place with heavy lag bolts. Someone had gone to serious trouble to tear them out.

But there were some colorful plastic toys in the sand area, and the jungle gym was a complicated playground of twisty poles, climbing bars, and dark blue platforms. Three teenagers were shooting baskets in the far court, fast and aggressive and laughing. One of them appeared to be a girl.

Finn wore plain black leggings and a sweatshirt, hood pulled up.

He started with jumps: burpees, lunges left and right, squats. Starting to warm up, he did four sets of planks, then handstand push-ups.

In the pen, nothing else to do, he'd gotten strong and balanced enough not to need a wall. But since getting out, he'd been busy. He tucked into the handstand in front of the jungle gym—no children were using it—and braced against its tower.

Down slow, faster up. Again . . . again . . .

At nineteen reps, arms starting to tremble, a voice interrupted.

"When does the blood come out your nose?"

Halfway into the next one, Finn instead dropped his legs, thrust off the ground, and half turned in the air to land on his feet.

"Emily." He grinned. "Why, does that happen to you?"

"Only after the first hundred, hundred fifty."

She wore a teal puffy jacket over gray pants and boots that looked more stylish than practical. Business casual, perhaps. Midafternoon and she'd said she was coming from a meeting.

"You mind if I keep moving?" Finn said. "I'll freeze if I start to cool down."

"You watched me climb, I guess I can watch you do some jumping jacks."

They walked to the chain-link fence behind the basketball courts. Finn put his back to it, reaching as high as he could behind his head, and grasped the wire. Shifting until comfortable, he raised his legs straight out, then up to almost touch his nose, then back down and held them there. Five seconds, six . . .

Emily nodded. "Don't feel you have to show off or anything."

"Of course not." He lowered his legs, heels just brushing the ground, and started a set of twenty lifts. "So what's up?"

"Wes is starting to fray. The calls come in all day. I see him in his office behind the glass walls, waving his arms and walking around with the headset on. The auditor's here—usually we don't get her team in until March. Everybody looks grim."

"You said cash flow was getting tight."

"It's worse now."

He caught her tone and finished up, dropping from the fence. "What's going on?"

"He's planning to fuck you over, Finn."

One of the teenagers missed a pass and the basketball slammed into the chain link just behind him. Startled, they both spun around. The boy gestured with one hand—*Sorry, bro*—retrieved the ball and went back to their two-on-one.

Finn worked his hands, sore from the wire. "I'm not surprised. We talked about that."

"If—when—you get into the vault, he's going to dial 911."

"What? While we're *inside*?"

"Yes."

"That doesn't make any sense." Finn frowned, feeling anger stir. "The whole idea here is to *not* get found out. He wants his counterfeits disappeared—not exposed for the whole world to see."

Emily glanced at the ballplayers fifteen feet away. "Come on."

They walked back toward the jungle gym. Wind gusted between the buildings, raising a chill on Finn's neck.

"How do you know this?"

"He needs my help." Emily shoved her hands into her coat pockets. "One of my jobs—now and then, Wes has to run some trades off the books. Anything through the company systems has a full audit trail. If Wes is doing something sideways, he might need some layers of deniability on the transactions."

"Is that legal?"

"Mostly. Depends on exactly who's getting cheated."

"And in this case?"

"He's setting you up."

Finn had undirected energy coursing through his system. He looked at the jungle gym, found a bar seven feet off the ground, reached up and started doing pull-ups.

"I don't understand," he said between breaths.

"He explained just enough so I'd know what to do. It has to be timed exactly right. Wes wants the guards to catch you in the act, right *after* you've switched the fakes into the neighbor's rack."

"*Why?*" Finn stopped at twenty-five and dropped off the bar. "We went over all this. When news breaks, that will just drive the price into the basement. He'll lose everything."

"He'll lose the rhodium, yes, but—"

"But?"

Emily glanced at him, then hopped up to take Finn's place on the bar. Much faster, she knocked off twenty-five pull-ups—then one extra, ostentatiously.

"He wants me buying deep out-of-the-money puts," she said, back on the ground. "In secret, small lots, not raising any flags."

Finn looked from her to the bar, back. "What does that mean?"

"Going short. Remember? They make money when the price goes down, not up."

"How much? Enough to cover what he loses on the inventory?"

"More than."

Finn tried to make sense of it.

"So you're saying he's, like, fuck *my* rhodium, it's all shit, but I can screw everyone else?"

"Exactly. He *wants* the price driven down."

"How much is he going to make?"

"Based on the numbers he's giving me, if rhodium falls to two-thirds of its starting price, Wes immediately takes home twenty-seven million dollars." Emily paused. "Down to half, and it's more like fifty."

"Holy *bat*shit." But one conclusion seemed obvious. "This is exactly what he did in New Mexico, isn't it? With the molybdenum?"

"I wasn't there."

"Too much coincidence—the exact same strategy."

"No." Emily shook her head. "It's not some big secret. People try to move the market all the time."

"Move it *down*?"

"Sure."

"Fucking Wall Street." Finn started walking, not going anywhere in particular. "Think you could find out for sure?"

"New Mexico—you want proof? Maybe in the old files. I don't know."

"It would help."

They stopped at the edge of the park. Finn leaned into the fence, stretching his legs. After a moment, he stopped, frowned, and straightened up.

"Wait a minute," he said. "Wes is actually buying these, uh, puts?"

"Yes."

"With what? He didn't even have a few thousand bucks for *us*. Where's he getting the money for this big play?"

Emily kept pace. "Why do you think there's nothing for you?"

"Mother*fucker*."

"He's been cleaning out accounts for weeks, setting this up. Sweeping pennies off the floor practically." She put a hand on Finn's arm, slowed him to a stop. "This has to be the biggest gamble of Wes's career. He's walking up to the blackjack table and putting everything on a single hand."

"That's too fucking stupid for words."

"Not if the wheel is rigged," Emily said. "And by the way? You're the ones rigging it for him."

CHAPTER TWENTY-SEVEN

David's day had been a long one. He'd spent the morning with a trio of company lawyers, sorting out December's termination proceedings—serious rule breaking always involved the security staff sooner or later. The afternoon was more meetings: a major shipper dissatisfied that some gang had looted his containers of flatscreens and video games, an HR manager looking for help with a harassment complaint, three performance reviews—he had to finish his entire staff before the end of the year, and time was running out.

To David's way of thinking, that meant he'd wasted eleven hours in completely nonproductive activity. But he was tired and hungry, and it was time to go home.

In the locker room, he ran into one of the operations managers changing out of stained, greasy overalls. For a senior manager, he was often as dirty and blackened as his crew.

"You're here late," David said.

"Repacking the bearing boxes for the special flatbed." The man rolled up his overalls and stuffed them into a plastic bag. "We're way over spec tolerances, so everything needs to be triple-checked."

"Problem?"

"Well . . . just the weight, really. Forgot about the load distribution."

David removed his uniform jacket and shirt—the latter into a laundry bag, the former into his locker. He didn't like going off the property looking like a rent-a-cop. "Load distribution?"

"Yeah. You ever seen one of these bucket-wheel excavators?"

"No."

"It's a monster. They have to take it apart for shipping—one set of treads on one flatcar, primary gearbox on another, all down the train. But the excavator arm is a single unit."

"That's the hundred-foot-long thing."

"Thirty-seven meters, actually. It fits on the articulated car they built. It's shorter than those aircraft fuselages we get sometimes."

"So what's the issue?"

"The weight. The bucket wheel is massive—this enormous toothed claw of solid steel. The pictures look like something out of a video game."

"Huh?"

"Robot warriors as tall as skyscrapers, you know the kind of thing." The man tightened the belt on his cleaner pants. "Don't you?"

"I'll ask my grandsons."

"Anyway, because the arm is so long, and the claw is at the very end, it has to sit entirely over a single truck on the railcar. Which means we've got three hundred tons sitting on the wheelsets."

"Too much?"

"Not for the railcar, no. They're driving it slow. But all that weight bearing down on one short piece of track—we had to go back and check the limits on every single crossing between Pittsburgh and here."

"The bridges have to be built for way more than that. Some of those old steam locomotives weighed four hundred tons, and they were in service seventy years ago."

"Okay, the bridges should be fine. But all the culverts? Grade crossings with utility conduits? Run a steamroller that damn heavy down the line, things might break."

"Huh." David finished changing his clothes and snapped his locker closed. "Glad that's not my problem."

"Yeah, thanks."

They walked out of the building. The night air was cold, wispy clouds beginning to blur the moon's bright circle.

"Smells like snow," David said.

"That'd be just the thing, wouldn't it? Get a blizzard for the holidays."

"The kids would love it."

At his car, David stopped for a moment before getting in.

"The weight," he said. "It's solved, right? The train comes in, you'll transfer it out with no trouble?"

"Yeah, I think so."

"Without a lot of extra delay?"

"Yep." The man shrugged. "Unless something goes wrong."

Finn thought that Nicola's hotel looked familiar—enough that several blocks away, he pulled his truck over and sat a minute, trying to figure out why.

The building was blocky and surfaced with flat, dun-colored stone, the windows blank and square. Dirt-cheap construction: code-minimum metal framing, synthetic chipboard, plastic and aluminum fittings, a skin of faux limestone. Any decorative feature would cost money, so there were none. It was night, and small spots illuminated the sign, the entrance, and the building's top corners.

Oh.

It looked a lot like the Albuquerque state courthouse.

Finn sighed and put the truck back in gear. His trial had lasted a week. The van from the county lockup took him directly into the underground garage, but he'd caught glimpses on the way in and out every day.

Both New Mexico taxpayers and huge-hotel-chain executives were apparently willing to settle for gimcrack construction, the cheaper the better.

In the parking lot, he drove to the rear and called Nicola's number.

"Be right down," she said. "North side entrance."

"North?" Finn looked around. "I forgot my compass."

"To the right of the main entrance as you walk in."

He parked the truck and waited until he saw Nicola appear through the glass door, coming from an adjacent stairwell. They arrived at the door at the same time, and she pushed the panic bar to let him in.

"Cheap, this place," Finn said.

"Doing my part."

"Every penny counts."

"Top floor." As they ascended five flights of stairs, she gave him a pair of latex gloves, putting on her own in the hallway.

Her room was at the end of the hall, the same plain materials as the building's exterior. Finn dropped into the single chair, a little out of breath.

"I told them I couldn't sleep with morning sun coming in," she said. "And I had to be on an upper floor because of noise."

"Did it work?"

"Take a look." She swept open the window shade. Finn rose and stood next to her, peering into the night.

The hotel stood right off I-78, at the far end of the mile-long rail yard. The classification tracks were visible, fading into darker distance, patches of stadium lighting dull on the containers and freight cars. The yard's perimeter fence stretched away from them, Caleb Street alongside it, warehouses and industry pressing in from the other side.

"I can't see our building," Finn said, squinting.

"It's down there. With this"—Nicola tapped a spotting scope mounted on a tripod—"I've got a nice view of the main lot and the operations center."

"You're right." He could see the dispatch tower in the distance, windows glowing.

"Though it doesn't matter too much. Mostly I'll be using the various video feeds."

She'd set up three computers on the desk—two laptops and a monitor connected to a smaller box—amid a tangle of cables, a keyboard, and a separate numeric pad.

Finn traced two of the network lines to ports set in the hotel's desk.

"You're using the hotel's internet? Is that safe?"

"There's an encrypted VPN tunneled to a remote server I set up as a secure node for this project. All my traffic goes through it, then out into the world. For the sensitive connections, I'm using a series of anonymous proxies. On the night, I'll switch them again, to one-time dark nodes."

"Right. Sounds great."

Nicola laughed. "Look, I'm the one sitting here, right? If I slip up and the opposition gets a traceroute, they're going to break down my door, not yours. Trust me, it's secure."

"That's what I mean."

After Emily's revelations about Wes's plan, Finn had thought hard about what to tell the rest of the team. In the end, he decided that saying nothing was the best approach. Emily told Wes the job was scheduled for Saturday night, January fourth, and Finn had confirmed that in a separate conversation. Wes could go ahead and plan whatever he wanted—Finn and his crew would get it done days before then.

No reason to worry the team with irrelevancies.

Nicola sat on the bed and Finn took the chair again. They went over details. Timing, fallbacks, what she was figuring out inside Penn Southern's mainframes.

"And they *are* mainframes, too," she said. "Some of that COBOL was probably written while Nixon was president."

"Huh."

"Lots of modern hardware overlaid on top, of course. But these huge companies just can't let go of the big iron."

"So everything's good. Ready to go."

"Uh, no." Nicola looked at him a little quizzically. "We haven't talked about Stormwall yet."

"Oh." The vault's rent-a-cops. "I thought you had that figured out."

"I can't get in."

Finn sat straight. "You can't?"

"They're a security company." Nicola, who'd been cross-legged on the bed, slid off and paced over to the window, staring out into the night. "Unlike many, they seem to know what they're doing. The NSA could probably force their way through, but so far, every attack I've made has been stopped cold."

Finn looked at her back. "If you don't take out the cameras, we don't go in. It's that simple."

"I know."

"So . . . what? Should I call Jake and have him cancel the rock drill?"

"Not yet." She turned around with an annoyed glare. Finn felt himself start to frown but realized she was angry at herself, not him. "No, there's one more thing we can try."

The pronoun didn't escape him. "We?"

"If I had physical access," she said, "that would solve the problem."

"Access? To what?"

"Their office."

"Ah."

"Stormwall has contracts with dozens of companies for, among other things, remote monitoring. All the feeds go to a central facility. They probably have some combination of pattern-recognition software and human screen-watchers keeping an eye on them all."

"So we need to break into a nerve center of a company whose entire business, whose whole reason to exist, is to keep us from doing exactly that?"

She smiled briefly. "It's not far away—Chalder, in North Jersey, one of those anonymous office parks. I drove by to take a look."

"And?"

"They seem to have one building all to themselves, with open paving all around. Brick, two stories, mirror-glass windows, guards at the door. Given the nature of their operations, I'm sure it's staffed around the clock. All power and cable comes in underground, probably through armored conduits."

"Oh, sure. No problem." Finn rolled his eyes. "That sounds *easy.*"

Nicola gestured out the window. "What you're planning over there couldn't be any harder." She rode over the comment he started to make. "But don't worry, there's an alternative. They have a front office in the city. Midtown. I couldn't actually *read* any of the traffic, but there's a substantial dataflow. I'm pretty sure they can access the remote feeds at the corporate location, too."

Finn was seven years out of date on monitoring technology. He'd never dealt with much more than a guy at a bank of TV screens with maybe a VHS recorder running under the desk.

"Like, separate cables all the way into Manhattan?"

This time Nicola's smile was broad. "No one uses dedicated copper anymore. It's all done over IP."

"Right." Finn pretended he knew what that meant. "Well, anyway, why would they pipe the cameras there, too? As a backup?"

"I assume so they can show clients the service directly. I bet the Manhattan office is a *lot* nicer than Chalder—tropical hardwoods and Persian carpets, you know. They probably have thirty-grand OLED screens set up like a starship bridge."

"And you think clients are fooled by that."

"Impressions count."

"True."

"Believe me. I sell work to the same kind of people."

And, of course, she'd sold *him* on her skills, too. Finn had to grin.

"So if we can get you into Stormwall's posh headquarters, you can . . . put in a wiretap or something."

"Something, yeah."

"Okay, then." Finn felt better. "How hard could that be?"

CHAPTER TWENTY-EIGHT

When Finn walked into the warehouse midmorning, it felt like a real operation for the first time. The once-empty, echoing space had been transformed, most obviously by plywood framing that walled off a large area next to the grid-cut and broken floor. A full-length trailer was backed through the far bay and loaded with dozens of concrete pipes a meter in diameter. Neat stacks of lumber sat next to the Kei truck up on wheel stands with pieces of metal and the welding kit unpacked on the floor. The table and chairs, cluttered with paper and small tools. A radio—sports talk, probably the only station everyone could agree on—buzzy at the volume it had been turned to.

And to complete the picture, two workmen arguing with each other.

"How could you forget? You're the fucking driller, for Christ's sake." Jake, arms crossed.

"I don't know. I don't know!" Asher's permanent scowl went even deeper. "You never made a mistake in your entire life?"

"I don't think I ever forgot to put my pants on before leaving the house. You know? When I get in the bathtub, I generally remember to fill it with water first. That's the kind of screwup we're talking about here."

"Yeah, well—"

"Good morning." Finn pitched his voice loud enough to be heard over both of them, the radio, and a train rumbling past. "What's going on?"

Jake pointed at the new construction. "That. See?"

Finn studied the curtain wall. It was simple enough: a two-by-four frame, sill plates bolted directly into the concrete floor, the far side faced with plywood and buttressed with diagonal braces every six feet. Crude but strong. All the spoil excavated from the jacking shaft would go behind it—otherwise, the pile of dirt would overrun the entire interior.

"Looks good to me. Corman put it up?"

"Me and him, yeah," said Asher.

"Two thousand cubic feet," said Jake. "That's what we'll take out of the pit. There's just enough room back there."

"Okay, that works," Finn said. "So what's the problem?"

Jake shook his head. "The tunnel bore. Where does *that* dirt go?"

"Oh."

"A hundred twenty meters, one meter in diameter. We need another twenty-five hundred cubic feet of dump volume."

Finn grimaced. "The microtunneler pumps it out in slurry. Can't we just leave it in the sedimentation tank?"

"I don't think so." Jake looked at Asher.

"No." Glaring, like none of this was his fault. "Maybe a fourth of that before the tank has to be cleared."

They could heap some muck above the height of the wall, but not all of it.

"At least you thought of it now. Be kind of obvious if we had to put it in the street." Finn looked around. "Okay, here's what you do. Build another wall, across that corner." He pointed to the opposite side of the warehouse.

"That's not exactly convenient," Asher said.

"Well, if you hadn't—"

"Never mind." Finn cut Jake off. "Look, the control unit goes here, right?" He held out both hands, indicating the area in front of the broken concrete. "Gantry for the pipe jack is going to stick out at least this far. Sedimentation tank behind it. That uses up almost half of the entire floor."

"Yeah, but—"

"The excavator can handle it if necessary."

Jake nodded agreement. Asher seemed willing to flounder on, arguing about anything, but no one wanted to listen. Eventually, grumbling, he found a measuring tape and went to check whether they had enough lumber for the second wall.

There was take-out coffee at the table. Finn sat, moving a coil of hose to the floor to make room. Jake leaned on the wall.

"Who brought in the concrete?" Finn gestured to the flatbed. "I thought you and Corman went to get the boring rig."

"We split up. He can handle it."

"Okay." The air had a faint, pleasant smell of resin and sawdust. Finn drank some coffee, staring absently at the jacking pipe.

"That doesn't look like enough," he said eventually.

"Nope. We're going to need another trailer. I was waiting until the curtain wall was done before unloading this load."

"Good point." The pipe would have to be stacked, ready for use, and close to where the gantry would sit over the entry shaft. "Actually, we might want to get the whole tunnel machine in place before that."

"I thought about that, but it'll be easier to run the excavator back and forth beforehand." The earthmover was not just for digging the pit; it would carry the pipes, one by one, in a sling attached to the scoop. At thousands of pounds each, the concrete sections were far too heavy to move by hand.

"Guess we should wait on the laser, too."

The bigger the project, the more complicated the dependencies. Back when Finn was on the legitimate side of the business, planning was driven by cost. Now it was all about speed. Once they started the drill, it had to run without the smallest hiccup.

Jake went to help Asher frame the second wall. Finn picked up the work area around the Kei truck. Another train went past, then some heavy trucks, loud in the street.

They were having lunch, eating sandwiches and arguing about football, when Corman walked in empty-handed.

"Hey." Jake looked at the closed bay doors. "I didn't hear a diesel rig."

"No." Corman helped himself to some tortilla chips from the paper sack Finn had opened.

Long pause.

"No . . . what?"

"No boring machine."

Finn sighed. "Okay. Why not?"

"Because it hadn't been returned yet. Crew renting it now, they were supposed to have it back already. But their job ran long."

"Fair enough. When can we get it?"

"Guy said tomorrow."

Jake looked at the roof, calculating, for a moment. "Well, that's not a problem. Still plenty of time to get it installed in the pit."

"Long as it's running right." Asher shook his head. "Who knows what condition it'll be in?"

Corman was eating a large handful of chips. When he'd finally swallowed, he wiped his hand on his jacket and said, "They're doing maintenance after they pull it out of the ground today. Should be done by tonight, they'll drive it back to the rental yard early tomorrow morning, we can pick it up then."

A lot of words at once for Corman.

Finn started to talk, had a thought, and stopped dead for a moment.

"Hang on," he said. "They're doing the refit on-site?"

"Easier that way. Clean everything there, they don't have to take it apart again at the yard." Corman shrugged slightly. "Could just be making excuses."

Finn looked at Asher. "Does that sound right?"

"Sure. Promise to bring it back all shiny and shipshape, sometimes they'll discount the rental."

"Good enough." Jake wadded up the paper wrapper from his tuna-with-everything and caught Finn's eye. "No? Not good enough?"

"Let me ask you something," Finn said, turning to Corman. "Do you know *where* they just finished up? The current job?"

He thought about it. "I think I saw the name of company that's got it now on the paperwork."

"Because, it seems to me—" But he didn't finish, because Asher started laughing.

Jake looked at him, annoyed. "What?"

"Because it'll just be sitting there," Asher said.

"Yeah, so wh—"

"All night long, clean and sharp and ready to go. Probably up on the trailer and everything. Right?"

"Ex*act*ly," Finn said. "Bootstrapping."

CHAPTER TWENTY-NINE

Late afternoon, sun already gone, long shadows and wind kicking grit off the streets. People on the sidewalks were hunched into their coats, most walking quickly, done with their workdays. Maybe a storm was coming—there was a bit of the manic energy that accompanies vertiginous swings in air pressure. The air had a winter snap.

Nicola, however, strolled along like a contractor on break, eating something wrapped in foil. Emily caught an occasional waft. Eggs? Chili?

"What is that, anyway?" she finally asked.

"Breakfast burrito." Nicola's mouth was full. "There was a Chinese taqueria at Grand Central."

"Seems early for dinner."

"Breakfast, like I said."

They stopped at a corner. "Where's mine?" Emily asked.

"Oops, did you want something? Sorry."

"Hmm." Emily pretended to think. "I guess I *did* have breakfast about ten hours ago."

"Sorry." Nicola laughed. "Wasn't thinking. I just got up."

"That's a hacker schedule? Work all night?"

"Nah, I'm just not a morning person."

They continued down Forty-Second. Rush-hour traffic, taxis weaving, buses coughing diesel.

"Thanks for coming," Nicola said.

"Finn said you needed help with something."

"Uh-huh." Nicola finished eating, scrubbed her face with a napkin, and dropped the crumpled ball of trash into a barrel at the entrance to Bryant Park. "Before we get to that, though . . ."

Warning flags fluttered. Emily eyed her warily. "What's up?"

"Don't take this the wrong way, okay? But I have to ask."

"Yeah?"

"Who are you working for?"

"Ah."

"For me and the guys, it's nice and clear. We're all on the same team. Done this shit before, do it again. But your situation is a little more complicated? Maybe?"

"Wes signs my paychecks."

"Yeah. See, that's what I'm wondering about."

Truth was, Emily had been wondering, too. She wasn't going to lie—some of Wes's assignments had put her on the far side of financial-sector regulation. Probably even the criminal code, depending on how ambitious the federal prosecutors might be. But breaking into a gold vault was quite a bit more newsworthy than some ambiguous insider trading.

"The thing is," she said slowly, "there may not be many more paychecks."

"I figured." Nicola didn't seem surprised. "Guy dreams up a scheme like this, it's not exactly long-term strategic planning."

"He's making bad decisions. Choosing bad options."

"And Finn is a better one?" Nicola studied her. "For you?"

Clearly the smartest one on Finn's team. "I could leave. Quit now and walk."

"Um, no, you can't."

"No?"

"Or I hope not. Because if you do, I'm out, and I don't know about the others, but probably the whole thing's off."

"I'm not doing anything essential." But Emily shook her head. "Never mind, I know what you mean."

They stopped near the fountain, long since shut down for winter. Leafless trees clacked their branches in the wind. An out-of-season skateboarder pushed his way past, but few other people were around.

"You're not threatening me," Emily said.

"Of course not."

"But you could if you wanted. And I'd take it seriously."

Nicola nodded. "You're right," she said. "But that's not me. I make choices, too, right? Too much grunting and dick-waving in the world already."

Emily laughed. "Sounds just like Wall Street."

"Still, I'd like to know," Nicola said. "I'd like to be . . . reassured."

"Fair enough." She waited while the skateboarder circled past them again. "One, Wes has done everything but slosh gasoline around the office and set himself on fire. I need to think about where I go next. Two, I could use the money. Three, those first two points are not unrelated and I'm really, really tired of Wes right now, and if life happens to fuck him over, well, that might make me happy."

"Uh-huh." Nicola paused. "And four?"

"Oh, four." Emily shrugged. "We don't really need to talk about four, do we?"

They left the park, followed by a few dead leaves blowing along the sidewalk.

"Good enough for me," Nicola said.

"I'm glad to hear it." And she was. She liked Nicola more every time they talked. "So what's the big secret? What do you need *my* help with?"

"It's up ahead. Not far now."

They crossed Fortieth and continued two blocks south. At the corner, Nicola stepped under the awning of one of the city's innumerable hardware stores and gestured slightly across the street.

"The tower," she said. "Eleventh floor."

Deconstructivist black metal with a half-exposed frame and a gash down the entire silver facade that would have been avant-garde twenty years earlier. It occupied the corner lot, butting up against the next building along. Eighteen floors was only halfway to the top.

Emily counted windows. "That floor doesn't look much different than the rest of the building," she said. "Are we going in?"

"Not through the lobby." The traffic light changed, and Nicola led the way across the zebra stripe, then down the street along the building's right side. They crossed over between taxis and radio cars bouncing over poor paving.

"Now take a look at the back," Nicola said.

Manhattan no longer had alleys, Hollywood to the contrary—everything had been filled in with development. The skyscraper here was flush with its neighbor: a six-story brownstone adjacent to a narrower three-story building, then a brick rectangle three times as high, and so on down the block.

The enormous, ragged notch, like the tower was splitting down the center, reappeared on its rear. Emily thought it looked stupid, but she was no architectural critic.

"Again, the eleventh story," said Nicola.

"Uh-huh." Emily crooked her neck. "So what's on that floor?"

"Stormwall Security Services."

"Aha."

"They have the monitoring contract for the vault," she said. "I need to visit their computers."

Emily studied the floor for another minute.

"There's a reason we're not looking at the front entrance, isn't there?" she said.

The fourth building down the block had a brightly lit health club above street level, rows of exercise machines visible through plate glass.

"The gym has an emergency exit just above the roofline of its shorter neighbor," Nicola said. "See? Like a fire escape, but it's just an ironwork platform. There must be a ladder to the street off the shorter building, around back."

"Okay."

"I've seen people out there smoking. I assume they're club employees, no doubt breaking all sorts of rules—members probably don't want to see their personal trainers puffing away. But if they can get out there, I figure we can, too."

"Really?"

"Might have to buy a day pass, but sure, once we're inside we'll figure it out."

Emily said, "We?"

"From there," Nicola said, not answering, "across the roof, then up the side of the next building. See that pipe? Not a drain; I think it's an electrical conduit, RCN maybe. With the window ledges alongside, it doesn't look too hard. Then over *that* roof, and we're alongside Stormwall's tower."

"And they're"—Emily counted again—"five stories above that."

"I'm an okay climber." Nicola held her hands up, like, *You know?* "I'm not good enough to do that alone."

"Fifty feet, unprotected." Emily shook her head slowly. "People free-solo insane heights now. A thousand meters, more. Not me. You fall off anything more than fifteen feet, you probably spend the rest of your life in a wheelchair."

"It's not really *climbing*," Nicola said. "See how the structural beams poke into the notch? More like going up a ladder."

"Uh-huh." Emily peered at the building. "Until you slip and fall and die."

"The design is deliberately irregular. Looks to me like there are plenty of places to stop and rest." The designer had done his best— no doubt he was a man—to make it seem jagged and broken. "That's why I think this is possible. It doesn't just make the climb almost as easy as a steep set of stairs, but it's dark enough to hide in. At night, we'll be invisible."

The corner traffic light changed, and another pack of cars accelerated past. A woman walked her dog along, and they fell silent until she was farther down the block. Nicola checked her phone but didn't unlock the screen. Emily decided she was doing something to not look like they were loitering.

"What about cameras?" she said. "The city has surveillance everywhere."

"Plenty, but all at street level. Look." Nicola began pointing them out. "At the intersection, on the traffic signal. Over the entrance of that store. The ATM machine across the street. The corner of the skyscraper—see? Two stories up, but it's pointed down. And so on. There are probably more, but they're all aimed where they expect to see people, not birds."

Emily studied the route. In fact, it didn't look that hard. She wondered if Nicola was selling herself short.

"You definitely need to do this?"

"The job doesn't happen otherwise."

"Uh-huh." The more she looked at it, the easier it seemed. "Why do you need me up there, too?"

"You're the climber. I'm an amateur." She forestalled Emily's objection with a gesture. "There's no way to know what's really up there. Not without doing it. And if I get into a jam, well—" She let her hand fall. "I'd like you there to get me out."

What the hell. She'd always wanted to be a nightclimber.

"When?"

Nicola looked at her phone again, checking the time. "How about six hours from now?"

CHAPTER THIRTY

Well, fuck me," said Asher.

Corman grunted.

"Just *once*, I'd like something to go smooth."

"If it was easy," said Finn, "anyone could do it."

The three of them sat in the cab of the Kenworth—which Gil had let them keep for a while longer—looking out into the night. The old truck was worn inside, the seat vinyl torn, the shift balky and not just because Finn kept banging the lever into Asher's knee. It smelled of cigar smoke and greasy food gone rancid.

"Maybe they're worried about the copper," he added. "Or the equipment."

"Fucking New Jersey." Asher shook his head. "Assholes here will steal anything, I guess."

The job site was a replacement bridge over a small river a few miles from Blairstown. Farms had given way to development long ago, even a two-hour drive from the city, and they could see lights of a McMansion suburb through trees at the bank.

The bridge was half done—abutments installed at either side, the roadways graded but not paved, a framework of steel erected across the span. A site trailer and a porta-potty sat to one side, and the drilling rig was lashed down on a trailer next to them. Presumably, the bridge contract required a parallel utility conduit under the ground.

As promised, the MTBM looked clean and ready to go: control unit, sedimentation tank, the cutting head itself under a tarp, jacking frame dismantled, stacked, and cabled in place. The trailer was even faced the right way, ten feet from the road. They could have backed in and been gone in five minutes.

Except the entire site was fronted by a temporary eight-foot chain-link fence, posts sunk into concrete footings and two strands of barbed wire at the top. The barrier wasn't complete—the fencing petered out close to the river—but it was more than sufficient to keep out any vehicles.

Like their truck.

"It's just some galvanized poles," said Asher. "We can drive right over it, flatten the son of a bitch."

Corman snorted.

"What? I don't see any alarm wires."

"Maybe not," Finn said, "but that means fuck-all. Anyway, we're sitting in the middle of Soccer Mom Acres here. Go crashing around, and we'll have SWAT teams arriving in about sixty seconds."

"All right, fine. We'll just cut the chain."

"It's one of those bike messenger locks." Finn put the truck in gear, hitting Asher in the knee again. "See?"

He drove past slow enough for all of them to admire the heavy black shackle securing the gate: a massive piece of tempered steel, its evolved design the result of a five decades' war against the most determined thieves in the Western world.

"Huh."

"Jaws of life might open it," Finn said. He kept going, wary of drawing attention idling on the road. "Too bad we don't have one."

"Diamond-tipped saw," said Asher.

"Shit, forgot that, too."

They drove back to the I-80 entrance. Finn pulled in to a sparsely occupied Park-and-Ride lot, putting the truck at the darker end. Traffic passed steadily on the four lanes of state road.

"Any ideas?" he asked.

And it was Corman who answered, pulling out his cell phone. "Call Nicola," he said. "She'll know."

✗ ✗ ✗

Nicola's heart raced—and not from exertion. Scaling the wall, hand over hand on the conduit and using the masonry clips for footholds, had been easy enough. But they'd gone as fast as they could, feeling exposed to the buildings all around. Fortunately, the entire side was dark, brighter light from the skyscraper casting deep shadows.

They'd gotten through the health club easily, for the cost of an introductory two hours each. After a tour, the trim young woman went back to the desk and left them at the locker rooms. Emily found the service door first and propped it open with a wedge that was clearly sitting on the iron landing for that purpose.

No one else was out there. After a moment, Nicola hopped the rail and dropped to the flat roof of the shorter, adjoining building. She checked the far edge, peering carefully over the parapet, and returned.

"The fire escape's back there," she'd said, looking up at Emily, still on the landing. "We can leave that way. About ten feet to the sidewalk."

"Good."

"Ready?"

"Just a minute." Emily closed the door and pushed the wedge beneath it. "Anyone tries to come out, it'll take an extra minute to dislodge that. Don't want them seeing us halfway up."

They ran across the rubber membrane of the roof, going around a blocky HVAC unit and the stub of an ancient brick chimney. Emily yanked on the conduit, which didn't budge, and after a quick look at Nicola—*Okay?*—she started up.

Nicola followed, and Emily pulled her over the top edge. A moment to catch her breath, and they dashed across the second roof to the far side, where it butted up against the skyscraper.

A weatherbeaten headhouse, basically a small shed for a door at the top of an interior stairwell, stood close to the modern steel and glass of the newer building. They ducked behind it, into deeper shadow.

As they settled on to their heels, a loud braying pierced the air.

"What the fuck?" Emily jerked around in surprise.

"Oh, shit, I cannot *believe* I forgot that!" Nicola unzipped a slash pocket on her jacket and pulled out her phone.

"I turned mine off, you know?"

"It's Finn." She hesitated for a second. "Ought to take it, I think."

They were alone on the roof, six stories above street level. Traffic noise drifted up, but it felt far away. The blank glass of the skyscraper was dark at their level. Behind the headhouse, they were well concealed.

"I'm going to check out the notch." Emily moved away.

Nicola clicked the phone's accept button.

"Got a minute?" Finn's voice.

"Keep it quick. We're in the middle of . . . you know."

"Right. So are we."

"Problem?"

"There's a fence we didn't expect." He described the lock. "Corman's got a plasma torch at the warehouse, but we can't drive all the way back for it."

"Might be kind of obvious, too."

"So I heard once, well, this guy inside was telling me you can open these things with a cap from a ballpoint pen. Corman thinks you might know how to do that."

"Sure, it works great, but only on the old tubular keyways. Kryptonite saw the YouTube videos, too, you know. They changed to flat keys, oh, fifteen years ago at least."

"Damn. Doesn't look that old."

"Well, there's other ways. You have a pair of hydraulic bolt cutters? That's what the bicycle thieves mostly use now. They're nice and fast."

"That's back at the shed, too."

"Okay. How about a tire jack? Messy but it works."

There was a pause, some muffled voices that Nicola couldn't make out.

Finn came back on the line. "Asher's going to check, but I doubt it. We're in a hauler, not an automobile."

"You're making this hard." Nicola thought for a moment. "Maybe a long steel pipe that fits over the crosspiece end, if you can get enough torsion . . . ?"

"Probably not." Another off-call conversation, his hand apparently over the phone's mic. He came back: "Asher found a sledgehammer."

"No jack, but a sledgehammer?"

"This thing's a real jalopy."

Emily came back, sliding into place alongside. She gave a thumbs-up, then pointed at the phone with a questioning look.

Nicola made a *just-a-minute* gesture with her free hand.

"I'd hate to drive away." Finn sounded frustrated. "It's just sitting there for the taking."

Nicola thought about the lock's design. Heavy, well-tempered steel . . . "Hey, wait," she said. "You're at a job site, right? Heavy equipment lying around?"

"Yeah, but we can't fire up a jackhammer. This has to be discreet."

"How about welding tanks?"

"A welding torch won't cut this. It wouldn't be hot enough."

"No, just the *tanks*. Oxygen, acetylene, whatever. Any gas, really."

"Actually, there might be, over by the site trailer—"

"Perfect." Nicola grinned. "You're going to love this."

Finn pulled on his cap as he got down from the cab. Corman had gone around the end of the fence at the edge of the property on foot, moving far more fluidly and quickly than his size would suggest. He came back carrying a dull metal tank in one hand—impressive, as it probably weighed well over one hundred pounds.

"This ain't gonna work," said Asher, exiting the truck from the other door. "Stupid."

"Just get the sledge."

They walked up to the gate. Finn glanced around. The site was illuminated by some bright security lights, sharp shadows at the edge. They were below a slight gradient leading up from the river and no houses were immediately nearby. Still, anyone could drive past.

"Don't look suspicious," he said.

Asher hooted, and even Corman might have cracked a fleeting smile.

"Right, then." Finn got out of the way. "Go ahead."

Corman tipped the tank toward the lock and opened the valve. A loud hiss as the acetylene blasted out in a narrow stream. Some of it vaporized immediately, creating a thin cloud. More condensed on the lock and the fence poles it was fixed around. Corman held the spray for thirty seconds, then abruptly stepped back and dropped the tank. He shook his hands in the air, grimacing

Finn bent down and twisted the tank's stopcock closed. It was subzero cold, like the metal tank itself. Corman had gotten freezer burn.

"Hit it," he said, and Asher swung the sledgehammer.

The lock shattered, its steel as brittle as glass.

"I'll be goddamned." Asher stared at the broken metal.

"Nicola said thieves use cans of compressed air. But a tank this size, under greater pressure, runs even colder."

"How does that work?"

"Uh . . . high pressure to low pressure, the system energy has to be constant . . . ? Something like that." Finn shrugged. "Who cares? Come on, let's hitch up the trailer."

Eleven stories up, and it felt like the temperature had dropped twenty degrees.

"It's like we're climbing fucking Everest." Nicola leaned back into the notch, resting her legs and warming her hands in her armpits. "This wind is *arctic*."

"Everest is in the Himalaya." Emily seemed comfortable, one hand on a beam, one foot on a joint with two-inch bolt heads, standing as easily as if they were on the ground.

Nicola gave her a look, which, in the shadowed darkness of the building's notch, she probably couldn't see. "We're not at the North Pole, either," she said. "But it *feels* like it."

"So how's the window look?"

"Well." Back to business. "Not good."

"No?"

Nicola flexed her hands, decided they were warm enough to try again, and eased back around the corner.

Wind whistled along the skyscraper's side. The lights of the city spread away in all directions. Traffic meandered in a neon gulley far below.

She started to freeze up, and not because of the cold.

"Don't look down," Emily said helpfully.

"I *know* that."

Stormwall's windows were six feet tall, running from about waist height to the interior ceiling. Slatted vertical blinds had been pulled to the side, and a few lights inside—computer monitors, equipment LEDs, that sort of thing—provided enough illumination to see. It looked like a typical office warren: cubicles, racks of equipment, some plastic ivy. Everything beige and gray, including the plants.

The problem was the narrow silver strip banding the entire window, just inside the frame. And the small black boxes mounted just below the ceiling, in every corner and across the middle of the room as well. And what looked very much like a pair of cameras near the door.

Not to mention the window itself was heavy tempered glass, permanently mounted in a three-inch metal frame.

She returned to the shelter of the notch.

"Four breaching charges might take out the window," she said. "I can't see any other way to get through it. And even if we had a magic glass cutter, there's about five different alarm systems in there. I wouldn't make it to the front desk."

"No go, huh?"

She shook her head. "Fuck."

"Oh well." Emily didn't seem too disappointed. "At least we got a great view. It's spectacular up here!"

Nicola shivered once, then again. "I'm fucking *cold*." She crouched on the beam, huddling into her jacket. The cat-burglar black fleece didn't insulate well.

"We'll warm up on the downclimb."

"If we had rope, we could just rap down."

"If we had wingsuits, we could jump."

That made her laugh. "Have you done that?"

"Of course not. Those guys are crazy."

They started to climb down. Emily went first, keeping an eye on Nicola above her—not belaying, because they had no equipment, but ready to arrest a fall. Nicola's arms, and particularly her hands, were hurting more than she wanted to admit.

A gust, almost a gale, buffeted the skyscraper. Nicola's nose ran from the cold, but she had to keep both hands on the beams. The adjacent roofline still seemed far, far below them.

Emily laughed. "I *love* climbing!" she shouted up, over the wind.

Nicola muttered and looked for the next foothold.

"Sorry you couldn't get in," Emily said.

"Yeah, well, on to plan B."

"You have a plan B?"

Nicola's hands were going numb from contact with the icy metal. Was that *snow* falling? She gritted her teeth and kept moving.

Finally, dropping the last meter to the roof, she bent to put her hands on her knees, breathing hard. Emily was right—the exertion had warmed her up. After a moment's recovery, she straightened.

"Yeah," she said. "There's *always* a plan B."

CHAPTER THIRTY-ONE

Finn got back to the warehouse midday, feeling like he'd never left.

They'd returned with the rock drill well after midnight. It might have been sooner, but Finn was feeling extracautious, so he had Asher and Corman drop him off nearby and drive away. He then lurked at the end of Caleb Street for half an hour, watching an occasional vehicle go by, before calling them back. By the time the truck returned, he had the bay open—Asher drove right in, Finn immediately rolled the door down, and with luck, no one at all saw a thing.

Hopefully, they'd all gotten a good night's sleep after that.

Asher had already arrived and begun to assemble the jacking frame. Two wrenches and loose bolts cluttered the floor around him.

"Good morning," Finn said, shucking his snow-dusted coat. He was cheerful: refreshed and energetic. "Afternoon? Nice to see the Christmas decorations going up everywhere."

"Fuck off."

"Excuse me?"

"I *hate* the fucking season."

"Right."

Finn thought Asher might have been sleeping here: a pile of blankets and coats in the corner looked suspiciously like a nest. But it wasn't his concern.

Nicola showed up next, face glowing, perhaps from the brisk, sleety wind.

"Awesome day!" She cleared the table of tools, fast-food Styrofoam, and a heavy loop of copper, then set down her laptop. She bumped the table leg by accident and something toppled. "Feels like winter for real."

"Yup." Finn picked up the rock chisel she'd dislodged onto the floor. "It's going to help, too—if the ground's frozen, that might make the drilling easier. Mud and sludge are the worst."

Asher finished the strut he'd been working on. His pipe wrench clanged to the floor. "Fuck," he said. "Gonna take a break." He headed out the back door, pulling a cigarette box from his pocket.

Finn pulled out a chair and sat across from Nicola at the table. "So how did it look?"

"Physical bypass is out," Nicola said. "That office is locked down tighter than the fucking vault."

"We've *got* to have you controlling the Stormwall monitors. The whole thing is impossible otherwise."

"I know, I know." She tapped at the keyboard, then pushed the computer aside. "I made an appointment for later this afternoon."

"An *appointment*? At Stormwall?"

"If you want to go through the front door, it's easier when they're expecting you."

"Huh." Finn looked at her. "That seems a lot simpler than climbing the outside wall."

"It's right before the holidays. Most of the staff will be on vacation or halfway out the door—usually it's the deadweight who get stuck on duty while everyone else is on their ski trips. Makes it a little easier for me."

"Why didn't you try it that way the first time?"

"Risk management." She leaned back in her chair. "I'd rather not have them capturing video if I can avoid it."

"Sorry."

"Whatever. Part of the job."

"And once you're in?"

A smile glinted. "Then I improvise."

The back door banged open. Asher kicked snow from his boots as he tromped in.

"Fucking *blizzard* out there."

"Long as they keep the roads cleared," Finn said.

"No shit." Asher shook out his coat. "You gonna help me bolt this motherfucker together or what?"

"In a few."

Muttering, Asher went back to the rig, clicking on the radio. Aerosmith blasted in, nice and loud. Like anyone after a couple decades roughnecking, Asher's hearing was none too good. As he began to uncoil a hose from the TBM's sedimentation unit, Finn leaned back in his chair, running down mental checklists again. His eyes drifted shut.

"God *damn* it!" Asher yelled, and a sudden gush of water sprayed around the room. He lost control of the hose, pressure kicking it like a lunging snake.

"Fuck." Finn jumped to his feet, as Nicola slammed her laptop shut and spun around, clutching it to her chest to shield it from the water. The lashing torrent knocked the radio off its perch, the music ending abruptly. Metal clanged and tools were blasted across the floor.

"Piece of *shit*." Asher wrestled the nozzle to the ground, pointed it away from all their equipment, and twisted the spigot handle. The flow trickled, then stopped.

"Jesus." Finn looked at the soaked floor. "Make sure it's tight next time, okay?"

Asher grumbled and looked for the fitting wrench. Nicola glanced at the wet table and rolled her eyes.

"Think I'll do this somewhere else." She began packing up again. "Oh, meant to tell you: I figured out what's happening at the railroad on New Year's Eve."

"Oh?" Finn put down the copper tubing he'd just retrieved from the floor. "What?"

"A special shipment. An open-pit mining excavator. I have emails and internal messages talking about the cutting blade, which is apparently huge. It's coming in on special railcars from a factory in Pittsburgh."

"That doesn't sound too unusual."

"Well—"

"Special trains can screw up the scheduling, but they're not uncommon."

"I don't know. They're expecting protests. Keegan's been telling his officers they all have to work that night."

"Who's Keegan? And—wait, extra police?"

"Keegan's their security chief. I found an internal directory." She got back to the point. "Listen, riot police are going to be there."

With the radio silenced, Asher must have been listening in. "*Riot police? What the fuck?*"

"There was talk of coordination between Newark and New York."

Asher started to sputter. "Any details?" Finn said.

"Just that they're locking down the yard, and police are going to be there. How many depends on how big the crowd is."

"Lockdown? Police? This is fucked," Asher said.

"Hmm."

"And I'm wondering about coincidence. The very same night we're planning to go in—"

Finn cut him off. "Let's get the story before we start making assumptions." To Nicola: "Can you get more details?"

"I'll try. Not until after I visit Stormwall today, though. Right now, I need to get ready for that."

"Right. Good luck."

She waved one hand, like, *No problem.* "Riot police, though?"

"I don't know," Finn said. His mind was off and running, considering options and possibilities. "But maybe we can work with it."

CHAPTER THIRTY-TWO

Heavy eyeglasses with light-sensitive lenses, the same dark gray suit she'd worn to Gladco but a different blouse and shoes, winter overcoat and scarf. Nicola went through the door looking down at her phone, tapping something out before she arrived at the reception desk. Not exactly a disguise, but she'd seen the cameras inside Stormwall. If they had them in the back, there'd probably be one or two in front, too.

The plan was to gain access, after which she could erase whatever was necessary. But it didn't hurt to be careful.

The receptionist was a man about Nicola's age with an extremely short haircut and what appeared to be a very fit build under his own charcoal suit. He sat straight in the chair, a stance no doubt drilled into him at Fort Benning.

Some companies put attractive young women out front. Stormwall was selling a different set of not-so-subliminal impressions.

"Here to see Kevin Jayne," Nicola said. "One thirty appointment."

"Certainly. I'll show you to the conference room." He stood, nodding politely to the corridor behind the desk.

She gave him a bright smile and paused long enough to put the phone away. When her hand came out, she held the tiny USB drive in a magician's thumb palm. Small as it was, the device nonetheless contained the sharpest, most lethal malware she was capable of coding. Plug it into any computer for just twenty seconds, and a razorfish would be loosed into the network, burrowing deep into its heart, erasing all traces of its passage as it went.

Any logged-in computer, that is. Stormwall's systems were protected by some of the most impressive external barriers she'd encountered. But inside . . .

All she needed was a half minute alone with someone's workstation.

"I'm a little early," she said as they walked back into the offices.

"Not a problem."

They entered the same cubicle warren she'd seen through the window, and Nicola scanned the desks as they passed. Fewer than half were occupied—maybe four or five people. Empty or not, all the cubes had screens and keyboards, sometimes more than one set. She glimpsed black and beige PCs under the desks, mostly towers.

Pretend to scuff her shoe? Ask for a bathroom? Her guide gave her not the slightest opportunity, and then they were at the meeting room, him ushering her through the door. Nicola hid an annoyed grimace and slipped the drive back into her pocket.

On to the next option, then.

"Mr. Jayne will be with you shortly," the man said. "Do you need anything?"

"No, thank you." She dropped her bag on the table.

"I'm afraid Wi-Fi and cellular won't work inside."

"I'd expect no less."

He smiled back. "The power outlets are available for use, of course."

When he'd gone, Nicola examined the room, trying not to be obvious about it. No cable jacks visible anywhere.

She sighed. *Next* option?

Nine minutes later, the door opened, and the tall, broad-shouldered, silver-haired vice president Jayne came in. He shook her hand with exactly the right pressure and duration—not too strong, not too long—and waved to the chairs. If, like most men, he was disappointed by her appearance, he covered it completely.

"A pleasure," he said.

"Thank you for agreeing to see me."

He made a not-at-all gesture. "You came very highly recommended. Paul Fincarlo at Gladco said you'd done an absolutely stellar job for them."

"I'm flattered." Nicola had called the interim CFO directly one week earlier. The international bribes-and-payoffs scandal had finally begun to disappear from the business pages. Mark Kells was still on the payroll somewhere, which was no surprise—either they feared he knew too much, or he'd gone ahead and blackmailed them outright. The new CFO had probably expected something similar from her and had been surprised when she'd merely asked for an introduction to Stormwall.

"That's *all* you want?" he'd said.

"Your check cleared." Nicola grinned, though he couldn't see her over the phone. "I like doing business with straight shooters."

He laughed. "It happens Stormwall does some monitoring work for us on the West Coast."

Which Nicola had already known, having seen the name in Kells's files.

"Maybe I can do something for them," she said.

"Uh-huh. I'll let Kevin know you're networking."

And now she had Kevin Jayne in the room, as suave and pleasant as any top business development executive she'd ever met—which was saying something.

"My specialty is penetration testing," Nicola said. "Full-spectrum external audits. If there's a weakness, I'll find it."

"Paul didn't say what you'd done for them."

It was a question, but she only shook her head slightly. "I can't tell you, either, of course. The only reason I continue to get business is that I honor absolute confidentiality."

"I believe we're in good shape here—it's basically *our* specialty, too."

She ran through her usual pitch—the adult version, leaving out the shiny stuff and dumbed-down metaphors necessary with people who didn't report to a CIO. Jayne was a professional, same as her, and she treated him that way.

Not that he was buying today.

"I really think we've got a handle on our own security," he said. "No offense intended, but you're trying to sell snow to Eskimos here."

"Perhaps." Nicola nodded. "On the other hand, maybe a simple demonstration? Just to show you what I can do?"

He couldn't help a moment of smug. "You tried hitting our network already?"

"More or less."

"And did you get anywhere?"

Nicola picked up her bag and stood. "Why don't I show you?"

Back down the cubicle corridor. The same people were at the same desks. She stopped at a vacant one.

It was clearly in use: papers and binders piled not very neatly, pictures of a dog and a child tacked on the cube wall, screen saver bouncing on the screen.

An LED glowed on the PC box below—the key indicator for Nicola. It wouldn't work without power—nor without being logged in.

Which was impossible to check, though. That was up to luck.

"Okay, let's see if it's still here," she said.

"What?"

"Hang on. It's in the back—"

She knelt on the floor and reached behind the computer. It was pushed under the desk, so she had to reach awkwardly around, moving it so Jayne could see the connector bus.

On her knees, facing away from him, the position put her ass square into his field of view. She was no supermodel, but in her experience, men were men. They couldn't help themselves. For good measure, she shifted her weight from one side to the other, flexing, giving him a nice look.

"Check it out." She backed away slightly and tipped the box forward. Numerous cables were hooked up—power, speakers, monitor, network, the usual rat's nest, concealed in the dusty reaches behind the humming equipment—and they made it difficult to move the computer far. Jayne had to kneel, close to her, to see.

"There." She pointed vaguely at the box.

The head of the flash drive was about the size of a dime, gray and shadowed, plugged into a jack at the bottom of the frame. Most people would never have noticed.

Jayne saw it immediately.

"Shit!" He leaned forward. "How did you get *that* in there?"

Nicola beat him to it, plucking the drive out of the computer. Her shoulder knocked the desk's edge and the entire cubicle rattled. Backing out she stepped on his foot.

None of it intentional, but the distraction was just sufficient.

They stood up and Nicola handed him the drive.

"Don't worry," she said. "It's dead. Not just wiped—I burned the memory beforehand."

He glared at the drive, holding it a few inches from his eyes. "We have an absolute rule against any—*any*—foreign hardware."

"That's a good rule." Nicola slung her bag across her shoulder, resettling it. "Seriously, don't worry. It's nonreactive junk. You can have it."

"I'm going to check this immediately." He closed it into his fist. "I'll ask again. How in hell did you place it?"

"After-hours social engineering."

"What—?"

"As a demonstration. I'd be happy to write it up, in a full and detailed report." She paused. "I mean, as part of a contract, right?"

He hesitated, and Nicola handed over a business card—a throwaway email and an IP address where she'd placed some promo material on a one-off webpage. Setting the hook, exactly the same as if Jayne had been a genuine lead.

"I'll be in touch," she said. "Thanks for the time." She left him still staring at the drive.

In the elevator going down, she moved the duplicate, genuine flash drive to a safe, metal-lined pocket sewn inside her bag. She'd plugged it in when she first reached behind the computer, of course, Kevin staring at her glutes. Then she took her time shifting the computer so he could see the jack panel, and as she reached in to pull the drive out, she swapped it with the fake she'd kept hidden in her hand.

Kevin got the fake. Stormwall's network got the most beautiful razorfish she'd ever written.

Twenty seconds.

Nicola *owned* them now.

CHAPTER THIRTY-THREE

Corman didn't use electronic maps. He found smartphone screens to be impossibly small for his blocky, work-roughened hands. Just dialing a call was a long and irritating exercise, let alone maneuvering through online directions. But he wasn't the sort of technological dinosaur who persisted in treating his phone like a walkie-talkie. You still saw guys all the time at worksites, too cool to put the damn phone to their ear. Corman at least tried to keep up with the world.

But he figured that if he could use his phone to follow a route, somebody somewhere could use the *phone* to follow *him*. Nicola confirmed this one day while they were sitting around the warehouse. In considerable detail.

That girl did love to talk.

So he'd bought a large-format street atlas, razored out the pages he was interested in, and taped them together into a sort of field survey. This ungainly compilation of paper was now unfolded on the pickup's bench seat beside him.

Today he was working out the best driving routes for their getaway.

The first stop was easy. A half mile from their warehouse, and there were effectively only two choices. Caleb Street was too busy, not to mention in plain view of anyone looking out from the rail yard. So: out the back, down the side roads, and into a narrow way between two industrial buildings. Finn had come to a short-term agreement with the owner of the complex—it used to be a large factory operation, but now just ran trucks and rented out container storage. They had their own temporary spot in the rear.

Good.

The second transfer point was only somewhat more complicated. Corman tried different alternatives, taking his time, backing up and going around the blocks. Distribution centers, heavily fenced lots, old brick industrial buildings, and small, blue-collar businesses. Busy during the day, trucks and diesel clouds everywhere. Hopefully deserted at night, especially during the predawn hours of New Year's Day.

In the end, the most direct road seemed best. Corman idled his truck and studied the spot Finn identified. It was a short access alley behind a utility substation, a squat brick building surrounded by chain link and barbed wire. ABSOLUTELY NO PARKING threatened several signs affixed to the fence, along with towing information and legal threats.

PSEG really didn't want their access blocked.

All the better for them.

From there, a short, straight drive took him to the ramp onto I-78. If they made it that far, they'd be free, driving into America with a truckful of metal more valuable than gold. And if not . . .

Corman didn't believe in thinking about *if not*. What was the point?

He went back and drove the routes he'd selected again, then a third time, memorizing every turn and stop sign and driveway. Finally satisfied, he stopped at Karl's for a take-out cheese steak. No reason to eat inside, let more people get a look at him. He sat in his truck, in a corner of the lot, trying not to drip grease while he studied the map again.

He had one other route to survey.

"Do you want to do it, or me?" Nicola pushed over a piece of paper with some names and numbers scribbled on it.

Finn, sitting across from her at the folding table in the warehouse, looked at the sheet. "You're sure these are right?"

"Nothing's one *hundred* percent." She shrugged. "But Lenape is the only current vendor that seems to have anything to do with linen supply. Stormwall's been paying invoices from them regularly, like at least once per month. And the budget code matches to a category called 'uniforms.'"

"Hard to argue that last point. And this is Stormwall's HR manager? Daisy Vanderweil?"

"One of several, according to the internal company directory. But her name is on the invoices."

"Okay." Finn considered. "You do it. I'm sure you're better at this sort of thing."

Nicola nodded—no false modesty for her—and picked up her phone. Finn hollered over to Asher to keep it quiet for a few minutes, then settled back in his chair to watch.

"Hi, this is Jen Fairmont at Stormwall? We have a rush order?" She pitched her voice higher, its usual edges gone. "Can I talk to whoever is in charge of the account? Oh, thank you." Pause. "Hi, Paula, thanks for— Yes, I work for Daisy, she'd normally be handling this, but she's so busy today, she asked me to just call it in if that's okay? Yes, you know, everything has to be done *yesterday*." She laughed brightly. "Three new hires, and of course they're starting next week, and there's barely enough time for the *background* check let alone the orientation . . . Right, exactly. Oh, I *know*. Isn't that how it always is?" Pause. "Okay, so what they need is the standard money-room jumpsuit. Yes . . . right, blue, the usual insignia? Really, just the same as all the others . . . Three. One large, one medium-tall, and one XXL." She laughed again. "Yes, *exactly* like ordering at Starbucks!"

Nicola rolled her eyes at Finn.

"Listen, Daisy asked me to send someone over to pick them up? Is that okay? Oh, wonderful, they need them for the orientation first thing tomorrow morning, that's excellent . . . Shall I have Chip ask for you?" Pause. "Chip Relleno, do you know him? He's in the cubicle next to me, but *he* gets to drive the company car, you know how that goes . . . Right, the usual billing." Nicola squinted at her notes. "Code it '34-STAFFUNI,' like always . . . Thank you, Paula, that is *so* helpful. One more thing off Daisy's plate . . . and onto mine, you're so right!" Laughter. "Okay, so Chip will be there late this afternoon. How late? Gosh, I don't know. Six or six thirty? Is that a problem? . . . Well, how about this, could you just leave them at the desk, and he can sign them out from the security guard?"

By this point, Finn was shaking his head with admiration. Another minute, then Nicola clicked off and set the phone on the table.

"You're all set, Chip," she said.

"Maybe we should put you on the phone to Penn Southern's vault," he said. "See if you can talk them into packing up all the rhodium and leaving it on the dock. Save us the trouble."

"People generally want to be helpful." Nicola tucked the paper away. "It's not so hard to take advantage."

"Helpful?" Finn looked over at Asher, who was sprawled in the excavator's padded seat, head back, eyes shut, mouth hanging open. "Maybe we travel in different circles."

"I hope the sizes are right."

"They'll be close enough." He stood up, pulling on his coat.

"You going to be back later?"

"No. I have to find somebody. Might take a while. I'll go straight to Lenape from there."

"Anything I can help with?"

"Thanks, but probably not." Finn zipped up and found his hat. "I don't think these guys leave electronic trails."

CHAPTER THIRTY-FOUR

When the sweep came through, Kayo's automatic instinct to run was so strong that he had spun around and started to jump down the stairs—until he remembered, *Shit, I'm clean!* He halted immediately, faked a sneeze, and turned casually back to the corridor.

No warrants. No bonds. No probation or parole. For once in his life, he was a straight-arrow motherfucker, absolutely no paper sitting out there whatsoever.

Millz, though, shit. Far as Kayo knew, there was at least a bench warrant out. For the most petty shit you could think of. Millz had been in court last summer after a stop-and-frisk, cops said he resisted—but they *would*, a guy as big and wide as Millz just *standing* there gonna count as resisting. Anyway, the judge dropped the case, eventually, but the court still charged Millz $135 for fees. Which he didn't have after a week in holding. So, a warrant.

Which meant Millz had to disappear. The patrol was in no-fucking-around mode: five officers and a fucking *dog* spread across the station's broad corridor in a shallow vee and moving steadily along.

Kayo didn't even have to do anything. He just took one step forward, away from the wall, and *looked* at them. Motherfuckers converged on him like they'd coordinated it.

"Hands out."

"Stop there. Don't move."

"Turn around!"

Kayo kept his head up, looked them straight in the eyes, one after another. "Don't move, or turn around? Which one you *want*?"

Closer to home, that would have been more than enough for a beatdown. But here in the heart of Port Authority, surrounded by curious commuters, the officers of the law were more restrained.

"Turn around and face the wall, *sir*."

The usual bullshit. They roughed him a little, discreetly, jabbing during the pat-down and twisting his arm. Kayo stayed meek.

From the corner of his eye, definitely *not* looking, he saw Millz fade away across the concourse. Gone in seconds. Unless the NYPD had blocked every single entrance—unlikely without the mayor being in the neighborhood or some shit—Millz would make his escape without trouble. Kayo grinned.

"So what's up, Officers?"

They took his name, flipped through his wallet, apparently unsurprised at the lack of ID.

"Traveling somewhere today? Waiting for a bus?"

"Uh-huh."

"Which bus would that be?"

The dog was sniffing around his legs. Kayo frowned and tried to step back.

"Yo, back that fucking mutt *off*."

Instead, the canine handler gave the German shepherd more slack. "This is a trained animal," he said. "Trained to find illegal substances."

"Ain't nothing *illegal* in my fucking pants."

"He seems interested."

"You mind if we have a look?"

Millz should have been clear by now. Kayo didn't have to distract them further. He shrugged and held out his hands. "People watching us, Officers."

"Oh?"

"Watching *you*." He glanced around—indeed, a few passersby had slowed, drawn by the confrontation.

Double take. One of the onlookers—shit, he *knew* him. Man just standing there, like it was the fucking zoo.

Caught his eye, the smallest shake of the man's head.

The senior officer—he had a sergeant's chevrons on his sleeve—turned to examine the bystanders. "On your way, people," he said loudly.

A few moved, a few didn't. A frisson of tension ran through the group, police and civilians alike.

A phone came out, a young woman pointing it toward the confrontation. The police stiffened. The dog noticed the mood and turned away from Kayo to face the new threat. Pressure built, almost palpable.

Kayo sighed and closed his hands protectively over his stomach. He knew *exactly* who was going to catch the most shit, starting in about five seconds . . .

Except, no?

The man in the crowd suddenly turned peacemaker. He gestured at the woman with the camera—"No need for that, miss, I don't think"—and nodded to the police. "They're just doing their job."

"*Thank* you, sir."

"But look at them—!"

"Nothing's happening." Pause. "Right?"

A long moment, and then it ended. The tension dissipated. The handler pulled in his dog, and the crowd—never that large to start with—began to drift away.

Perhaps disappointed, the woman lowered her phone, made an irritated noise, and walked off. The police finished up with Kayo, finding nothing. Some face-saving bluster, and then they were on their way, continuing through the station. Five minutes later, it was like nothing had happened.

Kayo knew better than to hang around. He settled his K2 sherpa coat and headed for the exit. Enough of *this* shit.

Of course the man was waiting for him, across the street. Kayo let him catch up, thinking, *Damn, what's that motherfucker's* name?

"You're welcome," the man said. He'd gone clothes shopping, the cheap Giants windbreaker replaced by a serviceable canvas jacket.

"Ain't nothing would have happened. Not there."

"Whatever."

"How was Bellevue?"

"The worst fucking place I ever slept."

Kayo had to laugh. "*You're* welcome."

"I was looking for you."

"Why?"

"How's business?"

"What the fuck do you *want*?"

They started to walk.

"I'm working on something," the man said. "Might be some opportunity in it."

"Uh-huh." They slowed at the corner, and Kayo glanced back at the station.

"Don't think you should be going back there," the man said. "Not today."

"Fuck them."

"How about, at least hear me out?"

Kayo considered. Motherfucker was right. The day was gone. Millz was gone.

"Come to the big city to make your fortune," he said. "How's that working out?"

"Well." The man grinned. "Why don't I tell you about it?"

CHAPTER THIRTY-FIVE

E vening.

Finn showed up after dark with ears hurting from the cold, some paper-wrapped sausage, and a bottle of hard cider.

"Artisanal," he said, handing the bottle to Emily. "Made right across the river in Brooklyn."

Emily looked at it, faintly puzzled. "Cider?"

"I thought we could heat it up." Ever since arriving in the city, he seemed unable to adapt to the cold. New Mexico might have ruined him for winter. "Sausage. Also from Brooklyn."

"You want that warmed up, too?"

"Couldn't hurt."

She'd apparently only just returned to the apartment herself. Finn could see a grocery bag half unpacked on the counter, eggs and milk sitting out.

"Kielbasa and potatoes," she said. "Where's the artisanal sauerkraut?"

"Missed that." He stepped fully inside. "I used to think *I* was an artisan."

He hadn't seen her since the park. After the revelation that Wes had been gaming him, Finn started off angry, a deep and abiding fury. Slowly, it had transformed into determination. The planning adapted. Wes was jerking them around? Fuck him. They were going to take their money anyway.

When Emily called to check in, he surprised them both by suggesting meeting at her apartment—and she surprised him by saying yes. Takeout and a strategy update. It wasn't quite a date.

But now that he was here, it felt like more than a business meeting.

"Have a seat." Emily pulled out plates, put something in the microwave. Finn removed his coat and sat on the futon couch. There was a heavy wool blanket folded over the back, and after a minute, he pulled it over himself.

He was weary, and it had been a cold day.

"How's Wes doing?" he asked.

"Holding it together." Emily came in and sat next to him, placing a tray on the coffee table. She curled her legs beneath her. "Barely. Manic most of the time, phone calls, yelling at us, banging on his computer."

"Still solvent, though."

"For another few weeks." She tore a piece of bread from a baguette—artisanal, Finn figured—and chewed slowly.

"That should be enough."

They ate, drinking cider in mugs from the microwave. The apartment felt peaceful.

"What did you do today?" Emily asked.

"Well." He hesitated, but only a moment. "I followed Asher around, actually."

"Followed him?"

"Like some cheap private detective. Yeah. It's harder than you might think."

"Why?"

"In Manhattan traffic? Cabbies cutting you off everywhere, every light timed wrong?"

"No." She smiled around a chunk of sausage. "Not what I meant."

"I know."

He couldn't let go of New Mexico. Emily had dug further in the archives, even asking the auditors if they'd kept any copies from that year, but she'd come up empty. So what Wes did or didn't do, possibly to profit off the botched robbery, remained unknown.

"Even if Wes had wanted to set us up, he couldn't have," Finn said. "I made damn sure never to tell him the details. I doubt he even knew which railroad we were targeting."

"So you think . . . Asher?"

"Or Jake, or Corman." He shook his head, frustrated. "But none of them makes sense."

"And did Asher lead you anywhere suspicious?"

"McDonald's and a Newark strip club."

"Uh-huh?"

He looked up, cheese in his hand. "I didn't go in."

They finished the dinner, such as it was, and the bottle, more slowly. Finn hadn't really gotten used to alcohol again, either. Seven years effectively without—occasional pruno didn't count—and his tolerance had gone back to nil. A mild buzz settled over him.

Emily had scrunched into herself, curled up at her end of the futon couch. Finn realized he'd wrapped himself in the blanket, leaving nothing for her.

"Hey, are you cold?" He lifted one corner of the blanket. "Here."

Emily studied him for a moment. Belatedly, he realized his invitation might have meant more than that.

She scooted over and eased under the blanket.

It was the most natural thing in the world to settle his arm around her. To shift position slightly, fitting themselves together more neatly. To turn his head, starting to speak, and then to catch her gaze, so close.

The first kiss wasn't even tentative, but long and slow and exploratory. Finn shifted his weight again, and Emily turned toward him, both arms all the way around now. He ran his hand along her side, under her shoulder blade, down between her back and the futon.

"Oh my," Emily said, eyes opening.

He eased both hands around her, lifted her head gently toward him again. Her own hands slipped under the blanket, then under his shirt, pulling it from his waist. How had she kept them so warm? So soft? His own felt calloused and rough on her skin.

There was moaning.

Matters sped up. Emily found buttons to unbutton, a zipper to yank. Finn located a clasp. Muscle memory took over, opening it one-handed, no fumbling at all. Skin on skin, the blanket tangling around them, clothes half off and askew.

"Finn."

He had one palm on an erect nipple, marveling at its tactile beauty, even as his mouth searched her face, her neck, her shoulder. He pressed her closer.

"Finn!" More insistently. With muddled reluctance, he pulled back, just enough to see her face.

"What?"

"I just . . ." She fell silent for a moment, and Finn kept roving, now loosening her belt, sliding one hand under the waistline, glorying in the smooth muscle of her butt. "*Stop* that for a second," she said.

"You really want me to?"

"No." But she stayed tense. "Is this smart?"

"Um."

"No, it's not smart." Answering her own question.

"No, I mean—" Finn gave up. "I don't care."

A long moment, and then Emily laughed.

"All right, then," she said and disengaged herself just enough to pull Finn up off the couch. "Me neither. But not here, for God's sake."

It was better than he could possibly have imagined—and he'd had seven long, long years of imagining.

In the fifteen feet across the floor and through her bedroom doorway, they managed to shed the rest of their clothing. Emily yanked up the duvet and slid under. Finn dove in after her. The sheets were cold to start but warmed up almost as fast as they did.

Oh my God, Finn thought, and that was the last rational flicker for a while.

They lay spent, breathing elevated, waiting for the world to return. Finn, still inside, encompassed her with both arms, face buried in her neck.

"Wow," Emily said finally.

"Uh." Finn worked on recovering his powers of speech.

"Seven years?"

He nodded, chin rubbing her shoulder. "Plus," he said, "or minus."

✗ ✗ ✗

Not much later, again.

In the quiet stillness of the small hours, they dozed, holding each
other. Each time Emily came awake, it was a revelation all over again.

They talked, short sleepy conversations that were about nothing
and thus, in fact, about everything. Soft laughter. The feel of each
other's skin, forever.

Dawn was late, light finally creeping in around seven thirty.

"Hey," said Finn, coming more fully awake. "Don't you have to
get to work?"

"It's Saturday."

"Oh. Shit, I totally lost track."

Eventually, they both realized they were hungry. Also thirsty,
and maybe needing a long hot shower. Though they still didn't want
to get up, the real world was finally having its way.

Before she pushed out from the covers, Emily thought of something from the night before.

"Are you going to keep following them around?" she said. "Like,
is that the plan?"

"No." Finn sighed. "Seems pointless, and it's not like I don't have
plenty of other things to do."

"Whoever betrayed you before—aren't you worried he'll do it
again?"

"No," he said again, but this time with certainty. "I don't know
who it was, but I'm sure of one thing: None of us wants to go back
to prison."

"So . . ."

"But it's possible that someone has another agenda, all the same."

"The money?"

"The metal." Finn stroked her back, one more time. "*Someone*
may be thinking about taking it all for himself."

"Isn't that exactly what you're doing?"

"Fucking Wes over, yes. Not everyone else."

"In this sort of situation," Emily said, "it seems like that might be
a frequent problem."

"It shouldn't be. We've worked together for a long time." Finn's hand fell still on her shoulder. "But yes, that's where I think we've ended up."

"Of course, now that you've figured this out, you'll make sure it's impossible."

"Oh, no." She felt, more than saw, him shake his head. "Not at all."

"What?"

"There will be an obvious opportunity," Finn said. "One chance to grab it and run. And if someone does so?—then I'll know. We'll *all* know."

"But that may not do you any good." Emily could see any number of things going wrong, no one getting what they wanted. What they deserved—good or bad. "You could just lose everything."

"You're right." He sat up in the bed. "In fact, I've been meaning to ask you about that."

"What?"

"Making sure we actually come out ahead on this operation."

Emily looked at him, the alertness now lighting his eyes, and realized he'd thought all this out already, probably long before. "You have a plan, don't you?" She laughed. "I mean, *another* plan. On top of all those other plans."

"I might," Finn said. "And you might be able to help out."

CHAPTER THIRTY-SIX

D ecember 30, eight p.m. Sixteen hours until they started to drill.

The warehouse was cold—no heat—but well lit by the work lights. The jacking shaft was fully dug and they'd installed the shoring timbers on Christmas Eve: heavy planks pounded vertically into the base of the hole, cross-braced and holding up its walls. Jake had cleaned and oiled the gantry machinery, and a heavy hook dangled from a two-inch chain run through its pulleys above the hole.

The jacking frame itself was built into the pit, the auger head in place, hydraulic and slurry lines connected. Additional shoring backstopped the heavy pistons, which would shove the pipes after the auger, one by one, as it drilled the bore forward.

Finn looked around, crossing off items in a checklist in his head.

The concrete pipe sections were neatly stacked alongside the shaft. Behind them lay two stacks of slide-belt sections, which would go into the pipe when it was all the way through. The Kei truck was put back together, alongside the excavator, which had its bucket scoop swapped out for a forklift fitting. At the far bay door, a two-ton box truck was parked—the sort of anonymous, graffiti-marked delivery truck seen all over the city. Its white metal walls were grimy and dented with faded Chinese characters hand painted on the door.

"Seaport Fruit & Vegetables," according to the guy who'd sold Finn the vehicle, and maybe it really did translate that way.

Finally, behind that truck, the same battered tractor they'd hauled the boring rig away with. It was hooked to a trailer, a tall gray semi with Arizona plates and California inspection stickers.

Jake, Asher, and Corman were out—sleeping, Finn hoped, resting up for the long day and night ahead. Nicola was in her usual chair at the folding table, laptop open.

"You're ready, right?" he said to her.

"Final checks. You know." She offered a small smile. "Same thing you're doing."

"I always worry that I've forgotten something."

"And have you, ever?"

"No."

"Well, there you go."

"Of course, it's the things I *haven't* thought of that always cause the problems."

Nicola rubbed her eyes. "Charge your phone."

"What?"

"In my experience? That's the most common oh-shit. Someone's phone runs out, suddenly they can't talk to anyone, everything goes to hell."

"Huh."

"Get some sleep, Finn." She closed the laptop and looked for her shoulder bag. "That's what I'm going to do."

Before they left, he unplugged the excavator and shut off the lights. The dark space smelled of dirt and oil, wood resin and bare metal.

"You know," he said, closing and locking the door behind them, "this is the biggest job I've ever put together. Biggest target, the most complicated plan."

"Good thing your team is up to it, then."

"Yeah . . ."

"Oh, I've got *my* shit together." She laughed. "I sure hope you all do, too."

X X X

Nicola was right, an early night would have been best. But Finn knew he'd just toss and turn and think about the endless list of things undoubtedly going wrong that very minute. He wouldn't sleep for hours.

So here he was sitting with Jake, whom he'd picked up, in the truck, windows cracked but the heater running, passing a bottle back and forth. At the edge of Bayonne, down a potholed service road between a tank farm and an industrial yard, chain link and barbed wire on both sides. But at the end, the turn-around faced out across the water. Nothing blocked their view of the New York skyline. Lights glittered across the low rolling waters of the harbor.

"Used to be we'd be out in bar somewhere the night before a job," Jake said. "Making noise, buying rounds. Now . . ." He grimaced at the plastic bottle. "Gatorade. Jesus."

"Used to be we were dumb, maybe."

"In case we got caught—I just figured it'd be a shame to waste the last night before jail."

"Me, too." Finn shook his head. "Easy to think that way before, you know, actually *going* to prison."

"I wouldn't mind a real drink."

"Plenty of time later."

A container ship moved steadily up the harbor, superstructure and bow lit up, the vast stacked waist of the vessel lost in shadow. An oil barge beat steadily the other way, the tug's engine loud even at a distance. As the noise faded, Finn could hear waves lapping at the shore below them.

"You and Emily, huh?" Jake handed over the Gatorade.

"I guess so. You okay with that?"

Jake laughed. "Only if you admit you're the moron."

Finn smiled in the dark. "Warned you off kind of sharpish, didn't I?"

"She's good. Smart."

"Yeah. Surprised me, too."

A vehicle appeared from among the oil tanks, driving slowly inside the fence. A white SUV with a lightbar and a blotchy logo on the door—private security. Its headlights swung over the truck but didn't stop. Finn watched it continue along the perimeter, moving away from them.

"What are you doing after?" he asked.

Jake kind of grunted. "Back to the shop, I guess. I'm settled in pretty good."

"Got the business to keep going, you think?"

"Enough. What about you?"

"Don't know."

"Maybe down to the islands, if I was you. With Emily. White sand beaches and rum all day."

"That's another one."

"What?"

"In the old days, when we were raising hell the night before? That's the kind of plan we'd talk about. Sunshine and loose women."

"Still sounds good to me," Jake said. "What are you gonna do now, stick it all in an IRA or something?"

"That wouldn't be the worst choice."

They watched the river traffic for a while. An overpowered boat sped upriver, its engines a loud, irritating roar even from half a mile. Lights twinkled in the distance.

"Thanks for coming for me," Jake said quietly.

"Huh?"

"Bringing me in. I really appreciate it."

Finn felt awkward, surprising himself. "No one else I'd rather work with," he said. "Twenty years, damn near."

"Minus seven."

"There's that."

"Anyway . . ." Jake shrugged, the motion just visible in the darkened cab. "You know."

"It's nothing." Finn drained the Gatorade, capped the bottle, and tossed it behind the seat. "Come on, we got to go back. It's late."

"Yeah." Jake sighed. "It sure is."

CHAPTER THIRTY-SEVEN

Morning, the last day of the year.

In the warehouse, the air was cold enough to frost their breath, the light thin and gray through the clerestory.

Jake looked into the jacking pit. "You can stop fussing already," he said. "We've checked everything about ten times."

Asher was at the bottom, fifteen feet down. The jacking frame was lowered into place and the hydraulic rams were aligned, ready to shove the huge drill head into the opposite side of the pit. Overhead, the first pipe dangled from the gantry chains.

"Just making sure," Asher muttered. He tightened a hose fitting one more eighth-turn, then coiled a few turns of cable. "Someone—I ain't saying who, but *someone*—bumped the laser. Had to get it back into alignment."

"How far off was it?"

"Half a degree."

"Doesn't sound like much."

"Yeah?" Asher twisted to look up at him. "Not *much*? Over a hundred thirty yards, let's see, that's only a diversion of four fucking feet, right? Who cares if we miss the entire fucking *building* anyway?"

They had the wireless triangulation units, too, of course, which set the target electronically. But Asher was correct: The laser had to be perfectly aimed for the system to work.

"Hey, you look good," Jake said.

"What the *fuck*?"

"I never liked that beard."

Finn had made Asher shave it off, figuring that real Stormwall employees probably wouldn't be allowed facial hair.

"Yeah, well, fuck you." Asher went back to his machinery.

Jake gave up. He looked at his watch. Three hours to go.

Corman was asleep, sacked out on some cardboard he'd scavenged. Jake considered, then headed for the big truck. He could nap in the cab, across the wide bench seat.

They were tired and short-tempered. Waiting was the hardest part.

They started drilling at eleven thirty, following an early lunch.

After two months of effort, long days, hard labor, and the constant tension from knowing they were breaking some serious laws, the start was anticlimactic. Asher settled himself in the TBM's operator chair, fired up the motors, and looked out. The auger's bore plate spun up to max rotation, the row of bits along its surface immediately becoming a silvered blur. Engines whined. Finn took one last, careful look, then gave a thumbs-up.

Asher eased back on a lever, and the hydraulic ram pushed the bore into the wall of the pit.

It was loud, but not *too* loud. Starting out, not all the spoil was captured by the slurry lines, dirt spattering out behind the auger. But as it slowly entered the shaft, the stream ended. During the remainder of the bore, all the displaced muck would be mixed with water and sent back through hoses to the sedimentation tank. There, the water would be filtered out for reuse, and the excavated dirt would simply accumulate.

"Looks good!" Jake, shouting a bit to be heard over the roar.

"So far."

It didn't take long for the ram to fully extend. Asher pulled it back, the pistons sliding into themselves, and the auger cooled to an idling rumble.

"Okay," said Finn, and he released the gantry's chain lever. The first section of jacking pipe, three feet across and ten feet long, descended into the pit. Corman, below, guided it into place on the frame.

"Go," he called, and Asher shifted the ram back to forward. It pushed the pipe against the base of the auger, and the bit roared again as it was shoved back into action. Slowly, the pistons extended, and the pipe disappeared into the hole.

And that was it. The sections were eight feet each, and they had to install fifty-one to reach the vault.

The hydraulics could shove the drill forward at a steady speed. It took another several minutes to reverse the jack, lower another pipe section into the frame, fit to the previous pipe, and start the rams again. Still, all in all, the attainment rate averaged to almost half a foot per minute. To Finn, who remembered the old days of open-cut trenching, it was nothing short of miraculous.

"I'm going to walk the perimeter," he said.

Asher waved one hand. "Gotta keep this moving."

"I know." Only constant forward motion kept the tunnel wall washed in slurry fluid, lubricating it for the growing pipe chain to be pushed forward. Halt for longer than a few minutes, and they might never get the drill moving again.

If that happened on a normal project, the foreman would have a bad day—they might have to drill an access bore from above to reach and free the auger. But it was a solvable problem.

If it happened here, they'd just have to walk away, completely empty-handed.

"Looks good," said Finn. Asher only nodded, focused on the job.

Outside, Finn could barely hear the machine. A faint, whining rumble. The buildings around them appeared deserted, closed up for the holidays, and no engineer on a train would hear anything but his diesels.

No problem.

He walked back to the door. They'd be at this, nonstop, for the next twelve hours.

Midafternoon, David looked at the sky. Snow had begun to fall, clouds low and ominous, and the day's light was already fading.

Standing next to the custom flatbed the operations crew had built, he felt small and insignificant.

The trailer was more than a hundred feet long, with three axles front and four back and a monster-size Tor tractor hooked to the kingpin. It glowed in the yard's security lights, which had clicked on automatically in the gloom. The foreman had brought it out and parked it next to the sidetrack they'd offload the excavator from.

"Looks real nice," David said. "Did your crew wax it or something?"

"Just a good washing. What can I say? They take pride in their work."

"Tractor all gassed up?"

"Of course." He looked offended. "Be kind of embarrassing to run out of fuel halfway to the docks."

"More snow in the mountains. Dispatch says they're still on schedule, but the storm seems to be getting stronger as it approaches us."

"I hope they highballed it."

"No, but it's getting bypass priority. The corridor's too crowded to shut everything else down."

A minimally muffled diesel engine clattered, and David turned to see a pair of cranes moving toward them, coming from behind the vast locomotive barn. They walked a dozen yards back, letting the operators begin to position the lifters alongside the special truck.

"Train's not due for ten hours," David said. "No need to rush."

"I like to be ready." The foreman squinted up, letting snow fall into his eyes. "Hard to say what this is going to turn into. We get a blizzard—"

"The forecast doesn't have it closing any roads, and we're less than two miles to the port. Once the excavator is through their gates, it's the shipping company's headache."

"Makes you wonder."

"What?" David zipped his hood. The temperature was dropping.

"These protesters." The foreman looked in the direction of the main entrance, a quarter mile down the tracks. The dispatch tower behind it was well lit, windows glowing in the murk.

"I don't think any have arrived," David said.

"Nothing to see yet. Maybe the weather will keep them away."

"I doubt it."

"Me, too, but that's the point—why us? Why not go pester the longshoremen? No one cares about *trains*, for Christ's sake."

"The port has federal security."

"So? You're saying they're better than your guys?" He laughed. "Surely not."

"No." David shrugged. "Better armed, though, and more of them. Also, we're closer to PATH. Who wants to walk through five miles of industrial wasteland?"

Wind blew snow into his face, and David decided he'd had enough. He'd be here through the night, maybe into the day, depending on how quickly the crew was able to shift the excavator from the train to the trucks. No need to stand out in the cold now, when nothing was happening.

"Come on," he said and started to walk back to his truck. "I'm going in. You should maybe get a nap, too."

"Yeah."

"You did a real nice job on that hauler."

"We'll have that thing on its way, no problem," the foreman said. "If you keep the hippies out."

"Don't worry." David felt fine. "It's going to be a quiet night."

CHAPTER THIRTY-EIGHT

—————

Dusk.

Corman eased the Seaport Fruit & Vegetables box truck into its parking space.

He snapped off the headlights, shut down the engine, and carefully double-checked the dashboard. It wouldn't do to, say, leave the fog lights on and run down the battery. As he got out of the cab, wind cut through his jacket. The temperature was dropping.

Around back, he opened the metal cargo door, just enough to confirm the slide rails were still properly placed, and let it bang back into place. The crash of the door closing echoed from the buildings around him. No one appeared. Everyone in the zone seemed to have gone home, eager to start the night's revelry.

He'd have to walk the half mile back, but Corman didn't mind. He liked being alone in the winter weather, left to his own thoughts, undisturbed by the clamor of people around him.

Finn said they were on schedule, good to go. When he got back, Corman would take the big hauler out to its own designated spot— a mile farther, alongside the utility substation. That was far enough that Jake would follow along, then drive them both back to the warehouse.

They'd been rotating the different roles on the boring rig: in the pit, moving the pipe sections with the gantry, running the drill itself.

That meant one of the four of them was always resting—or running errands such as this one. Nicola was off in her lair, hacking computers and phones and networks. Or whatever. Corman's understanding of her abilities was hazy, but he appreciated the results, and she was fun to talk with.

He clanged the door latch shut and started walking. No rush. The bore was on schedule, moving straight through the earth, the vault closer by the minute.

So far, so good.

Eleven p.m.

They ate a kind of dinner—sandwiches Finn had bought that morning with fruit juice and coffee. He'd also replenished the stocks of barbecue chips and Snickers and energy bars. The drill kept grinding away, but it was so deep in the tunnel that they couldn't hear it over the noise of the hydraulics, motors, and pumps.

After taking a look at the positioning system, Finn decided they were close enough to start getting ready. He called Nicola and handed around the radios they'd use from now on.

Some adjustments, and he put the phone away, pulling on the headset instead. Nicola's voice came through the earpiece.

"Okay, everyone, time for a comms check. You should hear me, but you should also hear everyone else answer. If that doesn't happen, speak up. Going down the list . . . Finn?"

"Loud and clear, Nicola."

"Jake?"

"Five by five."

"Corman?"

A rather bearlike grunt over the radio.

"Corman, is that you?"

"Yeah."

"Okay. Asher?"

No response.

"Asher? Asher, are you there?"

Finn put his hand over his mic but shouted loud enough that it carried through anyway: "What are you doing? Put the damn headset on." Muffled noises. "Yeah, I know, none of us like wearing them, but we need the ear protection. Anyway, something happens, I can't go waving signal flags at you . . . That's better."

"Fine, fine, I'm on."

"Thank you, Asher." Nicola was brisk. "Your batteries ought to last five hours. You've each got two spare sets, right? In your pocket, nice and handy?" Pause. "Right?"

"Yes."

Grunt.

"Yeah."

"Five *hours*? My ears are gonna fucking fall off."

"I'll take that as affirmative. Finn, visual check, please."

Finn would be first into the vault, and he had a camera mounted on his helmet. He reached up and flicked its switch.

"Excellent. You may turn it off now. The camera battery's only good for about ninety minutes."

"I'm sure you'll remind me."

"That's my job."

Asher: "None of this is any good inside the vault. Maybe you can punch radio through a little dirt, but that thing is wrapped in a meter of concrete and structural steel."

"Finn has a repeater."

They ran through a few more details. Nicola had assured them the radios were fully encrypted, and they didn't have to worry about eavesdropping scanners. But it still made Finn uneasy to openly discuss their plans. He kept it short.

"What do you see at the yard?" Jake asked.

"Hang on." They waited while she apparently moved to the spotting scope.

"Light snow for now. I can still see the tower and the entrance. Looks like protesters have begun arriving—some cars on the road, a crowd standing around."

"Police?" Finn asked.

"Some cruisers and a tac van. Hard to tell from here, but there might be a dozen cops at the gate."

"Official or yard security?"

"It's dark, and snowing, and I'm a half mile away."

"Okay." Finn considered for a moment. "I think it's time for a diversion."

"Yo."

"Kayo?"

"Who the fuck else be on this phone?"

"Where are you?"

"Down the road, where you said. Cold as shit out here."

"See any protesters near you? Police?"

"They all at the gate. We took the long way around."

"If it's safe, you might as well go ahead now."

"All *right*, then."

CHAPTER THIRTY-NINE

David stood with Sean alongside his cruiser, outside the ops building, watching a crowd gather at the gate.

"Not even midnight," Sean said. "They're in for a wait."

"The train's due in three hours."

"That's a long time to be standing around out here." He wore a uniform parka, insignia on the sleeves and a reflective TRANSIT POLICE on the back. Snow had begun to accumulate on their shoulders.

"They're probably nice and warmed up."

Sean laughed. "Wish *I* could be drinking bubbly right now. Ring in the new year."

The few dozen protesters were mostly young, men and women, in a motley of colorful winter coats. Several diehards had arrived by bicycle. Another had a drum, but the beat was muted by the softly falling snow, and he soon stopped. They milled around, no leadership evident.

Headlights appeared down Caleb Street, slowly resolving through the snow-filled darkness.

"What the hell?" Sean frowned. "A *field* trip?"

The vehicle was a large yellow school bus. It slowed and stopped a hundred yards away. The red blinking stop sign swung out. People began to emerge, straggling out—more demonstrators, some carrying signs.

"They must have chartered it," David said.

Ranged in front of the gate were the Newark crowd-control officers—a dozen men with vests and helmets. Boggs must have called in serious favors, because a larger number of New York police were also at the yard. At least, David assumed they were NYPD. All wore black armor and helmets, but some had masks as well—and no unit markings. The incident commander, a city ESU lieutenant, had been vague about their exact origins.

"This is shaping up great," Sean muttered.

"Nothing's going to happen until the train gets here."

David thought he noticed a smell of weed drifting from the civilian side. The riot officers stood relaxed but held a loose row, shifting and talking quietly among themselves.

"I might go inside," he said. "No reason to be out here freezing."

"Yeah, I guess—"

BOOM!

An explosion, muffled by the snow, but instantly recognizable. They swung around.

"What the—?"

A few hundred yards down the perimeter fence, a fireball bloomed. Shouts from the crowd and a wave of movement. A sharp clacking of batons and shields as the police straightened up.

"Fuck." Sean yanked open the door of his car.

"Okay," said David as he got in the other side. "Maybe I was wrong."

Finn stood next to Jake, looking over Asher's shoulder at the locator's screen inside the TBM cab. Corman was in the pit, having just fitted the next pipe.

"We're *there*," Asher said. "Look. Coordinates are lined right up. The nose of the auger is sitting about one inch away from the vault wall."

"Excellent." Finn clicked on his headset. "Nicola?"

"Yes." Her response was immediate and calm.

"Asher says we're right outside."

"I know."

"You do?"

"I've been watching the telemetry."

"Oh." Finn was still surprised by their new networked world. "Are you set to take over the monitor circuits?"

"I cut them over twenty minutes ago. Totally clean." With access to Stormwall's internal systems, it had been trivial to map out the feeds from the vault, record an uneventful half hour or so, and loop it in.

Or so she claimed. It still seemed like magic.

"You're sure?"

"No one has noticed a thing. I've got my own surveillance on every workstation that might get a picture of the vault, and it's plain business as usual."

"And you're watching the rail movements?"

"Of course." There might have been a little exasperation there, even over the buzzy frequencies of the wireless.

"Then . . . I guess we're set." Finn looked at Asher and Jake. "Time to change into the uniforms."

He pulled the Stormwall jumpsuits from the plastic dry-cleaning bags they'd been bundled in, waiting for him at the company's head-quarters. Asher took his with a look of distaste.

"Not exactly *styling* here, boss."

"Good thing you don't work for them, then."

While they changed clothes, Finn ran through his mental check-lists one last time. Latex gloves, bolt cutters, repeater, power . . .

If they were discovered, the likeliest occasion would be now, as they drilled through the wall into the vault. Normally, for a tunnel bore like this, a receiving shaft would be dug at the far end, a cradle waiting to gently catch the cutterhead as it appeared. Here, naturally, that was impossible. They had no alternative but to punch through and shove the drill all the way in until it simply crashed to the floor.

Moreover, there was the slope of the tunnel to consider. They needed the tunnel to be higher at the far end, so that gravity could pull their loot all the way back down the pipe. The ground had a natural descent that helped. But still, they'd started fifteen feet down and would end no more than a foot or two below grade. Because the vault was underground, they expected to arrive seven feet above the floor, almost at the ceiling.

When the auger smashed through and fell to the floor, it was going to be really, really loud.

"All right," Finn said as he finished retying his boot laces. "Nicola?"

Over the radio: "Yes?"

"Wait for a big, loud, heavy train. As soon as the locomotives are alongside the building, give us a signal, and Asher will put the mole on full power."

"You want to go outside and watch? Just to make sure?"

"Good idea."

Finn checked Asher and Jake. They both had their own radios back in place.

"You hear all that?"

"Yeah."

"Sure."

As he was walking out of the warehouse, pulling on his coat and raising the hood over the headset, Finn checked in with Nicola once more.

"How's the diversion going?"

"Like kicking a wasp's nest. Lots of movement."

"Excellent." Finn stepped away from the TBM's panel, leaving Asher to get ready. "Time for us to get moving, too."

CHAPTER FORTY

A minivan was on fire, cracked up against the perimeter fence and abandoned.

Sean's car arrived first by seconds, skidding to a stop on new snow. They got out, but the heat of the inferno kept them back.

"They don't usually burn like that," Sean said. "Not from a simple crash."

"I don't know where the tank is in that thing." David waved back the first onlookers, who'd arrived in a panting jog from the yard's entrance. "But probably not right in the middle of the passenger compartment."

Where the fire was concentrated. The flames might have been more visible because it was dark, but Sean was right: Running off the road shouldn't have caused it to explode.

"If you were emptying a can of accelerant, though, that might be where most of it ended up."

"Uh-huh."

Firefighters pulled up in an engine, stopping a good seventy-five feet away. They'd been unusually quick to respond because, like Sean himself, they were already stationed at the yard's entrance lot, only a quarter mile away. The first men off began unreeling hose from the redline.

More demonstrators drifted in. It was no stretch to assume that some of them had arranged the minivan's immolation—as a statement? A distraction? Simple amusement?

David didn't care.

"Think Newark can get an arson investigator here?" he said.

"Tomorrow morning maybe." Sean snorted. "Or the next day— the detectives don't like missing their time off, and New Year's Day is a big one."

"Unlike the uniforms, huh?" A Newark cruiser had pulled in next to the them, four of the riot officers getting out.

"They don't want to be here, either." Sean gestured them back. "Of course, now that they are, everyone's hoping for a big confrontation—make it worthwhile, you know?"

"Great," David said. "They might get their money's worth."

Finn stared at Asher. "What do you mean, it didn't go through the wall?"

"I'm telling you, I've pushed in an entire pipe section—five feet. But it's still boring through concrete and rebar. The wall must be a lot thicker than the plan said."

"How can you tell?"

"Cutterhead torque and face pressure." Asher gestured at the displays in front of him. "It's obvious."

"Nicola, did you hear that?"

"Yes."

"You've got Stormwall's interior camera feeds, right? I mean the real ones, not the fakes you're feeding them. Can you look around and see if you can spot anything?"

"Like, oh, a two-ton auger sitting on the floor in a pile of debris?" She didn't sound fazed. "Hang on."

Jake had just brought over the next pipe section with the excavator. He hauled on the gantry chains, rattling them up through the block and tackle.

"Should I put this one in place?" he said. "We can keep going."

"I don't know."

Nicola came back on the line. "Nothing. I don't have three sixty, but one camera sweeps that side. The corner looks normal—just some bins and a table inside one of the units."

A long moment. Finn ran possibilities through his head. "Asher, how sure are you about the positioning?"

He seemed offended. "We've got wireless triangulation guiding the laser, and it's only a hundred thirty yards away. We should be good to a quarter inch."

"Yeah, but—"

"And, anyway, I'm telling you it's in the wall. I can *feel* it."

Jake came over and looked at the control panel. "Maybe the plans are wrong. Maybe they put in six feet. Or eight, or ten. Who knows?"

"Okay." Finn made up his mind. "Drop in another pipe. No reason to stop now."

"Good." Asher began reversing the ram, readying it for the next section. "We've got, what, ten sections left? The fucker could be fifty feet thick, we'll still get through it."

"Fifty more feet, and we'll be all the way out the other side." Finn pushed a hand through his hair. "Just get us in, damn it."

CHAPTER FORTY-ONE

Emily had been watching rhodium for fifty minutes.

She had a trading window open on her home computer. Nothing fancy, not the high-powered ultrafast workstations the guys used at the office. None of that was necessary, and she didn't care about a fifteen- or twenty-second delay.

The markets felt a little off. Prices rose and fell without apparent reason. Someone would ask something ridiculous—6, 7 percent over the last cleared trade—and it would sit there, blinking, for a full minute before disappearing. Or there'd be an intense flurry of activity, volumes spiking so fast the chart couldn't refresh its axes, but everything clearing within a basis point or two.

Maybe it was the algobots, automatic trading systems making thousands of offers every second. They were always around, 95 percent of the market on slower days. Human day traders swam on the surface of a very deep, very murky ocean, with all the leviathans and turbulence far below. Faint ripples surfaced, sometimes long rolling waves, but always eons past the point that a slow-moving primate brain could profit.

On the other hand, New Year's Eve, it was probably drunk guys. Maybe showing off to girls they'd just picked up at the parties. Maybe alone in their trading dens, bottles of Macallan and no one to share. Maybe some significant fraction of the bots were off-line, given a rare vacation when their overseers wanted to go have fun.

Whatever, volatility was all *over* the place.

Emily stretched, looked away from the monitors, and closed her eyes for a minute. Resting.

Trying not to worry about Finn.

A soft ping from a preprogrammed alert. Emily opened her eyes. Rhodium twitched up, then down, then down again. Interesting . . . but not an opportunity. Not yet.

This was just killing time, anyway. She was waiting for something else.

For the phone call.

"Ten feet past the edge of the fucking wall." Asher stood before the control panel, arms crossed. "Still grinding away at concrete."

"I don't know, man," Jake said. "I don't know."

Finn looked at the jacking frame in the bottom of the shaft as if it could tell him something. "Maybe one of us can crawl up the tunnel . . ."

"There's nothing to see. That's the *problem*."

Kayo stood in the cold, shivering though he tried to keep it to himself, more and more pissed about the entire experience. He looked at Millz.

"What are these assholes *doing*?"

"Dunno." The first TV news truck had shown up thirty minutes after the car fire, but by then, it had burned down to an unimpressive pile of blackened metal. Apparently disappointed in those visuals, the Channel Three team had parked their van near the demonstrators at the entrance. Now it was closed up tight, engine running, no one visible.

"All I know is, they're inside all warm and dry and probably drinking hot rum from a thermos, and we're out here with the fucking kermits."

They were standing closer to the demonstrators than to the row of riot police, but almost as wary of both. The rail yard parking lot was dusted with snow, more falling, lights farther away blurred by the precipitation. Trains rumbled past in the yard, usually invisible behind the closer rows of cars but occasionally appearing on the mainline. Up in the dispatch tower, faces were looking down at them.

After the explosion, the police had gotten serious, setting their shields in a row, no more smoking or standing idly around. A few weapons appeared: tasers, shotguns, and, in the rear, some assault rifles. When he saw that, Millz was ready to turn and leave immediately, but Kayo had talked him down.

"Who they gonna arrest first, they see us running off? All we're doing, we're lawfully *assembling* and peaceably expressing our First Amendment *rights*." Kayo looked at the scraggly protesters, mostly young people with irregular haircuts and North Face jackets. "Don't know what they're afraid of, anyway. Couple of bicycle cops could keep those fuckwads in line."

"All I'm saying—"

"The man *paid* us. When's the last time somebody paid you without you having to fuck them up first, huh? Plain cash and more to come, and all we got to do is stand here."

"That ain't *all* we got to do."

Kayo ignored that, though there was still a smell of gasoline on his gloves. "Anyway, who knows what might fall out of a boxcar, huh? We could go home with a carton of iPhones."

"iPhones?" Millz laughed, all phlegmy, and spat. "Bag of coal, maybe. Bucket of oil if we bust open a tanker. These are fucking *trains*, not FedEx vans."

The TV truck's door opened and a guy in a nylon jacket over a hoodie stepped out. The protesters looked over like cattle hopeful for feed, and one of the leaders tried to get a chant going. But no one had much energy for it, and the camera operator—certainly not the reporter, not in those clothes—walked about twenty feet from the van and opened his fly.

At least he had the grace to put his back to the crowd.

Kayo's feet went numb. He stamped them up and down, which didn't help much.

"Gotta walk around," he said.

Millz followed. They ended up by the school bus that had brought in a few dozen demonstrators. The driver was standing in its entry, arms crossed, sheltered from the snow.

"Hey," said Kayo.

"'Sup."

"Cold, huh?"

"Naw, don't mind it much."

"Guess not. Was me I'd be *inside*, running the heater."

Kayo pulled out a smoke, offered one, lit both. Millz wandered away.

"You with them?" said the driver.

"The Million Man March over there?" Kayo shrugged. "Kinda."

"Well, you don't look like the stormtroopers."

"No shit." The police had pulled down their visors and unlimbered batons and tear-gas guns. Black armor gleamed. Kayo shivered. "Those motherfuckers, best stay real clear."

"Yeah."

"What you doing here anyway? Waiting to take them all back?"

"They paid for eight hours, they get eight hours. Charter."

"Uh-huh." Kayo took a drag and discovered that snow had put it out. He frowned, tossed away the butt. "Seems like they might be going back in a *different* bus, you know? The kind with bars on the windows."

The driver laughed. "Least they could warm up inside."

"Except those ain't got heaters."

"Or windows, now you saying. Sounds like maybe you know."

"Could be." Kayo grinned. "Sometimes they let you go, sometimes they haul your ass to Tombs."

They stood companionably for another few minutes. A few unmarked cars drove in and out of the yard, the police shifting each time to make room, then closing ranks again.

"Maybe it's time to leave," Kayo said. "Worst party in the world still be more fun than this."

"Oh, yeah." The driver pulled out his phone to check the time. "Happy New Year."

CHAPTER FORTY-TWO

Y ou idiots!" Nicola's voice burst over the circuit. "I figured it out!"
"What?"

"You drilled into the corner of the vault, right?"

"That was the plan." Finn straightened from where he'd been, kneeling at the shaft's edge. "It seemed like the clearest area, and right next to where we want to—"

"It's the *corner*." She paused. "Don't you get it?"

Finn, Jake, and Asher all looked at one another. Asher made a face, like, *What the fuck's she on about?*

"What the fuck are you on about?" he said.

"Did you take into account the width of the wall?"

"Yeah, I know, three feet—"

But Finn broke in. "The *other* wall."

"What?"

"Son of a gun." Finn was shaking his head.

"Right," Nicola said. "You hit the corner dead square. I can see the coordinates here, plain as day. But then you drilled straight into the perpendicular wall, right down its center." She laughed. "The tunnel pipe is three feet wide. You should have been six *feet* from the corner—not eighteen inches."

"Oh shit." Jake caught on. "We're running parallel, aren't we? Digging down the length of the side wall."

"Yes. Exactly. I mean, I think so."

It took Asher longer, but he was first to ask the obvious question.

"Okay, fine. But now what?"

"Huh?"

"We can't turn the auger. It doesn't make right-angle bends. So how do we get in?"

"The wall is three feet thick," Finn said slowly, "and the pipe is three feet wide, right?" He paused. "Hey, Nicola?"

"Yes?"

"Scan the cameras back. Can you see anything from the inside? Like maybe just the edge of the pipe sticking through on its way past? Maybe gouging a rip along the wall?"

A few moments of silence.

"Yes," she said. "Missed it the first time—these things are too low res. But there's a long crack, and some dust in the air. That's what happened, all right."

"Right." Finn looked down at the pipe opening at the bottom of the pit. "We're going to have to go in, all the way to the end, and bust our way out sideways."

"How?" said Jake.

"Um . . ."

"The pipe wall is just concrete, but it's two inches thick. Can't swing a pickax in there."

"I *told* you we needed semtex," Asher said.

"That'd be as likely to collapse the tunnel as open it. No."

"Tire jack," Jake said. "One of those must have one." He pointed at their row of vehicles: the Kei truck, the delivery truck, the tractor trailer. "Set it up crossways inside the tunnel, where we want to break out."

"Good idea." Finn turned it over and around in his head. "Might work."

"Formed concrete is fucking strong," said Asher.

"True," said Finn. "So we'll have to weaken it first."

Emily had gone to get some dinner earlier—take-out Thai in a plastic sack. A hole-in-the-wall on Greenpoint, open like it was any other night. Maybe it was for them.

Now she pulled out the aluminum flat of *rad na* tofu and a plastic container of soup. Someone had music on, bass thumping through the entire building. But almost no traffic noise. Either everyone was inside somewhere having fun or the snow was muffling all sound.

Eating, wrapped in the wool blanket on the futon couch, she checked her laptop one-handed. A simple search got her video from Channel Three: a field reporter in falling snow, hatless, a crowd of demonstrators behind him. From a half hour earlier. The story title, above the news ticker at the bottom of the screen, was "Car Bomb at Anti-China Protest."

"Jesus, Finn," she muttered.

Searching Twitter brought up some near-real-time photos. One cell-phone shot, blurry and with bad contrast from the glare of security floods, nonetheless clearly showed a line of paramilitary police: balaclavas, armor, shields.

He'd said there would be some kind of demonstration, nothing to do with them but a convenient distraction. This, however, looked like it had gone beyond that.

She checked her phone again for messages.

Nothing.

CHAPTER FORTY-THREE

Finn was jammed into the tunnel, breathing his own carbon dioxide and thinking he really ought to have a respirator.

The pipe's inner diameter was only thirty-four inches. Corman couldn't even have entered. Finn wasn't huge, but the space was tight and claustrophobic. After crawling more than a hundred yards from the warehouse, his knees and elbows were sore, scraped right through his clothing.

"Can you hear me? Anyone?"

Nothing but static, as Asher had predicted. Finn had the repeater with him, but it required line current, and they weren't ready to unspool a power cable all the way up the tunnel.

And the reason for *that* was the gallon jug of hydrochloric acid he'd brought along. Leftovers from the galvanizing tank. No matter what, things were going to get messy. He didn't want to accidentally burn through a power cord, cause a short, and blow himself up.

He stretched the goggle strap over his hat, readjusting the headlamp, then squirmed a little farther and twisted himself back around. The slope was modest but unmistakable, and he wanted to be uphill when he started pouring acid.

Another minute to place and set the breaker. It was a cheap scissor jack, perpendicular in the tunnel, one end against each side of the pipe. The jack handle scraped the base of the pipe, but did turn all the way around. Barely. Finn tightened it, then pressed as hard as his posture's poor leverage would permit. With luck, the concrete would break and he wouldn't have to . . .

No luck.

Finn sighed. He recovered the jug from the other side of the jack, where he'd placed it out of the way, and studied the pipe wall.

Nothing complicated here. He hesitated a few moments, then took and held a deep breath, opened the cap, and started pouring.

Nicola peered through her spotter's scope. She had the hotel's room lights turned off, and her computer screens faced the other direction. There was no reflection, and her view through the window glass was clear.

She'd been wearing latex gloves for ten hours now. Changing them now and then, sure, but still. She didn't know how heart surgeons kept them on for similarly long shifts, day after day.

Snow filled the air outside, dancing in the wind, glowing in the soft globes of light around the streetlamps fading into the murk down the avenue. The control tower was a faraway luminescent blob.

She adjusted the reticle, trying to focus on the parking lot in front of the blob. Half the time, snow gusted across her field of vision, obscuring everything. But the other half, she could see the ranks of dark officers, the bright security lights glinting off their shields and helmets. The protesters were a vague mass of color and movement, shifting restlessly just inside the fence. Vehicles occasionally came and went.

Halfway between her hotel and the dispatch center, the vault building sat dark and unnoticed at the edge of the property. From her distant vantage, it seemed even closer to the yard's boundary, barely enough room for the single line of track separating it from the fence.

She moved the scope slightly, sliding her focus across the street to the warehouse. It was dark, too, just another anonymous industrial building, one among many.

Finn had gone into the tunnel fifteen minutes earlier. They'd heard nothing since.

✗ ✗ ✗

"Jesus *Christ!*"

His voice startled them all. Nicola had turned the gain all the way up on her headset, and he came through at about ninety decibels, distorted and painfully loud.

"Finn!" She hastily spun the dial back down. Obviously, he'd gotten the repeater running at some point.

"Yeah—" but Asher and Jake were talking, too, everyone overriding one another.

"What happened?"

"Are you in?"

He was coughing, almost retching. Nicola returned to her computers, found the mouse, and panned the internal camera toward the corner. Finn was crouched on the floor, hunched, pieces of rubble around him, a dark jagged hole in the wall above his head.

"He's all right," she said to the other two. "I can see him. He's inside the vault."

"I hate that fucking stuff," Finn rasped.

"Hydrochloric acid," Jake said. "I told you: It'll strip chrome."

"I think it might have stripped my lungs."

But after a minute, he was back on his feet, looking around. His coughing diminished. He found the camera and stared up at its lens.

"Nicola, can you see me?"

"Yes."

"And is, ah, anyone *else* watching?"

She checked the other screen, scanning through the surveillance she had running on Stormwall's servers, operators, and remote monitoring staff. "All clear, so far as I can tell. There's some extra attention on the Penn Southern account, but it's focused on the demonstrators in the parking lot."

"Good." He paused. "I can't believe we're *here.*"

"Awesome." Jake's voice. "We ready to continue?"

"Yeah." On Nicola's screen, Finn looked up at the hole he'd made. "I'll expand the opening and clean it up. Jake, head up here with the winch. Asher, start getting the conveyor sections ready to go."

"Right."

"On it." Even Asher sounded energized.

They got to work. Nicola kept track, glancing occasionally at the interior feed to see what Finn was up to. He soon had a four-foot pair of hydraulic cutters in action, snipping through the cage barrier to the next unit. Jake appeared at the opening after five minutes and began setting up the winch. Asher, after feeding Jake the power cord while he was crawling up the tunnel, began stacking conveyor sections in the pit.

Nicola thought of something and frowned. She checked the time on her phone.

"Hey," she said into the wireless. "Where's Corman?"

CHAPTER FORTY-FOUR

David had to get out of the tower.

Boggs's usual posse of yes-men was larger than usual, many of them clearly unhappy to be taken away from their parties. At least when the CEO wasn't looking at them. They milled around the control room, peering at the route screens, bothering the dispatchers, generally getting in the way. Boggs himself was stationed at the east bank of windows, glaring down at the protesters in the parking lot. A Newark station commander, the man supposed to be in charge of at least his officers, stood alongside. Boggs elbowed him.

"Why don't you just arrest all those pissants?"

"The First Amendment? Due process? They haven't committed any crimes?"

"Bah."

David beckoned Sean across the room. In a low voice he said, "What do you think?"

"The Newark guys are doing fine. Grumbling and all, but you know." Sean had been outside, walking among the various police forces. "Those ESU cops from the city, well, honestly they kind of scare *me*."

"Their lieutenant called them his 'warfighters.'"

"Shit." He grimaced. "'Warfighters.' Great.'"

"Look, I need a break." David glanced at Boggs, who was reprimanding one of the technicians because his coffee wasn't hot enough. "Let's go check the perimeter. They might be planning another firebomb or something."

"Good idea." They slipped through the rear doors, down the fire stairs.

"The train's only a couple hours away," Sean said. "They're making up time."

"Can't get here soon enough." David zipped his coat as they approached the outside door. "I just want to get this over with."

"I'm right here," said Corman. His voice came over the radio, so Nicola heard him as well, but he was walking into the warehouse.

A blast of snow came in with him, and he pushed the door hard to close it. Asher stuck his head up from the shaft—he was standing on the jacking frame, pulling over the rattling conveyor sections and dropping them in front of the tunnel opening. Each one sounded like a can-collector's shopping cart going off a cliff.

"Where the fuck have you been?" *CRASH.* "Starting to wonder." *CRASH.* "Because *some* of us are doing all the fucking heavy lifting around here." *CRASH.*

"Getting a smoke."

"Where the fuck's your radio?"

"Dunno. Didn't work out there."

"The weather," Finn said from inside the vault, over the wireless. He sounded a little out of breath himself. "Still snowing, I assume. How do the roads look?"

"Slow."

"Hope it doesn't get worse than that. Nicola, what's up at the yard?"

"More vehicles," Nicola said. "More troops. And more protesters—another bus."

"There's PATH service out here?"

"No, a charter. School bus or something. Only it wasn't a football team. They were carrying signs."

Asher gestured to Corman. "Hey, help me out here. Get the rest of the roller slides."

The last sections didn't fit into the pit, which was already too crowded. Asher crawled out. "Your turn," he said.

Corman clambered in. Jake had dragged the winch to the top of the tunnel, unrolling steel cable as he went. Its end was fixed to the jacking ram. Corman examined the hook. He clipped it to the first ten-foot section of the slide and shoved it into the pipe.

"Go," he said.

A pause. "You mean me?" Jake, on the radio, from inside the vault.

Grunt.

"Right." A moment later, the winch cable tightened and slowly pulled the section up the pipe. As it went past him, Corman picked up the next piece of the conveyor, snapped it onto the end, and fed it in. Asher helpfully pushed in the last sections down to him as they began to run out. He missed Corman's head by six or seven inches easy.

In less than ten minutes, they'd installed the entire belt. It poked from the opening of the tunnel pipe, and ran up to the top, by the hole into the vault. Now they had their extraction mechanism: Anything dropped at the top end would slide and rattle all the way to the warehouse. More than one hundred yards, like a kid down a waterslide.

That, at least, was the theory.

"Better try it out," said Asher, who was watching from above. "Things start to get jammed up in there, gonna be a fucking nightmare going in to unclog it."

"Good idea." Finn, on the radio. "Give me a minute here . . . Jake, try this."

Some muffled noises and muttering, apparently as Finn handed something up to Jake and he cleared the top of the belt for it.

"Ready?"

"Just send the fucking thing down already."

A faint noise, increasing after a few seconds. The spinner wheels clashed and rattled. The object came closer, closer . . . and Corman reached in and grabbed it, just as it reached the end of the pipe.

"What's that?" Asher, peering down. The conveyor's little roller-skate wheels spun to rest.

Corman held it up. The ingot was small but bright silver, glinting in the ceiling lights.

"Damn," said Asher.

Finn, over the radio: "Did it work?"

"Like a UPS warehouse."

"Good. Asher, come on up. You have trouble scooching along the conveyor, Jake can send the winch cable down for you. It'll be fastest to shift the metal into the tunnel with a bucket brigade. Corman can catch."

Asher looked at Corman. "Shouldn't we both be here? One to grab the bars, the other to load the truck?"

"I want to get out of here as quick as we can." More rattling began, suggesting that he was wasting no time. "It's going to take an hour at least. Once we're done up here, we'll all come down and help with the transfer."

"Whatever." Asher began to climb into the pit. "How much is that one little ingot worth, anyway?"

"Assuming it's not one of the counterfeits, about sixty thousand dollars."

"Mother of fucking God." Asher held it for a moment, then reluctantly handed it back to Corman and boosted himself into the pipe. "I'll be *right* up."

Despite how tense she was, Emily began to doze off on the futon. Some long, late nights recently, and full-time at Heart Pine during the day. She didn't want to behave abnormally while Wes was around—or Finn, every one of the last three nights. She hadn't been getting nearly enough sleep.

A ringtone, blaring unexpectedly, jerked her awake. She grabbed the phone, already standing up and turning toward her trading computer.

"Yes?" A moment later, "Awesome. We are *go*."

CHAPTER FORTY-FIVE

Now that they were in, Finn only wanted to get *out* of the vault as fast as possible.

"Three racks here," he said. "Lots of shelves, lots of weight, but it should go easy."

Jake stayed up in the tunnel opening, ready to take each rhodium ingot from Asher and send it on its way down the belt. The bars had to be centered and pushed off with a consistent velocity—a level of finicky detail that Asher might be inclined to let slip.

Finn enlarged the hole through the cage, removing bars until his hand hurt from the cutters. The remaining security was equally light: a few padlocks and, on the racks, a pair of vertical bars that slid through holes aligned in each drawer, more to keep them in place than to keep thieves out. He'd already taken the one ingot, and the first drawer hung open. He studied gleaming rows of metal.

"We can probably carry eight or ten at a time," he said. "No need to overload Jake."

Asher ran his hand across the small, smooth, rounded blocks. Their top faces were like neat silver tiles. "Beautiful," he said and lifted the first ones out.

They emptied the first two drawers at a steady pace. The rattle of the conveyor wheels never stopped.

When Finn slid open the third drawer, he paused.

"You know," he said, "these don't seem to be fixed into the frame."

Asher crouched next to him and peered along the slider. "Lift it up and maybe push back. There's a bobbin latch."

They tried it, and after one false start, the drawer came right out. It was heavy—eighty or ninety pounds, but the two of them could carry it without trouble.

Manhandling it through the pipe opening, seven feet above the floor, took some effort.

"Just the right width," said Jake. "About two inches narrower than the belt."

"Give it a try." Finn clicked on his mic. "Corman? Watch out, we're sending down an entire flat."

Jake aligned the tray and pushed it off. The rattle was louder, then diminished.

A minute's silence. "Got it," Corman said over the radio.

"We'll do this way from now on."

It only took another half hour. When they were finished, Asher dropped on a chair.

"Need to rest a minute," he said. "Those things get heavy."

"We're done!" Jake looked out from the broken hole in the wall. "Let's get *out* of here."

Finn checked his watch. "Yeah . . ."

"Corman's gonna need help getting everything into the truck."

Back to the radio. "Nicola?"

"Yes?"

"How's everything look?"

"I think the special train might finally be approaching. Chatter on the yard frequencies—they use all this jargon, it's like Navajo code talkers, but it sounds like something's happening. Hang on a sec."

"I want a beer," said Asher. They'd gone through a number of water bottles, which Finn had been collecting in the large plastic bag they'd use to carry out all their trash. Same thing for the granola bar and Snickers wrappers. Also several latex gloves, torn or damaged while they worked, which they'd exchanged for new ones.

"Looking forward to sleeping about fifteen hours, myself," said Jake.

Finn sat on the floor, waiting. "We're not done yet."

"Okay." Nicola's voice. "I've got a reasonable view to the front of the yard, and the snow seems to be lightening up some. The train's definitely on its way. I think they're escorting it in—I can see blue lights. Is there an access road running alongside the tracks?"

"I don't know. Corman, you have any idea?" Pause. "Corman?"

"Yeah." He sounded winded, which was maybe no surprise. He'd been loading the same material that had required three people in the vault. "Not sure in that direction, but probably. Line to the north has a service road."

"So they're protecting it from demonstrators." Finn considered. "Are the police at the yard moving? Doing anything?"

"Hard to say, but nothing major. A car goes in and out now and then."

"Right." He stood up. "Listen up. Everyone on the wire?"

"Yes."

"Yeah."

Grunt.

"So we've got all of Wes's metal out. That's our payday." He paused. "But . . . Wes is only one of the people with space here. There are other racks, in other units. Who knows?"

Asher was on board immediately. "Let's do it!"

Jake hesitated. "We have a schedule . . ."

"And we're running well ahead of it right now. We've got, uh, twenty-three extra minutes."

"I guess if nothing unusual is happening upstairs, maybe."

"Corman?"

"Yes." No questions.

"Nicola?"

"On one condition: If I see or hear anything that looks the least bit odd, you stop immediately and leave. Okay?"

No one disagreed, though Finn privately thought Asher might have trouble just walking away from the treasure horde if it came to that. "Immediately," he said. "Yes."

"Then let's go ahead."

"Okay." Finn turned to the next cage. "Back to work. Let's see what we can find."

CHAPTER FORTY-SIX

They were in Sean's patrol car, a half mile down the road, when David's cell phone rang.

"Hello?"

"Chief? This is Hagan." The Newark commander, presumably still in the tower.

"What's happening?"

"The special is a mile away. They'll be entering the yard in a few minutes."

"Where are you?"

"Still in dispatch. We can see it out the windows. Somebody gave them an escort—must be a half dozen cruisers driving alongside."

"Which fucking moron's idea was *that*?"

"Not ours. I thought maybe you."

"No." David cupped the phone and said to Sean, "Who the hell ordered a ticker-tape parade?"

"What?"

He passed on Hagan's description. "If we can see it, the protesters can sure as hell see it. They're going to be all over it now."

"Chief"—Hagan spoke up—"we've got movement. People getting into cars . . . Something's happening at the entrance portal." He broke off.

David rubbed his eyes. "Back to the yard," he said. "Might want to use your siren."

Sean backed the car over a rubbled stretch of asphalt, turned, and hit the accelerator. "Trouble?"

"Sounds like it." David clicked off his call with Hagan and redialed the chief dispatcher's line.

"Yeah?"

"This is Keegan. Are you on the special?"

"Of course."

"Send it through receiving track five."

"The old line?"

"That gate's a little farther from the road—might help keep the mob clear of the locomotive."

"Got it." Indistinct noises as the dispatcher conveyed the order. He came back a moment later. "They're doing it. Where does that track go, anyway?"

"Past the vault building," David said. "Between it and the road. Hardly ever gets used."

Another muffled conversation. "That works," the dispatcher said. "We can switch it right back to the transfer siding on the other side of the vault."

"What are the hippies up to?"

"They're stringing out along the road, next to the yard perimeter. Is it still snowing where you are?"

"Some." Sean had left the wipers on, but they were squeaking against mostly dry glass. The car careened through a red light, siren blaring.

"Not here, either. The riot cops are staying put. I guess they figure the fence is good enough to keep them out."

"Anyone tries to go over the razor wire, they're going to regret it."

"We'll be there in two minutes." David braced as Sean squealed through a turn, wheels finding pavement to burn rubber on even through the snow. "Or maybe less."

"No hurry," Sean said. "It's under control."

"Protesters are on the road," Nicola said over the radio. "Police still holding their positions in the lot."

Finn and Asher were hauling a tray of gold ingots, working as fast as they could. The first unit next to Wes's had been a bust: racks nearly empty, a few platinum bars. But the one beyond—jackpot.

"Hearing anything from the FBI?"

"Their traffic's encrypted."

"Railroad security, then."

"It's confused. Half are trying to deal with the incoming freight, half are still with the protesters at the entrance. Some of the guys are getting snappish."

"Excellent."

"Wait a minute." Nicola went silent.

Finn helped shove the tray up to Jake, who sent it down the belt, and immediately turned back with Asher for another. "What?"

"The special is just entering the yard, but it's taking a sidetrack. The one . . . It looks like they're going to come right past the vault building."

"It is? Which side?"

"The track along the fence. Close to the road."

"Fuck." Finn stopped dead and hollered, "Time to go! We need to get out of here!"

Asher, who was already back at the rack they were pilfering, looked up with a frown. "What? We're not half done!"

"Don't waste time with that. Go!"

"There must be a hundred more gold bars!" Asher yanked at the drawers, revealing row after row of shining gold ingots. "There's a fucking million dollars here!"

"Guys?" Nicola's voice, losing some of her cool. "Is there a problem? Because the train is almost on top of you."

"Jake, shove off!"

"What's going on?"

"A *million fucking dollars!*"

And then Nicola was shouting, all control gone. "Don't go down the tunnel!"

"Nicola?"

"Stay there," she yelled. "Don't leave! Don't *move!*"

CHAPTER FORTY-SEVEN

The special train was short. Two SD70 locomotives, an empty gondola as a spacer, then the articulated flatcar carrying the excavation arm. The huge mining claw was eighteen feet tall, well above the height of the rear locomotive, and its long mechanical arm extended to the very end of the bed. Another spacer gondola and several more flatbeds with other components lashed down under steel bands. The equipment was all oversize gears and massive metal struts and long, heavy hydraulics.

Snow had covered the horizontal bits and accumulated on the flatbeds' decking. The locomotives rumbled slowly through the yard. The police vehicles that had joined it a few miles back stopped at the perimeter fence, blocking any demonstrators who might think to chase the train through the portal on foot.

Dispatch had cleared the train's way, making sure there was a free line straight through to the transfer siding. The operations crew waited there, stamping their feet and trying to keep cigarettes lit in the wind, ready to begin shifting the machinery to the next leg of its journey. A hostler in a switcher pulled a cut of boxcars and containers down the next siding. Somewhere outside the yard, a train whistle blew.

Asher's tunnel bore was just under the track next to the vault building. They'd started deep in the ground, but in order to maintain the angle, the jacking pipe was almost at grade ten feet from its destination. Just a few inches from the surface of the earth.

Just a few inches below the crossties of the sidetrack. So close that it had cut through as much ballast gravel as clay.

The locomotive engineer didn't know it, but he was about to pilot his two-hundred-ton behemoth over a patch of ground that was supported by nothing more than a thin concrete pipe wall.

A rustle of movement went through the throng of demonstrators. Some loud talking, not quite shouting, though Kayo couldn't make out the words. The police straightened their lines, readied their shields, displayed their weapons.

"Something happening," the school-bus driver said unnecessarily.

"No shit." Kayo thought he could see the tension build, an almost tangible force in the air. "You might want to saddle up, huh? Start the engine, know what I'm saying?"

"Uh-huh." The driver nodded, threw his own cigarette into the snow, and climbed into the bus.

Kayo caught up to Millz, who'd been trying to make time with a girl with dreadlocks and a bright green coat. She saw him coming and skittered away.

"It's about to happen," Kayo said. "Maybe we leave soon."

Millz shrugged. "Ask me, it's fucking *been* time to get the fuck out of here."

"Not quite."

They drifted closer to the protesters.

"—ought to be here any minute," a tall, bearded man was saying. He had a phone in one hand, glove off so he could operate the screen. "Coming from over there."

"What are we going to do?" People around him began to move.

"Go tell Channel Three to get their camera out!"

"Where's Laney?"

"Come *on*."

The police line shifted to form an arc that blocked the demonstrators from going any farther into the yard, toward the rails. Kayo finally started to get nervous.

"Don't like this," muttered Millz.

"Yeah, okay, maybe we—"

Sean skidded to a halt, scanning the scene before them.

They were halfway along the perimeter road, paralleling the yard's exterior fence. Warehouses stood blankly behind the opposite side of the street. The parking lot and dispatch tower were two hundred yards to the right, demonstrators starting to move in the swirling snow, leaving the lot and headed their way. Police followed. A lightbar strobed the scene.

To the left, a locomotive's painfully bright headlamp glared, growing in size and intensity. The horn blew, a long, painfully loud blast. The train materialized from the snow against a backdrop of endless railcars in the yard behind. It was traveling on the track closest to the fence, ten feet from the boundary.

Ten feet from the protesters, who'd begun to assemble themselves along the fence, pressed against the chain link. Many were shouting.

The train wasn't moving fast, not even close to the yard's twelve-mph limit, but it was suddenly upon them, the enormous mining claw looming overhead.

Much bigger than a double-stack. David wondered how they had fit it through the tunnels.

"What are they doing?" he said aloud. Some of the demonstrators had begun climbing the barrier. "There's *razor* wire on top."

"Don't know." Sean pulled the handbrake and opened his door. "But we need to—"

CRAAAAASH!

The locomotive abruptly stopped, like it had run into a wall. An impossibly thick, heavy wall. Banging shattered the snowfall as all the cars behind slammed into one another. Sparks flared. The flatcars jackknifed, loads suddenly free, bogies and four-inch beam iron collapsing like balsa. Metal screamed and tore.

"Holy *shit*!" David saw a coupler break. The excavator arm rose up, impossibly high as its car buckled into the air.

The front locomotive toppled, smashed in its rear by the second. Everything in slow motion, but clearly going over. Screaming and yelling from the demonstrators, now scrambling away from the fence.

The loco's headlight beam dazzled the snow on the ground before it, then turned up, blinding David as it swept over their vehicle. The SD70 collapsed in a thunderous roar, smashing through the fence and onto its side.

Something struck Sean's windshield and shattered it—a chunk of metal, flung from the juggernaut as it struck the earth. Cars wrenched along behind, the huge excavator arm next to topple, falling almost on top of the second locomotive. The enormous claw flattened the fence and its cutting teeth gouged the roadway, cutting deeply into the asphalt. Flames exploded as diesel and hydraulic fluid sprayed from crumpled engines.

Sirens. Two police vehicles tore out of the parking lot toward them.

David swung out of the car, almost falling as his knee collapsed in pain but pulling himself upright. Shouting was audible over crashing and banging. People fled past him, running as fast as they could from the blast and tumbling wreckage.

"What the fuck *happened*?" he yelled, but he received no answer.

CHAPTER FORTY-EIGHT

Inside the vault, it sounded like an air raid. A distant rumble, growing louder, then an enormous crash, a shock wave rolling from the tunnel. Jake screamed. Dust flew out the opening, and he followed a moment later, dropping to the vault's floor like he'd been kicked.

The lights flickered, once, twice. They came back on full, then went out completely.

Emergency lighting snapped on. Battery-powered LEDs hung in corners, next to the cameras. The vault's interior turned black and white in their inadequate beams.

"Nicola? Corman?" Finn clicked his mic switch. Nothing. The repeater was dead, and their signal couldn't penetrate the walls and earth.

"I'm okay." Jake, groggy, being helped up by Asher. "I'm fine."

Finn pulled himself up to the tunnel entrance and peered down it. Jake's headlamp was on the pipe floor, still shining. He squinted, trying to see through the pinging cloud of dust.

"Shit." He dropped to the floor. "The tunnel collapsed."

"What?"

"Completely filled with dirt and rock."

"Collapsed?" Jake, still dazed.

"From what?" Asher let Jake go. "It sounds like we're being fucking *bombed*."

"I don't know."

"Can we dig it out?"

"I don't know." Finn tried to think. "I don't think so."

"Then—"

"I don't *know*."

"We're trapped!"

They stared at one another.

Nicola saw the train wreck as it happened, through her spotting scope. Despite the distance, she had perhaps the best perspective of any observer: from above, at some remove, and with more knowledge than anyone of exactly what was happening.

"Corman?"

"Yeah." At least his radio connection still worked. "What—?"

"Big train just collapsed the tunnel pipe, right outside the vault."

"Collapsed—"

It took all of Nicola's self-control to keep her voice steady. "Disaster zone. Protesters everywhere, police moving in." She hit a switch again, futilely. "I've lost radio contact."

A moment while Corman took that in.

"Police," he said.

"You can go out the back. Is the truck loaded?"

"Half. Two-thirds, maybe."

"They won't bother you." She looked through the scope again. "Everyone's focused on the wreck. There's a crowd around the locomotive—they must be trying to get the engineers out."

"What about Finn?"

"Working on that." Nicola dropped to her chair and pulled the keyboard toward her. "I can see them on the monitor. I just don't have sound or radio."

"I don't—" He stopped.

"Nothing you can do." She pulled up the Stormwall feeds, checked her access again. "Just get the truck out of there."

"Time?"

"What?" She looked up at nothing, then figured out what Corman meant. "Yes. Five, ten minutes. After that, they'll start paying attention again."

A moment. "I'm going to finish loading."

"You sure?"

"Yeah." Nicola heard it in his voice: Like her, he knew how to focus.

"Five minutes, *max.*"

"Uh-huh."

Nicola went back to her screens. First: Were the Stormwall monitors still seeing the dummy feed, all normal in the vault? Yes. Lots of traffic on the monitor circuits, but it was all messaging and VOIP. No one had triggered an alarm.

Rapidly, she called up the vault's maintenance panel. Stormwall had remote access not just to the cameras but to the fire alarms, HVAC, and electrical as well. Especially in case of a fire, someone needed to be able to shut down circuits that might contribute sparks and power to a blaze.

Nicola hadn't spent much time studying the maintenance controls, but they weren't hard to figure out. She opened a dialog box, scrolled through a matrix of options, and moused over a command.

Then she hesitated.

On the screen, she could see Finn and Asher helping Jake off the floor. Finn had already looked into the tunnel, then turned his back to it, which she took as confirmation that it was impassable. Now they stood, looking around, clearly not sure what to do.

Nicola clicked her mouse.

The vault's emergency lights went off.

David wanted to help extricate the engineers, but more than enough younger, fitter officers were available. Instead, he policed the crowd. Most of the demonstrators had sensibly run the other way, but a few came closer, and he shooed them back.

The lead SD70 was on its side, the second nearly so. The rails had buckled underneath them, derailing both locomotives, and momentum had pushed them over. A pair of policemen wrenched open the cab door, lifting it up like a tank hatch. One disappeared inside.

Flames were rising in the engine area, and the excavator claw, thirty feet in the air, hung over them like imminent death. David called to Sean, and they began pushing people farther away.

"Is the engineer okay?"

"What?"

They could barely hear each other. Groaning and hissing and creaking from the wrecked train, wind whipping snow everywhere, and more and more vehicles arriving, including the first of the yard's fire engines. Sirens wound down, but more rose in the distance. David could smell diesel and oil.

"Was it sabotage?" Sean shouted.

"Don't know." David shook his head. "See how the ground collapsed there? It looks more like, I don't know, a culvert or something."

"An explosion could have done that."

"Maybe." David didn't think so, but he wasn't an expert. Not much call for the bomb squad in railroad security.

"Hard to believe it *wasn't* some black-bloc anarchist."

"Maybe. I hate to admit it, but Boggs may have been right about the protesters." The two engineers limped away, arms over the shoulders of their rescuers. They must have been worried about the possibility of fire, because normal protocol would have called for backboards. "Must be a hundred million dollars of equipment damage. I hope Boggs kept the insurance up to date."

"I don't feel like asking him."

"No kidding." David looked at the chaos around him. "What *else* might go wrong now?"

"Hey, Corman?" Nicola said into her mic.

"I'm not done loading the truck yet."

"No, that's fine, I know it's going to take a few minutes."

"What?"

"Does Finn know Morse code?"

CHAPTER FORTY-NINE

It wasn't until the lights went out that Finn had his first moment of real fear. Until then, reacting to the explosion, whatever the hell that was, and the tunnel collapse—it was all moving too fast. He was just trying to keep up, no time to worry.

But in the pitch black, a wave of bad memories returned. Trapped inside thick concrete walls, no escape. Prison.

The only sound was scraping as Jake moved, then a clang when one of them knocked something to the floor. Ventilation had been whispering in the background the whole time, but Finn hadn't noticed it until it was gone.

The silence was almost as oppressive as the darkness.

Finn stayed in one place, trying to remember what was around him. He didn't want to whack his head or his knees.

"Uh, Finn?" Jake said.

"You all right?"

"Sure. But, you know—"

"*Fuck* this." Asher's contribution.

And then the lights came back on. Still just the emergency floods, but it seemed like daylight after the absolute blackness.

"Well, that's better—" Asher started, and the lights went out. "Ah, *mother*fucker."

And switched on again, then off—then on for a few seconds longer.

The blinking continued for a minute before Finn got it.

"What the fuck are you *laughing* about?" Asher sounded aggrieved.

Finn looked around for a camera and waved at it. The lights blinked once.

"Hi, Nicola," he said, and then to Jake, "Can you find a pen? And a big sheet of paper?"

Emily was doing fine until the train blew up.

She leaned forward, head inches from the monitor, as if she could extract more details from the news video that way. But, of course, it only dissolved into meaningless pixels. "What the fuck are they *doing*?" she said out loud, almost groaning.

Channel Three in one window, Twitter in another, Instagram in a third. The incident had already been hashtagged: *#trainbombing*. A local news crew had been on the scene, bored, waiting for something to happen. Well, something sure as hell *had* happened.

Finn, Finn, where are *you?*

For distraction, she glanced at the trading screen. Up another 2 percent, just while she'd looked away.

Whatever else was going on, she was getting incredible prices.

Corman shoved the last tray of ingots into the Kei truck's cargo area and stepped back. The load was messy and not that big, a pile of loose metal bricks and some trays on top, the entire heap less than three feet high. But it was massively heavy. The truck sagged close to the ground, wheel wells scraping the top of the tires.

He pushed the door closed, gently. So overloaded, the truck felt fragile to him.

"Nicola," he said into his mic.

"Yes."

"Going now."

"Let me talk you out, okay?" She'd spot for him, watching through the scope, to keep an eye out for police vehicles or unusual activity that might suggest a problem. "Just until you're through. After that, the view is blocked."

Corman gingerly fit himself into the driver's seat. Normally, the truck would have sunk several inches from his weight, but it was already at the suspension's full extent. He closed the door, hoping the reinforcements they'd welded into the chassis would hold.

The bay door was already open, all lights extinguished.

"Ready," he said.

"Give Finn a minute." They waited. "Hey, Corman?"

"What?"

"You did a good job today."

He didn't know quite what to make of that. "You, too."

A few more seconds passed. "All right," Nicola said.

"They ready?"

"Coming out in thirty seconds," she said. "You're all leaving together."

"One more time," Finn said. "We're plain old Stormwall security. There's a fire alarm, we have to get out of the vault before the halon is released. Someone tries to stop us, we just keep moving." He looked at Asher. "Be polite."

"Yeah, yeah."

To Jake: "You okay?"

"No problem." But Jake's face was pale, and he rested little weight on his right leg. The fall had injured his ankle. Not a break or a sprain—he would have needed a crutch—but bad enough. They wouldn't be able to run—if it came to that.

"We only have to get out of the building," Finn said. "And another hundred yards. There will be police and demonstrators and emergency crews everywhere. We'll blend in, and then we'll disappear."

"Are you sure Nicola can pull this off?"

Command presence. "Absolutely."

He took one more look around. Emptied racks, broken carts, holes in the walls, debris strewn everywhere.

"Another satisfied customer," he said, then looked up at the camera. "You all ready?"

Jake and Asher moved close to the exit door. Finn glanced at them, then did a double take.

"What the fuck! Asher!"

"What?"

"Put those *down*!"

Asher had two gold ingots in each hand, trying unsuccessfully to conceal them at his side. "Come on," he said. "They're worth thousands of dollars! *Each!*"

"Do you *want* to go straight back to jail? We're about as suspicious as possible, running out of the vault, sirens everywhere, like some fucking jailbreak. If you're carrying those bars, they won't even ask questions, they'll just shoot you on sight."

"But there aren't any pockets in these fucking uniforms!"

"And now you know why." Finn glared at him. "Put them down or stay here."

Grudgingly, with an almost physical manifestation of pain, Asher laid the four gold bars on a cart.

"You're making me cry," he said.

Finn shook his head. "All set?"

He looked up at the nearest camera and raised his hand, fist closed.

After a moment, the lights blinked. Finn made one last check, then counted it out, raising his fingers one at a time:

One.

Two.

Three.

A klaxon pierced the air. The lights went out again. And Finn shoved through the door, shouting "*Fire!*" as loudly as he could.

CHAPTER FIFTY

Kayo kind of stutter-stepped at first, starting to follow the crowd when the train finally appeared, then backing off and looking at the battalion of riot police. It felt like every single one of those blank gleaming helmets was turned his way. He had no idea which way to go.

"Now what?" said Millz.

"I don't—"

By coincidence, Kayo happened to be looking down the track, so he saw the locomotive crash. One second it was moving along, slow and steady, the next it was falling to the side. A moment later, the noise rolled over them, a long banging roar. Flatcars splayed left and right behind the engine, vast pieces of iron and steel thrown into the air and collapsing into one another.

"Fu-u-u-ck." Millz breathed it out, awestruck.

And Kayo's indecision vanished completely. He knew exactly where they needed to go: as far away as possible. He grabbed Millz's arm and pulled him aside just as the first police began running past, intent on the protesters.

"We're *done*," he said. "No, don't fucking run, keep it smooth."

Sirens everywhere. One of the gray tactical vans rumbled into life and turned toward the road. A plain old fire truck and an ambulance appeared from somewhere, headed for the wreck.

Snow stung his eyes. Shouts and screaming became audible under all the other noise.

"That was fucking cool."

"This way," Kayo said.

The school bus was just cranking over when they arrived. Kayo hammered on the door's window glass, and after a moment, the driver turned the handle to open it.

"Catch a ride?" said Kayo, leaning in.

"Where you going?"

"Anywhere."

"You didn't have nothing to do with that shit, did you?"

"Us? Fuck no." He ascended to the first step.

"I got to give them a few minutes—anyone was on the bus before, they can get back on now."

"How long you planning to stay?"

They both looked back, over Millz's head. Whatever order had existed in the parking lot was gone—civilians running around, police no better organized, vehicles tearing this way and that. Kayo saw the first batons in action, three armored cops subduing a kid curled into a ball.

"Maybe not so long," said the driver.

"Thanks, brother." Kayo and Millz climbed in and stood in the aisle. "Guess you can turn the heater on now, huh?"

The driver obliged, and a guttering draft of warm air began to flow. They watched the confusion for a minute.

"Didn't think they had it in them," the driver said.

"I don't think it was your group. They were just standing there. Had to be some kind of special-ops ninja squad blew up that shit."

"Maybe it was an accident," said Millz.

"Don't think so, but it don't hardly matter."

Something struck the back of the bus with a thump. Rock? A stray bullet? Kayo hunched involuntarily.

"Okay, fuck this shit." The driver put the bus into gear. "Eleven an hour ain't exactly hazard pay."

Kayo dropped into the front seat. "Better than we're getting," he said.

✗   ✗   ✗

David was at an ambulance, helping the medic lift in one of the engineers on a gurney. The other EMT knelt on the ground, working on the other engineer with Sean.

In David's experience, not too many people kept their heads in a crisis. But those who could pitched in.

His phone rang as the gurney rolled to a stop inside the truck and latched down. He dug it out of his pocket.

"Yeah? *What?* When?"

Neither medic allowed himself to be distracted, but Sean stared at him. "What?"

"You good?"

The first EMT nodded. "Yeah, no problem. We'll transport in a few minutes."

"Thanks." David looked at Sean. "Fire in the vault."

"The *vault*?"

"Maybe the train wreck hit something—it was right out front. But we've got a level-three alarm going off. Mandatory evacuation, maximum fire suppression. Let's go!"

They moved toward the vault, going far around the massive train wreck and the firefighters just starting to lay down foam. Twisted metal and broken debris littered the snow-covered ground. The fence and its razor wire had been smashed flat, leaving a way in.

"Unbelievable," Sean said. "What's next? A meteor strike? Angels with flaming swords?"

David slowed, his knee in agony. He pulled out his service radio and turned up the volume. "This is Keegan," he said, holding down the transmit switch. "Forget the demonstrators We've got a ten-eighty at the vault. Respond immediately."

He released the key, and static returned, followed a moment later by several brief acknowledgments.

Sean stepped over a gash torn in the earth by a skidding iron wheel. "How many?"

"All of them, probably."

"Not too excited, I hope. We already got enough lunatics waving loaded guns around."

"Firearms safety," said David. "Priority number one."

At the vault's rampway, a fire had indeed started, though it seemed to be outside, not within. Flames were rising from the fallen locomotives. A thick cloud of oily smoke mixed into the snow, falling lightly again. More riot police had arrived, and they'd begun to push the spectators farther back. The crowd itself had grown—protesters, the news crews, yard employees, and the usual mass of idlers who somehow materialized at any accident scene, no matter how deserted or remote.

They stopped, looking down the ramp.

"Doesn't seem like anything's on fire down there," said Sean, voice raised above the roar of the fire behind them.

"It was the monitoring company pulled the cord. Tried calling them, but their lines are busy."

"Busy?"

Emergency lights had gone on at the base of the ramp, inadequate to fully illuminate the loading bay. The receiving office window was dark. Falling snow further obscured their view. Acrid smoke drifted from the burning locomotive, and David's eyes burned.

Three men appeared from the haze. They struggled up the ramp, coughing, half running.

"What's going on in there?" David didn't recognize them, but all wore Stormwall uniforms.

One of the security employees was supporting another, limping badly. The third looked at David and said, "Fire alarms. Bad smoke. All the lights went out and we had to evacuate before the halon went."

"Is anyone still in there?"

"Didn't see anyone." The man goggled at the burning train. "What the hell happened out *here*?"

"Not really sure." David looked back down at the loading bay. "Are the doors still open?"

"We pulled them shut, but, you know, I didn't take a lot of time double-checking the locks. We got an injured man here."

"Okay. There's an ambulance out there—and more arriving. Get him looked at."

"Thanks."

David looked at Sean. "There's gold bullion in that vault," he said. "Boggs is going to be pissed if we don't make sure it's still locked up nice and tight."

"The only fire I see is over there," said Sean. "And it looks contained to me."

"All right." David started down the ramp. "Let's find out what's going on here."

CHAPTER FIFTY-ONE

A sher walked briskly away, snow and wind stinging his eyes. The uniform was cheap polyester, completely inadequate to the cold. If he'd had pockets, he'd have shoved his hands into them. Instead, he concentrated on keeping them from curling into fists—warmer, but odd-looking—and his back straight. Forward and confident.

Clean up right and no one looks twice.

Not that anyone was looking at Asher. He'd separated from Finn and Jake as soon as they were past the officers at the top of the ramp, no good-byes, pushing through the crowd. Conveniently, something exploded in the fallen locomotive as he passed, a deep thump, a fireball flaring out. Bystanders oohed, like they were watching fireworks. Armored police shifted and shoved back. No one noticed a solitary figure moving away into the snow.

Or so he hoped.

He turned from the avenue, putting the yard to his back, and then it was a quarter mile through deserted, snowy streets. Sirens and crowd noise faded. Asher thought about jogging but decided against it, just kept moving steadily. His ears and fingers slowly went numb.

The Seaport Vegetables box truck was undisturbed, its windows covered in snow. Asher fumbled under the bumper for the magnetic key case, fingers barely able to recognize and pull it out. Inside the cab, he started the engine—the diesel didn't catch or hesitate, thank fucking God—and put the heater to max.

When feeling returned to his hands, he retrieved the headset from under his jumper, where he'd had to carry it. To keep it from sliding down his leg, he'd shoved the radio unit into his underwear. But it snapped to life as instantly as the truck, and he caught half a transmission as he fitted the earpiece into place.

"—in the block. Clear, far as I can see." Nicola's voice, controlled as ever. "Where are you?"

"Corner of Fairwell and Sixth." Corman, driving the Kei truck full of loot.

"If Asher's there, you'll see him in less than a minute. No other traffic?"

"Car going the other way." A moment's static. "I might have picked up some attention, though."

"Where?"

"Dark SUV, driving along the yard fence. It stopped when I passed—couldn't see exactly in the mirrors, but it might have followed."

"I'll check the scope."

"It looked old-fashioned. Roof rack, tire on the hood." Corman, paying attention.

"Hang on."

Asher found the transmit switch and clicked it to active. "I'm in the truck," he said.

"Asher!" Her calm broke for a moment. "You made it!"

"Yeah, of course."

"What about Finn?"

Not Jake, Asher noted, but that was for another time. "They're out. We split up."

"Corman is almost there."

"He got it?" Asher felt a grin start. "How about *that.*"

"Get ready. If there's someone following him, you have to move fast."

"Right." Asher hated to leave the warming cab, but he hopped out and trotted to the rear of the truck.

The door slid up with hardly a rattle, thanks to the vast quantity of grease they'd filled the tracks with. Almost as smoothly, he pulled out the two tire ramps, letting them thump to the ground. And just in time—headlights turned the corner and accelerated toward him.

The Kei truck moved fast, speeding alongside the warehouse. Asher yelped and jumped out of the way. At the last moment, Corman braked, just enough, and hit the risers dead on. The Seaport truck bounced, slammed forward by the impact, and the Kei truck shot up and into the cargo area. A split second later, a great rending crash.

"Holy fuck!" Asher grabbed at the risers, unhooking them from the bed and dropping them to the ground, all the while staring at the Kei truck's rear. From what he could see, the front was collapsed into the forward wall. Had Corman survived the collision?

Yes. The driver door wrenched open, banging against the compartment's side wall, and the man himself emerged into the narrow gap.

"Aarghh!" It was a tight squeeze, and something dark obscured Corman's face—blood, as he came into the light.

"You okay, big man?" Asher reached up a hand, but Corman ignored him and dropped off the bed.

"Close the door."

Asher was already pulling the chain, the door sliding down and crashing into place.

"Fucker actually *fit*."

Nicola's voice on the radio. "Dark green SUV, tearing up Fairwell," she said. "*Move!*"

Asher ran to the cab, glancing once at Corman. "Can you walk?"

"Yeah." Corman wiped his face with a handful of snow. "Go."

"All right." He shoved the shifter into gear and eased the clutch—too fast, the truck almost stalled. He tried again—*nope, not panicking!*—and the truck started forward.

Corman disappeared into the snow, not looking back.

At the end of the alleyway, Asher turned the corner without stopping. In one last, quick glance at the mirror, he thought he saw a glow of headlights.

"Nicola? We clear?"

"Maybe. I don't have line of sight anymore."

"Fuck."

One more turn and Asher was back on Fairwell—the other end, past the industrial complex where they'd parked. Traffic light, a few cars and trucks. As Asher accelerated down the street, an unmarked with its flashers on came the other way, fast.

His heart thudded. He concentrated on keeping his speed exactly the same.

Two hundred yards behind him, the cruiser turned into the alley he'd just exited.

"Jesus, that was close," he whispered, more to himself.

"You okay?" Nicola must have heard.

"Yeah, but—"

"Stick to the plan." Nicola went away for a moment. "Finn says he'll be there."

David stood, shocked into immobility. Even Sean fell silent, mouth open.

The interior of the vault was a disaster zone: racks tipped and empty drawers tossed aside, debris and dust, bent metal, a gaping hole torn in the wall. They still had only emergency lights, beaming weakly in the haze.

Sean moved first, over to the gash in the wall. He pulled himself up and peered inside.

"Tunnel," he said. "Some kind of conveyor belt. You got a flashlight?"

David handed him a Maglite from his utility belt. Sean braced himself on one arm and pointed the light down the opening.

"Looks collapsed about twenty feet in." He dropped back to the floor, stumbling as he landed on a chunk of concrete. "Shit."

David coughed in the dust. "I guess we know what derailed the loco."

"Those three guys . . ."

"Yeah." David pulled out his radio but muttered in frustration a moment later. "No signal. We have to call from outside."

They moved quickly toward the doors and up the ramp, David limping more and more heavily. Sean had his own radio out.

"Might have a lead," he said.

"What?"

"Radio car saw a funny little truck drive out of one of the warehouses on Caleb Street—right across from the train wreck."

"A funny truck?"

"Funny looking. They're following."

"Could be something. Could be nothing."

"They're looking for it now." A pause while Sean waited for an update on the radio and David wondered what to do next.

Sean said, "You should contact Boggs, shouldn't you?"

David looked at his phone. "Fuck," he said.

CHAPTER FIFTY-TWO

There's no tail," said Nicola over the comm. "I don't think."

"How do you know?" Asher's voice, jittery.

"I don't see the SUV."

"They were on the other side! Not the SUV, some other police car."

"Did they backtrack you?"

"They went into the alley."

That stopped her for a moment. "Okay, then they'll meet in the middle," she said finally. "And find nothing."

"The rails are on the ground."

"Nothing that will help them for the next ten minutes." A note of exasperation. "That's all you need."

Asher muttered.

"What?"

"I said I fucking *hope* so."

Finn listened with one ear. He and Jake were in Finn's truck, driving as fast as was both safe and reasonably discreet through the dark, snowy industrial zone. Ancient brick buildings and modern, blank metal ones passed on both sides. The wipers kept up with the falling snow, but their headlights were almost useless, reflecting back nothing but glare from the flurries in front of them.

Finn felt good about one thing: Corman was clean.

He could have driven the Kei truck away—tried to escape on his own. He didn't, so he wasn't the turncoat.

Now it was Asher's turn.

The man himself squawked onto the radio. "I'm . . . four minutes away."

"We'll be waiting," said Finn. "Corman okay?"

"Banged up some, but you know—fucker would hardly notice if you hit him with a cinder block."

"Not with you?"

"Left, like we planned."

No one said anything. Corman on foot, two police vehicles converging directly on his vicinity.

Nothing they could do.

They left Finn's truck two blocks away. Jake could barely put weight on his leg at all now, unable to move at all without his arm across Finn's shoulder. The distance took longer than it should have.

"You get the engine started," Finn said, easing Jake to the driver's door. "Can you operate it with that leg?"

"It's a lever shift. Shouldn't be a problem." He opened the door and pulled himself up with both arms.

"Okay." Finn jogged the length of the tractor trailer all the way to the rear. Gil's battered hauler, hitched to the tall, enclosed the trailer they'd fixed up over the last two weeks. He unlatched the door, shoved it up and open, and pulled out the ramp.

The Seaport box truck appeared a minute later, headlights looming out of the snow. Finn looked around. The utility substation had a permanent security light at one corner, glowing dully in the snowfall. No other lights were visible, no noise except Asher's engine. Though it was hard to tell, the snow muffling everything.

The tractor roared to life, and then he truly couldn't hear anything else.

Good enough. Finn watched Asher approach, squinting into the glare.

"Cut the lights," he said into the headset.

"Right." Asher switched them down to fog. He approached at moderate speed, no hesitation, and bumped onto the ramp.

Finn stepped back, and the delivery truck surged up the incline, engine roaring with sudden effort. The trailer shuddered and rocked, the ramp gouging through snow into the pavement.

The Seaport truck forced its way into the trailer, loud squealing as its front edge scraped along the interior's ceiling. A pair of loud cracks sounded like metal breaking. The truck's rear wheels begin to skid, its engine roared—and then it was in. Six inches past the back door.

Just enough.

Asher shut it down and came out, leaving his own door hanging. Together, they pulled the rear door chain, spinning it through its pulley. The door crashed down. Finn slammed the latch and stepped back.

The last *matryoshka* was ready to go. And Finn thought to himself, *Asher's clean.*

Like Corman, he could have skipped his rendezvous, driven off with the entire haul for himself. Like Corman, he didn't.

And that put it on Wes. New Mexico, here—every fucking betrayal.

Wes.

"All set," Finn said into his mic. "Nicola, we still good?"

"What I can see is clear."

"Excellent." He gestured to Asher and they moved up toward the cab. "Let's make sure Jake's leg is good enough he can still drive."

"I just want a coat." Asher strode forward, arms pressed across his chest, shivering. "And a hat."

From behind them, headlights swung into the road, a muted glare against the falling snow. Finn spun around as an engine whined, the vehicle roaring down at them.

A dark, olive-drab Land Rover.

"That's it!" Nicola's voice, stress breaking through. "The one following Asher earlier!"

No time to react. The Rover braked hard, fishtailing to a halt ten feet away. Finn started to run, slipped on the snow, and stumbled. By the time he'd regained his balance, the Rover's door opened and Wes stepped down.

Carrying a handgun.

He pointed the pistol at Finn and Asher, holding it with practiced familiarity.

"Stay where you are, boys."

Finn slowly straightened up. Shock and dismay roiled his head. But another emotion slammed through also—anger. Anger at Wes, but also at the snow, the wrecked train, the police and the street-fighters, the protesters and the riot squad. Everything that had gone wrong.

And under it all, anger at himself.

Biting the words, Finn said, "I should have known."

"Oh, don't—"

But he wasn't being rhetorical. "Corman practically described a Land Rover," he said, disgusted.

"He saw me?" Wes shrugged. "I thought it might be too obvious, but I needed something I could trust in the snow."

"What's the plan, Wes?"

In response, he lifted the pistol and fired three times.

"Fuck!" Finn twisted around again, expecting to see Asher down—but Wes had shot Finn's old pickup truck instead. Both tires. The truck sagged into the snow.

"Sorry." Wes moved forward, skirting them by fifteen feet. "Guess you'll have to walk home."

He was headed for the tractor's cab, clearly intending to drive away with the entire haul.

Did he know about Jake?

More to the point, Finn realized, was Jake capable of *anything* with his bum leg?

"*Fuck* you," Asher said.

"You were keeping secrets." Wes was energized, almost bubbly. "You told me the date was January fourth."

"Last-minute change." But that was a good point. How had he—

Wes backed to the cab and looked up, still holding the handgun pointed at Finn and Asher. The door swung open and Jake hopped out.

Six feet to the ground, and he landed as lightly as a gymnast.

"Well, shit." Finn felt another wave of anger roll over him.

"Sorry, man."

"What the fuck are you doing?" Asher growled.

Wes immediately aimed the gun back on him. The tractor's diesel rumbled beside them, fumes drifting down from the stack.

"You did a hell of a job," Wes said.

Jake looked at Finn, his expression hard to read in the falling snow. Sadness? Regret? "I need the money," he said.

After Corman, then Asher, proved themselves, Finn had started to think he was wrong. Paranoid, worrying about betrayals that didn't exist. Jake had been with him for more than twenty years. More than half his *life*. Ups, downs, for better and for worse, Jake stuck with him.

Until now.

No, Finn amended. *Until New Mexico.*

"Need?" he said.

"The machine shop is bankrupt." Jake sounded bitter. "Whole damn world has moved on."

"So you're out of business. So what?" Finn wanted to keep him talking. "Your share is still more than enough to retire on. You don't have to do this."

"It's not just that."

"What?"

"I tried to save it. Thought I could turn things around. I got in too deep."

And Finn understood. From the corner of his eye, he saw Asher tensing up and put out one hand to restrain him.

"You went to *him*, didn't you?"

Jake didn't say anything. Asher grunted in surprise, turning to look at Finn.

Wes grinned, still on a high. "He sure did. Of course, we've always kept in touch."

Finn ignored him, keeping his gaze on Jake.

"Maybe you even put a little threat on the table? Wes gives you the money to keep going, you keep your mouth shut about New Mexico."

"I'm sorry, man," Jake said again.

"New *Mexico*?" Asher said.

"Yeah." Finn watched the gun. "Wes double-crossed us seven years ago. Figured out how to make more money from having the molybdenite theft discovered, in a very public way."

"What?"

"Wall Street. Tell you later. But the thing is, Wes couldn't have just called the cops. He didn't know any of the details—which train, where, when." Finn turned his gaze to Jake's face. "He needed someone on the inside."

Talking about him like he wasn't even there. Wes started to interrupt, but Jake overrode him.

"No one should have gone to jail! It would have been barely more than misdemeanors if those damn narcos hadn't shown up. Things just . . . got out of hand."

Finn sighed. "You are such an asshole, Wes," he muttered.

Asher was half enraged, half confused. "You're saying Jake *turned us in*? On the train job?"

"Wes was playing it sharp," Finn said. "If we'd just taken the ore and sold it, he would have made a quarter mil. But when it blew open instead—maybe four times that."

"You two *fucked* us."

"Just business," Wes said cheerfully. "Nothing personal."

Jake started to say something more, then just shook his head slightly. He turned and pulled himself back into the cab, leg working just fine now.

"Don't try to follow," Wes said. He swung into the cab, keeping the pistol pointed steadily in their direction the whole time.

Even before he pulled the door closed, the diesel rose in volume, gears ground, and the truck started to move.

Asher roared and started to run. Wes fired twice, the shots loud, and Finn ducked toward the ground. The tractor trailer picked up speed.

A few seconds later, they simply stood and watched it go, taillights dimming in the snow, engine noise racketing off the brick walls around them but fading quickly.

"Those sheepfucking *bastards*! Cocksucking butt*fuck*—" Asher raged into the sleet, still chasing the truck.

"Calm down," Finn called.

"What? That pile of *shit*—"

"Let it go."

Asher kept yelling, but he stopped following the tire tracks and just stood, fists clenched, glaring down the road. Finn went to check his truck, clicking on his mic.

"Nicola? Did you hear all that?"

"Yes. What the hell did you let him go for?" Anger filled her voice, too. "Why didn't you *stop* him?"

"Later." Finn looked at the shredded tires and decided his pickup was indeed undrivable. "We have other problems. But one thing first—the railroad police chief, what's his name . . . Kruger?"

A moment of silence, Nicola forcing herself back into control. "Keegan," she snapped.

"Do you still have his number?"

CHAPTER FIFTY-THREE

Boggs finally arrived at the crime scene, his black Escalade almost running down several civilians and two officers as it slewed to a stop at the police line. He got out, followed by some underlings, and they all trotted toward David.

The CEO was in a dark blue parka with Penn Southern's logo emblazoned on the chest. He left the hood down, snow immediately beginning to accumulate in the collar.

"What the fuck?" he shouted, waving both arms. "The vault was *robbed*?"

"I don't want to jump to any conclusions—"

"Where the hell were your people? How could this happen?"

David started to explain what he'd begun to figure out: the break-in and everything else happening that night mere distractions. He'd already dispatched two men across the road to see which of the warehouses the tunnel might have started from.

"I can't believe you were so in*comp*etent—" Boggs sputtered. "Are they still *in* there?"

David made a calming motion with both hands. "No, no, they're gone. The vault's empty."

"*Empty?*" Boggs's voice was almost a scream.

"Of people." He saw Sean stifle a grin.

"You." Boggs couldn't even get a sentence out. "You . . ."

David's phone rang. As he pulled it from his pocket, he said, "Police are establishing the crime scene. Detectives and a forensic team are on the way. The mayor's been called. It's under control ... Yes? Hello?"

For a moment, the men all were silent. Emergency lights strobed around them. People yelled here and there. Newark's hazmat truck continued to spray foam on the locomotives. Sean, best attuned to his boss's moods, picked up David's increased alertness first.

"What's up?"

David took the phone away from his ear and looked around. His officers, the few of them visible, were fully occupied with the crowd, but one of the Newark sergeants was nearby. He hurriedly gestured him over.

"Yeah?"

"Are your guys mobile? Or should we give it to the ESU?"

"What?"

David indicated his phone. "We have a description of their truck, a plate number, and a location as of two minutes ago," he said. "What do you think? You or the NYPD?"

Nicola broke down her equipment fast, pissed off and practically throwing stuff around. First, the operating-system thumb drives, straight into a degaussing box that was plugged into the wall, waiting. In the few minutes it took to thoroughly burn them clean, she yanked all the cables out and stuffed them into Ziplocs. Monitors, computers, and other equipment went into their padded carry-bags, then into a larger rolling suitcase.

Another satchel for all the miscellaneous stuff—radios, headset, the scope.

And one last step: She broke the newly demagnetized flash drives out of their plastic sheathes and fed the internal media into a small, portable shredder. It made a noise like a blender. The little confetti-size pieces, she dumped into a plastic bag.

One last scan through the room, checking under the bed, in the trash can, the drawers, anywhere a stray, incriminating bit of hardware might have fallen.

In the hallway, she stripped off her latex gloves and held them balled in her fist. They'd go into a trash can far away from the hotel.

Her credit card was a burner, good for the cost of her stay but little more, and associated with completely false personal data. Once she drove away, they could go over the room with a microscope and never get closer to her than some useless surveillance video from the lobby.

All standard housecleaning. But she didn't feel good about it, not at all.

They'd lost the entire haul. Finn hadn't been able to take out a single ingot, a single dollar.

What a fucking waste.

It took time get the school bus moving.

First, they had to wait while people kept running up, having decided they really did want to leave after all. Then a slew of emergency vehicles got in the way—ambulances, fire engines, police. More police. They were all going the other direction, and none were inclined to wait a minute while the groaning yellow bus eased around them.

Finally, though, the driver got them pointed the right way and in a clear lane. The seats were only half full, but everyone had stayed toward the front, so Kayo stood in the well next to him. Millz had a seat of his own, no one inclined to ask him to share.

"Fuck, *that* went to shit in a hurry," Kayo said. Looking out the back, he could still see scuffles, though most of the remaining protesters had been efficiently rounded up and flexi-cuffed.

"Just be glad we're on our way."

They continued through dark, snow-covered streets, few other cars out. A half mile down, a black Suburban tore past, portable blue light on its dash. A few minutes later, a dark sedan, also with a removable lightbar, followed it.

"What you think they're up to?" Kayo said.

"Ain't nothing I'm interested in." The driver kept them moving steadily down the avenue. "At *all*."

They stopped at a red light, no traffic on the cross street. The bus's engine rumbled quietly, the wipers pushing snow off the windshield.

Kayo noticed someone at the corner—no, two men. They wore plainly inadequate clothing, some kind of blue uniform, no coats.

They watched the bus warily, half hidden under a bodega's shuttered awning.

The light changed, and the bus started to move.

"Hey." Kayo leaned forward to peer through the window glass. "Hold up."

"What?"

But Kayo had already yanked the door lever. He leaned out into the snow as the driver, muttering, stepped on the brakes.

In the open air, no mistake. He gestured as the two men looked up at him, one frowning, the other shaking his head and starting to smile.

"Yo," Kayo called. "Need a lift?"

CHAPTER FIFTY-FOUR

Jake started to feel better. The cab heater was on full blast, melting snow off the windshield right through the glass. The tractor trailer moved easily in the storm, heavy enough to cut through the snow on the roads. He had to keep their speed down, but that was all right. Finn and Asher were two miles from any of their other vehicles, Corman was gone, Nicola was stuck in the hotel. They'd be on the interstate in another two blocks, and that was as good as disappearing off the face of the earth.

"That went okay," he said.

"Okay?" Wes looked at him from the passenger side of the cab. "Just okay? That was fucking *perfect.*"

"I'm glad no one got hurt."

Wes wasn't paying attention. "And I didn't think we'd get the metal at all. This is like a hundred-million-dollar bonus."

Jake had never understood that part of it. From the beginning, Wes had wanted the theft discovered while it was happening. He didn't know if Wes ever really thought Finn would go to all the trouble of breaking in and then not actually *take* anything—but for Wes, it worked out either way. The point was to tell the world that a significant portion of its rhodium inventory was both counterfeit *and* vulnerable to theft. Somehow Wes had figured to make money off that.

A *boatload* of money.

No. Jake shook his head. The amazing part was that Finn actually got the goods out—and Jake took it away from him. They had millions of dollars in untraceable metal, a nine-hundred-mile driving radius, and a heavy winter storm to disappear into.

He'd be drinking piña coladas under palm trees for the rest of his life, and he couldn't wait to start.

"Up ahead," Wes said, pointing the gun through the windshield.

"Can you put that away, for Christ's sake?"

But Wes was right. A sign announced I-78 and Jake could see the on-ramp. The road was deserted, snow blowing across the pavement, but headlight beams glowed from the highway. Traffic was moving. He downshifted and turned toward the ramp.

Suddenly, flashing lights turned the corner a few hundred yards ahead of them. More lights strobed into his mirrors from the rear, momentarily dazzling.

"What the fuck?" Jake's confidence disappeared. A sick feeling stabbed through his torso. He tried to accelerate, but the vehicle was far too heavy to rocket forward.

"Don't stop!" Wes yelled.

A dark panel truck appeared from nowhere, sliding across the road to stop a hundred yards in front of them. Another came up on the side, and more lights from behind suggested at least one or two vehicles in pursuit.

Figures leaped from the panel truck. Jake saw assault rifles and helmets and armor—they looked like every special-ops soldier from every video game he'd ever played. They spread along the road, not in his path, but perfectly placed to fire zillions of high-power rounds through his windshield.

No bullhorn, no sirens, no more noise than the usual—engine, wheels, weather. But it was obvious they wanted him to stop.

"Keep going!" Wes shouted, waving the handgun.

"What? Don't be fucking crazy!"

"I said *keep going*!"

"They'll shoot us!"

Wes swung the gun around and put it six inches from Jake's head. "We can break through. We're not giving up now." He jabbed Jake's ear with the barrel. "*Floor* it!"

For one perfect, crystal moment, Jake confronted his choice.

Then he ducked, punched the brake, and swung wildly sideways, trying to knock the handgun away.

"Nooo!"

BLAAAM!

Jake's window shattered. For a second, he and Wes struggled, sliding around the bench seat, the truck going out of control as the steering wheel spun.

Another gunshot. Reflexively, Jake shoved his feet down, trying to leap away, and slammed the accelerator. The truck slewed again, then picked up speed.

"Motherfu—!"

Jake swung again, clouting Wes by pure accident. For a moment, he was free, and he looked up to see the black van looming in front of them.

The soldiers began to fire.

Jake glimpsed the muzzle flashes, everywhere, an instant gauntlet. He even thought he could see the bullets. Wes screamed.

Then the window glass exploded all around them.

CHAPTER FIFTY-FIVE

We were completely screwed over," Nicola said, arms crossed and glaring at nobody. "And the worst part is, I still don't understand *why*."

They were in the same salvage yard they'd used two months earlier, before the job even started. The same guy let them in, gave them the same warning about the Dobermans, and left them to it. A cold wind nipped through the metal walls. Nine p.m. and the yard was mostly quiet, just an occasional truck growling past.

Asher slumped in a brokeback chair he'd pulled from the day office. Corman stood impassively near the door. Nicola sat on the same crate she'd used last time, back straight.

One man missing, though.

Finn leaned against a stack of pipes strapped to a pallet, under the weak overhead light.

"It's confusing," he said. "Took me about ten tries to really get it."

Jake and Wes were dead. The official story was they had tried to break through a police line, refusing to stop, and force was required to keep the semi from hurting anyone. Maybe it was true. All the rhodium and gold they'd extracted with such backbreaking labor was in the trailer, and the truck-inside-a-truck-inside-a-truck images had elevated the story to peak viral.

Finn and his companions had nothing.

"Wes planned to betray us all along," he said.

"But why?"

"His story about the counterfeit ingots was true enough. In fact, I think most of his stock was fake. He'd gotten swindled but good."

"Yeah, and *fuck* him." Asher, not in a forgiving mood.

"So it was plausible that he'd want us to switch his bad metal with good ingots from his neighbor in the vault. Meanwhile, his business elsewhere began to implode. Remember, he'd been betting big on all that rhodium. So big that his other investments were hurt. And when other investors—hedge-fund managers, bankers, the usual bastards—started to hear rumors, they went after him hard. He was in a serious cash crunch."

"Makes you wonder how he planned to pay us," Nicola muttered.

"He didn't, of course. More to the point, Emily looked through the records later and discovered that he'd stopped paying premiums for the insurance on his holdings."

Finn paused. Nicola got it first.

"That's why he didn't want us to simply take everything out!"

"Exactly. From his side of the table, if we just stole it all, he'd lose twice. The metal itself would be valueless, and he'd get exactly zero from the insurance company. Forget the cash crunch, he'd be instantly and utterly bankrupt. And facing civil suits for the next ten years, too. Wes was acting as fiduciary for *his* investors, and getting scammed by shady African commodities dealers is a big no-no."

"So, the swap." Nicola frowned. "But you said . . . ?"

"Yeah." Finn nodded. "Here's where Wes got too clever. Remember, he told us that if the counterfeits are discovered, rhodium's value plummets. Everybody gets worried about their own inventory, panic selling starts, the price drops through the floor. That's bad, right?"

"Um . . . right?"

"Bad for most people, at least if they own rhodium. But not for *everybody*."

Corman grunted in annoyance.

Finn acknowledged him. "You ever heard of selling short? No? Emily had to explain it to me, too. What you do is, you sell something *before* you buy it from somebody else. Only on Wall Street can you do shit like that, I guess. But the point is, if you sell short, then you actually make money when the price falls—not when it goes up."

Maybe Nicola read the *Wall Street Journal* every day. Or maybe being fifteen years younger meant she'd gotten a better education. Or maybe she was just smarter. "The cash crunch," she said. "It wasn't just his investments going bad."

Finn smiled. "That's right. He took every single dollar he could get his hands on—including our front money—and bought rhodium puts."

"Going short, you mean."

"In the biggest, riskiest way possible. Yes. Everything he had, and a lot of his investors' money, too, on one last gamble."

Asher scrunched his face, trying to make sense of the story. "So even though he got nothing from us, even though he lost everything in the vault—the motherfucker still would have come out *ahead*?"

"Depending on how far rhodium's price fell, he could have made fifty million dollars."

Shocked silence.

"Wow."

"*Fuck.*"

Finn nodded. "Exactly."

"And we're digging tunnels and getting shot at and having fucking *trains* fall on us? For fucking pocket change?" Asher shook his head. "I gotta get an MBA."

"Wait." Nicola was still following the thought. "Sure, he makes a fortune, but only if the price actually falls. What if it doesn't change? Or goes up?"

"Then he's done, and probably in jail, too."

"So he has to make the price drop." She uncrossed her arms. "The fakes—he was counting on them being discovered. But not in *his* vault. In the other guy's!"

"Yes."

Corman rumbled out a long, angry growl, but Asher was still paddling. "Wait, what? Then why did he . . . Wes was going to call the cops while we were still inside?"

"After we swapped the metal, anyway. We'd spill everything,

news of the counterfeits would put rhodium into free fall, and Wes would walk away with fifty million dollars."

What really galled Finn was that Wes had used the exact same strategy in New Mexico: set up the caper, tip off the authorities, watch everyone get arrested—and laugh all the way to the bank with profits from Wall Street's bizarro-world derivatives.

"That . . . that . . ." For the first time Finn had ever seen, words failed Asher.

"No," Nicola said. "We'd spill everything, like you say—including Wes's involvement!"

Finn shrugged. "He'd deny it all, and he was careful to allow nothing that could connect him. Who'd believe us? The story's preposterous. Anyway, fifty mil buys you the best lawyers in the world—or at least a very nice retirement in some tropical country with lax extradition laws."

"The news didn't have any of this shit," Asher said. "Counterfeit metal, Wes—none of it." All of them had been following the reporting very, very closely. "Just said they killed the ringleaders in a shootout and recovered everything that was stolen."

"Yes."

"That was *ours*."

"Well . . ."

Nicola stirred. "What happened to the price? The rhodium?"

"Ah." Finn felt a small smile begin to form. They were getting to the important part. "Wes was so focused on the counterfeits that he didn't really consider the other option. What happens when the theft is discovered—but the fakes aren't?"

"I think I just asked you that."

"The answer is that the price goes up. Maybe not *up* as much as Wes was hoping it would go *down*, but any hint of an interruption in supply—say, by an entire vault being frozen during a forensic investigation—gets people worried. Manufacturers order ahead of their usual pattern, just to be safe. Speculators close down short bets, which are apparently far more risky than the reverse, and that puts more upward pressure on. Other speculators see the price rising and jump on the bandwagon. Computers, watching for trends, do the exact same thing. Emily said it's all technical trading, whatever that means, but the result is the same. The price goes up."

"So Wes's inventory actually ended up being worth *more*?" Asher was incredulous.

"Sure. If he'd lived, he might have been able to pay the lawyer's fees out of it."

"Fuck that. We put in damn near months of hard labor and what did *we* get? Jack *shit*."

"Not exactly. Wes gave us eighteen to start, remember? And we got another two forty for his cars. Some expenses, but we really did this on the cheap. Close to a quarter million dollars, free and clear."

Asher snorted. "Divided five ways, that's nothing. Fucking minimum wage."

"Actually, I gave it all to Emily."

"What?"

Grunt—more than annoyed, this time.

"Fuck, did you just say—"

Finn, with a flourish: "When Wes was out buying all those puts, who do you think was *selling*?"

A long, gratifying moment.

"Ohhh." Nicola's acknowledgment was almost a sigh.

"And then—remember, unlike Wes, we had a pretty good idea where the price was going to go afterward. Namely, up. Emily took everything, including the seed money, and put it all into a, um, *heavily leveraged long position*." Repeating her words.

"Huh?" Asher's mouth was open.

"Like, Emily went into the casino and put every single chip she had onto double zero."

Nicola cut to the chase. "How much?"

"What?"

"The croupier hit double zero, right? How much did Emily win?"

"I don't think she'd say *she won* it." Finn looked at each of them, slowly. "*We* all *earned* it."

And then he told them the number.

CHAPTER FIFTY-SIX

W ere they happy?" Emily asked.

Sleet lashed the tall glass windows next to their table, but the interior of the café was warm and smelled of bread and chocolate. The place was actually a gallery, down on Twenty-Fourth Street. Maybe the art wasn't selling well. The owners had gradually expanded the coffee bar into a full-service dining area, and young people with odd clothing filled the sleek wooden chairs.

In other words, the kind of place that an earlier Finn wouldn't have entered in a million years.

"Seven hundred and forty-three thousand each? Yeah, I'd say they were happy." He considered a moment. "Always hard to tell with Corman, of course."

"They didn't mind that you gave me a share?"

"It was only fair." Finn sipped his hot cider. "For a while, they all thought they were getting nothing."

Ice rapped at the windows. Conversation burbled from the people around them. Finn could see into the better-lit gallery area from his seat, a rather stark room of bare white walls and a plain wooden floor. A series of dark red panels, slashed open with strips of shredded cotton dangling, occupied one wall. Opposite were a half dozen paintings of lily pads and watercress.

Finn assumed they were by two different artists, but he was no critic.

"Actually, Corman," he added. "It's not for me to say or anything, but . . ."

"What?"

"When we're all done, we leave, right? Asher gets in his piece-of-shit truck, drives away. And that's when I notice there are only two other vehicles. One is mine."

He stopped, didn't have to wait long.

"No way."

"Yup. Him and Nicola. The same car. She kind of waved at me when they got in."

Emily started to grin. "Good for them."

"My thought exactly."

The waitress passed by, checked in, moved on. Emily added more cream to her complicated coffee drink.

"Kind of ironic," she said.

"What's that?"

"You kept telling me how you were the last of the cowboys—the rangelands are all fenced, the gunslingers all dead." She caught his look. "Like, only dinosaurs are still out there stealing physical, tangible *things*. Today's thieves are online, millions of dollars with a few taps on the keyboard."

His own words coming back.

"And in the end, that's how *we* make our haul." Finn smiled and shook his head. "Yeah, yeah, I got it."

"On the other hand, you're still alive. Unlike the gunslingers and dinosaurs."

"Good point."

"What are you going to do?"

"Do?"

"With the rest of your life."

"Yeah." He finished the mug. "Been considering that."

"And?"

"I think I might settle on a business."

"Oh?" Her tone was hard to read.

"It turns out," he said, "there's this machine shop in New Jersey that might be for sale."

"Ah."

"Seems the owner died, and the estate's a little confused, but if someone's willing to move quick? They might get it for a good price."

Emily considered. "Didn't you say he couldn't make a go of it? Which is why he went to Wes in the first place?"

"Jake." Finn sighed. "Jake was clever, and he could mill steel better than anyone I ever knew, but you know . . . he wasn't very *smart*."

"And you are?"

"Smart enough not to take dumb jobs anymore." He turned the question away. "What about you?"

"I quit."

"I know."

"But the attorneys taking Heart Pine apart, they're paying me as a consultant. Wes wasn't exactly good with the paperwork. So I've got a few months there, helping them figure out the records."

"What about the government?"

She shrugged. "The lawyers say the SEC has made some calls, but no one seems too concerned. Wes lost a barrel of money, but it was mostly his. No widows and orphans in sight."

"That's good." And it was. "I'm glad it's all working out."

"*Hmm.*" Emily withdrew her hand and sat a little straighter, studying Finn's face. "Is it?"

For the first time in a long while, Finn felt good.

"Yeah," he said, and took her hand back. "I'd say that it is."

ACKNOWLEDGMENTS

Despite what I may have told our children a few times, I don't know everything. Neither, surprisingly, does Google. So I needed advice on any number of technical questions—and fortunately, people were willing to help out. Aaron Pickarski convinced me a tunnel-boring machine could do the job. Josh Larson explained how to surreptitiously tap high-voltage power lines. Pete Horstmann helped steal all those cars. Michael Mathison described dubious Wall Street maneuvers. Claudia Ramirez got some wording right. Joel Johnson shared all kinds of inside information about vault security.

Lynne Heitman, Kim Ablon Whitney, and Samantha Cameron were unfailingly supportive, and back when our writers' group actually talked about, you know, writing, provided ever useful feedback. My sisters, Sophie Littlefield and Kristen Wiecek, continue to offer advice, encouragement, and first-reader services. I couldn't have done it without all of you.

Of course, nothing would have seen the light of day without the hard work of Janet Reid. Super thanks to Otto Penzler, Rob Hart, and the team at Mysterious Press for knocking the manuscript into form—not to mention establishing the contest in the first place.

Finally, Lisa, Sonia, and Elliot: This wouldn't have been any fun at all without you.

ABOUT THE AUTHOR

Mike Cooper is the pseudonym of Michael Wiecek, a former jack-of-all-trades whose jobs have included stints with Boston's transit agency, on an ambulance, and at a food co-op, capped off by a graduate degree from the MIT Sloan School of Management and a job with Fidelity Investments. Wiecek's work has received wide recognition, including a Shamus Award, an International Thriller Writers Award nomination, and inclusion in *The Best American Mystery Stories 2010*. He lives with his family outside Boston.

MYSTERIOUSPRESS.COM

Otto Penzler, owner of the Mysterious Bookshop in Manhattan, founded the Mysterious Press in 1975. Penzler quickly became known for his outstanding selection of mystery, crime, and suspense books, both from his imprint and in his store. The imprint was devoted to printing the best books in these genres, using fine paper and top dust-jacket artists, as well as offering many limited, signed editions.

Now the Mysterious Press has gone digital, publishing ebooks through **MysteriousPress.com**.

MysteriousPress.com offers readers essential noir and suspense fiction, hard-boiled crime novels, and the latest thrillers from both debut authors and mystery masters. Discover classics and new voices, all from one legendary source.

FIND OUT MORE AT
WWW.MYSTERIOUSPRESS.COM

FOLLOW US:
@emysteries and Facebook.com/MysteriousPressCom

MysteriousPress.com is one of a select group of publishing partners of Open Road Integrated Media, Inc.

THE MYSTERIOUS BOOKSHOP, founded in 1979, is located in Manhattan's Tribeca neighborhood. It is the oldest and largest mystery-specialty bookstore in America.

The shop stocks the finest selection of new mystery hardcovers, paperbacks, and periodicals. It also features a superb collection of signed modern first editions, rare and collectable works, and Sherlock Holmes titles. The bookshop issues a free monthly newsletter highlighting its book clubs, new releases, events, and recently acquired books.

58 Warren Street
info@mysteriousbookshop.com
(212) 587-1011
Monday through Saturday
11:00 a.m. to 7:00 p.m.

FIND OUT MORE AT:

www.mysteriousbookshop.com

FOLLOW US:

@TheMysterious and Facebook.com/MysteriousBookshop

OPEN ROAD

INTEGRATED MEDIA

CPSIA information can be obtained
at www.ICGtesting.com
Printed in the USA
BVOW10s0347140717
489330BV00002B/4/P